D.S. CRAIG

Reincarnated as a Familiar Volume 3

First published by Ranobe Press 2021

Copyright © 2021 by D.S. Craig

All rights reserved. No part of this publication may be reproduced, stored or transmitted in any form or by any means, electronic, mechanical, photocopying, recording, scanning, or otherwise without written permission from the publisher. It is illegal to copy this book, post it to a website, or distribute it by any other means without permission.

This novel is entirely a work of fiction. The names, characters and incidents portrayed in it are the work of the author's imagination. Any resemblance to actual persons, living or dead, events or localities is entirely coincidental.

D.S. Craig asserts the moral right to be identified as the author of this work.

D.S. Craig has no responsibility for the persistence or accuracy of URLs for external or third-party Internet Websites referred to in this publication and does not guarantee that any content on such Websites is, or will remain, accurate or appropriate.

First edition

Illustration by Yura's arts
Editing by Greythorne Edits

This book was professionally typeset on Reedsy.
Find out more at reedsy.com

Contents

Acknowledgement	iv
The Story Until Now	v
Prologue	1
Lesti's Challenge	4
Sparring Match	15
Gardens and Letters	27
Malkael's Magic	40
A Lonely Nightmare	51
Rose	55
Fever and Progress	68
Getting Closer	79
Rose's Situation	90
Gathering Info	103
Secret Summons	116
Requesting Assistance	126
Finding a Spy	135
Bets and Tours	144
Elliot's Party	157
Aurelia's Battle	169
Battling Assassins	180
Rose's Resolve	195
Decisive Battle	199
Reunited	211
Epilogue	224
Newsletter & Social Media	230
Artist Information	231

Acknowledgement

If there's one thing I've learned over the last few years, it's how important a good support network is. This third volume of Reincarnated as a Familiar met quite a few challenges, personal and craft related, during production. It's only thanks to my friends and family, who supported me along the way, that I was able to keep going and get it finished. Thank you all for always being there for me.

The Story Until Now

My name is Astria, and I'm an Astral Cat. I actually used to be a human, a grade school teacher, in fact. However, one day, I died in an accident and found myself surrounded by darkness. I thought that would be the end of me, but suddenly, a strange voice started talking to me.

The next thing I know, I'm in a completely different world, with magic and everything. Even more unbelievable is that I was stuck in the body of a cat! A young red-headed girl called Lesti broke the school rules and summoned me as her familiar. In fact, she almost got kicked out of school. Thankfully, it turned out that I was pretty special, and they let her stay.

It took me a while to adjust to this new world, but every day was exciting. I slowly got to know more about Lesti and my new powers. Skell, a massive black dragon that lives in the caves under the school, trained me. Lesti and I even managed to discover a new way to use magic circles to learn instruction-based magic more quickly.

But not everything went smoothly. A jealous classmate of Lesti's kidnapped me. Of course, she rescued me, but in the struggle, a malformed summoning circle was activated, and an archdemon named Thel'al showed up. We fought hard and nearly defeated him, but my power ran out at the crucial moment, and he escaped.

After that, Lesti passed her practical exam with flying colors, earning herself the second seat in her entire year. With her ranking shooting up, she moved into the first class, where she met Aurelia.

Lesti quickly became friends with the girl, and we quickly found ourselves dragged into her problems. Not only was Aurelia secretly raising an elemental hound named Fang out in the city, but she was part of a smuggling operation too. However, that wasn't her choice.

It turned out that Aurelia was actually the head of the Mori clan's daughter. She was being used as a political prisoner by Lord Dawster, who was behind the smuggling ring. Even worse, his smuggling ring had been infiltrated by Thel'al's agents.

After discovering this, we laid out a plan to crush the smuggling ring and save Aurelia, but our opponents struck before we could. A man named Ulrich brought all the gathered beasts to attack the school. He also enslaved Fang, transforming him into a massive monster.

Lesti, Aurelia, and I managed to barely rescue Fang and turn him back to normal, thanks to a little intervention from whoever had sent me to this world. However, we couldn't save the other magical beasts that had been enslaved. The headmistress was forced to put them all down to protect the school, and Ulrich got away.

It wasn't the victory we wanted, but it wasn't a complete loss either. We managed to save Fang and free Aurelia from Lord Dawster's grip. We also managed to help Fang become Aurelia's familiar. I'm sure more challenges are awaiting us, but now that we've got some new friends by our side, I'm confident we can overcome them!

Prologue

A young girl stood before two sturdy wooden doors, staring at them as she fidgeted with the hem of her skirt. The excessively large hallways of the manor only helped fuel her feeling of isolation. She wanted to run away, but her feet wouldn't move. Deep down, she knew she would have to face them eventually. That hardly made her feel any better.

Finally, after standing there for some time, she summoned her courage and knocked on the door.

From inside, a man's voice called out to her. "Come in."

By the tone of his voice, she could tell he was already irritated, which didn't bode well for her. That realization caused her to tense up, but she didn't hesitate. Doing so would only raise his anger. With a deep breath, she pushed the door open and stepped into the large office.

Directly in front of her, a man wearing noble clothing sat behind a desk reading through several documents. For a long while, he ignored her existence and continued reading. While he did that, she scanned the room for the other presence that always accompanied the man, but it was nowhere to be found. The girl let out a sigh of relief, then straightened and said, "You called for me, my lord?"

Hearing her voice, he crumpled the paper in his hands, tossing it into the fireplace behind him with a sneer before glaring at her. "So, you've finally arrived. Has your time at the academy made you forget your manners already?"

The girl quickly but fluidly reached down and tugged gently on her skirt as she curtsied. "My apologies, my lord. I came as soon as I received your message. However, being unfamiliar with the city as I am, I struggled to find the location. Please forgive my tardiness."

"That's better. Very well, I'll forgive your rudeness this time." Despite his words, the irritated look on the man's face didn't relax at all. "Well, let's get down to business, then. I haven't got all day. Have you managed to make any progress in using that ability of yours?"

The girl's heart sank at his question. There was no way she would be able to produce results so quickly. She hadn't even been enrolled at the academy for a year. Between orientation, tests, and the chaos that happened in the fall and winter, she barely had any time to focus on the task the man had given her. Still, she knew it was pointless to make excuses.

Lowering her head, she curtsied once more. "I'm sorry, my lord. I still haven't managed to make any progress as of yet. However, I do have some ideas that I'm going to try now that spring has arrived. I plan to start a gard—"

"I don't care how you get it done, girl!" The man slammed his hands on the desk, cutting her off. "Just get it done!"

"Yes, my lord. I will not disappoint you."

"I know you won't." The man's reply was filled with confidence, carrying a dark edge that only the girl would understand. He stared at her for a brief moment, the disdain clear on his face. However, his look soon morphed into something more akin to concern—or more accurately, fear. "At any rate, I've heard that there have been a number of disturbances at the academy as of late. You haven't been getting yourself involved in anything risky, have you?"

His question brought memories of a particular night in the fall racing back to her. It still felt like a complete dream, that insane battle between the tiny Astral Cat, her master, and the archdemon that seemed to appear out of nowhere. It was all too much to believe, but she had seen it with her own eyes.

The Astral Cat's master had already been relatively famous at the academy. But since then, she had become a rather hot topic amongst the first-year students. Not only had she fought toe-to-toe with an archdemon, but she

PROLOGUE

had taken second place in the fall practical test. From that day forward, she had gone out of her way to avoid meeting the girl. Attention was the last thing that she needed right now.

"No, my lord. If anything, the chaotic events of the last several months have helped to draw attention away from me."

"I see." At her words, the man's irritation seemed to finally lessen somewhat. "That's good to hear at least. Plus, there's the bonus of that Gambriel brat getting knocked off his high horse." The man smiled, seeming to relish the woes of the former second-ranked student that the Astral Cat's master had displaced. "Speaking of which, he hasn't approached you at all, has he?"

The girl shook her head. "No. Master Elliot continues to keep his distance. I haven't had any contact with him outside of greetings in passing."

"Very good. Let's hope it stays that way then." With that, the man reached over and picked up another piece of parchment off the desk, beginning to read it. "I have no further questions. You're dismissed."

"Yes, my lord." Seeing her chance to escape, the girl quickly curtsied and spun on her heel, heading for the door.

Just as she reached for the handle, the man called out from behind her. "Oh, yes. Rose, one last thing."

"My lord?" The girl turned and looked back at him, her hand still partially outstretched.

The man didn't look up from his paper, but his dark tone said everything it needed to. "My patience is not infinite. You'll need to produce results soon. Otherwise…" He didn't bother to finish his sentence. He didn't need to. She already knew what would happen if she failed.

Taking a deep breath to steel her nerves, she squeezed out the best reply she could. "Yes. I promise that I will succeed." Then, without waiting for a response she pulled open the door, fleeing the manor as quickly as she could.

Lesti's Challenge

Fang and I stared each other down. Each of us stood on desks on opposite sides of the classroom we were in. Lesti and Aurelia were the only other people in the room, but neither even looked at us. A quiet, calm sort of tension filled the air as we each threw ourselves into the tasks we were assigned.

Nearly a month had passed since we had performed the bonding ritual and turned Fang into Aurelia's familiar. She now sported a purple crest in the shape of a howling wolf on the back of her hand, similar to the silver one that Lesti had. With the ritual completed, the headmistress gave Aurelia her permission to keep him on campus.

The whole incident had caused quite an uproar, from my understanding. Not only had another student gained their familiar early, but it was a close friend of Lesti's. Many of the noble families complained about favoritism. However, with time, the complaints had faded into the background. Some of the students looked at Aurelia and Lesti with disdain and whispered rumors behind their backs, but the girls ignored them. They had more pressing matters on their minds.

Our failure to save the magical beasts that Thel'al had enslaved had left a significant impression on the pair. With everything else settled, they had immediately gotten back honing their skills. In fact, I was worried they might be going a little overboard at times. If they had their way, almost every waking minute they weren't in class would be spent training. On several occasions, I stepped in and forced them to take a break, lest they burn out.

LESTI'S CHALLENGE

Lesti had been studying the magical runes inscribed on the collars and anklets Fang had been wearing, not to mention any other examples the headmistress would let her get her hands on. Of course, she wasn't working with the genuine articles. Due to how dangerous they were, they had been left in the care of Frederick, and he had transcribed the runes onto parchment for her.

With those in hand, she had been working her way through deciphering the runes at a breakneck pace. Apparently, she only had a handful left. Still, there was something strange about the structure of the spells that she didn't understand. This was especially true in the case of the runes that had been on Fang's collar and anklets. The crazy effects of those spells were so complex that Lesti couldn't wrap her head around how it all worked together, even though she now understood the individual runes.

On the other hand, Aurelia continued with the training that I had given her back before the attack, manipulating her own magical energy. Unfortunately, she hadn't made nearly as much progress as Lesti had in her studies, but at the very least, she was now able to vaguely sense her own magical energy. When she wasn't working on that, she was training with Fang to build up their combat synergy. It was honestly a sight to behold. The pair were so in sync that it would be easy to believe they were of one mind.

As for Fang and I, we had been sparring regularly to train our own combat skills. The pup had grown faster and stronger as time had passed, and with all the training we had been doing had finally gotten past his clumsy puppy stage. He had become a force to be reckoned with, striking at his opponents using a surprising amount of agility and coordination. The reason I was focusing on him so hard right now was that we were in the middle of a training session. I couldn't afford to take my eyes off him for a second.

Showing his youthful vigor, the pup decided to make the first move, dashing toward me with a sudden burst of speed. I was ready for his attack; as soon as he moved to jump across the gap between the desks, I struck. Lunging with all my strength, I slammed into the pup mid-air and wrapped my front legs around his neck, and we both fell to the ground.

Once we had landed, he let a small surprised yelp as I dug my back paws into his soft belly and bit him right on the neck. Of course, I hadn't extended my claws or bitten down enough to injure him, but I took his yelp as a sign of surrender and released him. Standing up and shaking off, he walked over and laid down by Aurelia to review our session.

Aurelia looked down at him with a soft smile as he laid next to her, pouting. "Of course you're gonna lose if you rush in. You have to be smarter than that."

Fang's only response was a soft growl, but it caused Aurelia to giggle. Unlike me, Fang wasn't considered a high level familiar, so the only person he could speak to telepathically was Aurelia. Still, I had a good idea of how he thought after spending so much time with him and could guess what he was saying.

"I'm not going to let you win, Fang." I shot him a stern glare as I cleaned myself. "That would defeat the purpose of the training and cause you to let your guard down when it really counted."

The only response I got was him turning his gaze away from me as if I didn't exist with a snort. *What are you, some sort of defiant teenager?* He had been acting like that a lot more lately. It probably had something to do with him transitioning out of his puppy phase, but man, was it annoying.

Ignoring him, I turned and headed over to Lesti to check on how her research was going. She sat at one of the desks near the front of the classroom staring at a large piece of parchment while scribbling notes. Her focus was so intense I wasn't sure I should interrupt her, but as soon as I approached, she looked up at me and sat her pen down.

"Are you done bullying Fang?"

"It's not bullying! It's training!" I swatted at her in mock anger.

"Rarf!"

"Oh, don't give me that! You know I'm doing my best to be gentle." I glared at Fang quickly before turning my attention back to Lesti. "And you, stop encouraging him like that!"

"Haha. Sorry. It's just way too much fun to see you get all flustered." Seeing her bright smile, it was hard to stay mad at her. Once she was done teasing me, her face lit up with excitement. "Anyway, listen to this. I think I'm close to making a breakthrough!"

"Really? That's great!"

"Yeah! Remember those runes that I couldn't figure out the purpose for? Well, it turns out they're a form of joining clause," she started explaining her findings excitedly as I did my best to follow along. "You see, I think the spells that we're dealing with here aren't single spells at all. Instead, I believe they are a series of simpler spells that are joined together by these other runes with different conditions and outcomes!"

Tilting my head to the side, I tried my best to come up with an example to make sure I understood the concept. "So, you could combine spells like my Power Cat and Speed Boost into a single spell?"

Lesti nodded, eyes still lighting up with excitement. "That's absolutely right! Although it is perhaps the most simple example. A more complex example would be to break down a spell into its components and then enhance it. Take Aqua Sphere, for example. If you break it down into its components, it will look something like this."

I watched as Lesti drew three magic circles in on her parchment. I still didn't know how to read magic runes, but I could tell these circles were different. For one thing, they contained fewer runes than most of the spells I had seen. This also allowed them to be written in a more compact form.

"So, these are the components of Aqua Sphere then?" I asked Lesti as I continued to examine the circles. "What do they do?"

She began excitedly pointing at the circles she had drawn. "This one just gathers the necessary water for the spell. Meanwhile, this one will shape the water into a sphere and hold it there, and this one controls launching the sphere toward the specified target."

"Okay, that all makes sense so far, but how exactly is breaking it down like this useful?"

"I was hoping you'd ask! If you just combine them like this with these runes…" With a massive grin on her face, Lesti once again started scribbling on her parchment. When she pulled away, there was a magic circle, unlike anything I had seen before scribbled on the page. A single large circle had the three circles she had written before copied inside it, with several of the runes from Thel'al's devices copied between them.

"So, if I'm correct, this circle would allow you to cast Aqua Sphere. Amazing, isn't it?"

"Yeah! It seems really amazing. You managed to write out Aqua Sphere in a more complex format." I stared at Lesti, not even trying to hide the sarcasm in my voice. I just couldn't see how this was useful.

"You don't get it at all!" Not one to be stopped by a single quip from me, she continued with her enthusiastic explanation. "Now that I've broken the spell down into components, each one is reusable! Any spell that gathers water can use this same circle, and any spell that requires targeting can use this one."

Slamming her finger down on one of the runes between the circles, Lesti grinned even wider. "Even more importantly though, with these runes, I can specify the number of targets and the spell will gather more water according to the number, shape that many spheres, and launch them all at their targets. I could go even further and separate the target count from the sphere count, but that can wait for a future test."

"So, with this, you could make multiple aqua spheres all at once? You don't have to cast the spell multiple times?" I looked at Lesti, hoping that I wasn't making a fool of myself.

Fortunately, she just smiled back at me and nodded. "That's right. I knew you would understand."

"O-of course I would." I averted my eyes to try and hide my embarrassment. However, my twitching tail gave away my true feelings. "Still, why do I feel like I've seen something like this before?"

I sat there pondering Lesti's example for a bit. Meanwhile, she excitedly explained the whole thing once again to Aurelia, who had come over to join us. I thought back through everything that I had been through in the last few months, all the way back to my training with Skell, and that was when it hit me. A specific memory from my training flashed before my eyes. A terrifying nightmare of countless Aqua Sphere spells being launched at me by a massive black dragon.

I found myself suddenly suspicious of Skell and Frederick. I knew they were both strong, but as Lesti learned more and more about magic, I found the things the pair were doing defied this world's common knowledge. First, it had been Frederick with his advice to Lesti on the familiar pact; now it was Skell with his repeating spells. Just where did those two learn all this?

"So, does the summoning circle not use runes like these?" I returned my attention to the girls as Aurelia asked Lesti about the summoning circle. Her question was something I was curious about myself. Why was Lesti only discovering this just now if she initially learned about magic runes from the summoning circle? It was one of the most complicated spells in the world. Surely it had to use the concepts she was describing here.

"Well, that's the odd thing. It doesn't use these runes at all." She quickly pulled out another piece of parchment from her things that had a miniature version of the summoning circle on it. "Based on what I've seen, it uses some of the same concepts, but in a simpler form. Instead of relying on runes to chain the spells, it separates the circle into separate rings for each portion of the spell. They then appear to activate, starting from the inner ring and making their way to the outer ring. If I had to guess, I would say this spell pre-dates the runes we're looking at, and no one bothered to update it once they were created."

"So, you think the summoning spell could be simplified then?" I looked at the circles on the parchment as my curiosity began to pull me in.

"Yeah, it could probably be broken down into its components just like Aqua Sphere." Lesti furrowed her brow. "I wonder why no one ever bothered though?"

Lesti gazed at the parchment that the summoning circle was written on with a thoughtful look on her face. I knew that look. If I didn't step in now, she would start trying to break the entire thing down here and now. Knowing we didn't have time for that, I stopped her.

"You can worry about that later. For now, it's time to get packed up. We have to get back to class." I turned and headed for the door. "If we're late again, Malkael is going to get mad at you for sure."

"Alright. I'll get packed up, so just wait for me, okay."

Lesti started packing up all her materials. Once she was done, we all headed back to the classroom for afternoon classes.

***

"So, in closing, while imagining the final product of your spell is important, understanding the individual steps needed to get to that outcome will increase spell performance and produce overall better results. Now, any questions before we end for the day?" Malkael scanned the classroom as he finished his lecture.

Lesti, for her part, wasn't paying any attention. Since she already used instruction-based magic, most of these concepts were already familiar to her. On the other hand, I found it incredibly fascinating. I could see how Malkael was slowly laying the foundations for students to transfer over to using instruction-based magic by getting them to think about the necessary steps their spells had to accomplish along the way.

"Well, then, if there are no questions, then class is dismi-"

"Instructor Malkael, did you not have a special announcement you wished to make at the end of class today?" Alex cut off Malkael before he could end the class.

"Ah, yes. Thank you for reminding me, Mr. Bestroff." Malkael opened the notebook that he always kept his class notes in before continuing. "As you all are surely aware, with spring arriving soon, a major event will soon be taking place here at the academy, the spring tournament."

Malkael paused his speech and looked up at the back row where we were sitting. "First, I've been asked to pass on a special ruling from the headmistress. Ms. Vilia and Ms. Aurelia, both of you will be forbidden from using your familiars during the tournament. This is to maintain the integrity of the competition since your classmates have yet to receive their familiars."

Lesti grinned and puffed out her chest. "Trying to level the playing field, huh? Fine by me. I'll win it all anyway!"

"I'm glad to see you understand," Malkael replied in a sarcastic tone, causing a wave of chuckles to pass through the class. "Anyway, my second piece of news is that we'll begin holding special classes to prepare for the tournament beginning tomorrow. We'll go over the rules of the tournament, practice our practical applications of magic, and even have a few sparring sessions."

At Malkael's mention of sparring sessions, a wave of excitement passed through the class. It was understandable, seeing as they rarely got to compete against each other directly. Outside of the practical exam, most of their time was spent learning magical theory and refining the power and control of their spells. This would be an opportunity for them to see how well they measured up against their fellow students on the field of combat.

Malkael waited for the excitement to pass with a smile on his face before continuing, "Therefore, starting tomorrow, classes will be held on the training grounds in the afternoon. The other classes will also be using the space for their own practice, so make sure to be on your best behavior. As members of the first class, you all act as representatives of your year."

"Any questions?" Malkael paused and scanned the classroom one last time. "No? Then class is dismissed for today. I'll see you all bright and early tomorrow."

Upon being dismissed, the class broke out into an excited fervor as everyone began talking about the tournament preparations. Several of the nearby students glanced over at Alex as they chatted amongst themselves. It was clear they were worried about having to spar against him. Being the top of their year by a rather large margin, he was an intimidating foe. Most students would want to avoid fighting him.

However, there was one student who was an exception to this rule. Before I could even react, Lesti confidently marched down to the front of the class. With her usual fearless grin, she pointed her finger at Alex. "I hope you're ready, Alex. I'm coming for your number one ranking!"

Alex let out a heavy sigh before looking over at Lesti with an unamused expression. "What are you even talking about? You know the tournament doesn't affect our class rankings, right?"

"O-of course, I know that!" Lesti sputtered, clearly flustered by Alex's response. "Still, if I win, then everyone will have to acknowledge me as the strongest student in our year, even if I don't actually get the first rank until the next practical exam!"

Alex's gaze turned hard at Lesti's words. "I see. That's only if you win, of course, and there's no way that's going to happen."

"What did you say?!" Lesti slammed her hands on Alex's desk and glared at him directly in the eyes.

"I said that you won't win. In fact, I doubt you'll even make it to the final."

"Oh, is that so? Then why don't we test that theory of yours? You and me, a sparring match, tomorrow."

"You really don't get it, do you?" Alex let out a heavy sigh. "Fine. Have it your way, but don't come crying to me when you embarrass yourself in front of the entire school."

Silently, Alex stood up and walked out of the classroom. Not willing to let him get in the last word, Lesti shouted after him, "The same goes for you! Don't complain when I beat you in front of everyone!"

Once the show was over, the rest of the class filtered out and went about their day, leaving only Lesti, Aurelia, Fang, and me in the room. Lesti was hurriedly packing up her books and notes, which she had strewn about her desk. Recently, she worked on learning more about magical runes and theory instead of listening to Malkael's lectures. It was quite rude, in my opinion, but Malkael never scolded her for it, so I hadn't said anything yet.

However, challenging Alex to a sparring match was something else altogether. It seemed rather reckless. Lesti had no physical combat skills and relied purely on manipulating the world around her to attack and defend. Even with her incredible casting speed and efficiency, there was still some lag. Which meant fighting someone with proper training and powerful enhancement magic like Alex was bound to end in a loss for her.

"Are you sure that was a good idea, challenging Alex?" I jumped up on the desk and looked Lesti in the eye. "It's a terrible matchup for you."

Aurelia nodded as she absentmindedly ran her hand through Fang's fur. "Mm. I agree. This doesn't seem like a fight you can win. Why challenge him like that?"

Lesti puffed her cheeks out and pouted at us both. "Wow, you two, thanks for the vote of confidence. I'm really motivated now."

"Oh, knock that off." I reached up and poked her in the face, deflating her puffed-up cheek. "You know I have absolute confidence in your magical abilities. I just think it's too soon to be challenging Alex. It feels like you're being reckless again."

Lesti stared at me for a long moment before letting out a heavy sigh. "Maybe you're right, but I have to do this. I need to experience weakness for myself and find some way to overcome it. Otherwise, I'll just always be counting on you in the crucial moments."

"Counting on me? That's not true—" I tried to reason with Lesti, but she held up a hand to cut me off.

"It is true. In both the fight with Thel'al and the incident with Fang, you did most of the fighting. All I could do was throw a few spells around. I wouldn't have been able to hold my own like you." She turned her head to meet my gaze, her usual determination burning brighter than ever. "That's why I have to get stronger. In order to help you fight and protect the things that I care about, I have to overcome this weakness, and this is my first step toward that."

Seeing her gaze so full of resolve, there was no way I could tell her to back down now. "As long as you know what you're getting into, then I'm fine with it. I'll be here to support you the whole way, so don't even try and think about doing everything on your own."

"I wouldn't dream of it." With a brilliant smile, Lesti picked me up and cradled me on the crook of her arm before scratching me behind the ears.

I leaned into her hand, enjoying the affection. "Still, you didn't have to go and pick a fight in front of the whole class. There are other ways you could have gone about this, you know."

Aurelia giggled. "Isn't it just like her to come up with such an extreme answer, though?"

"It definitely is."

Lesti puffed her cheeks out and pouted once more. "You know, sometimes I can't tell if you two are teasing me or praising me."

I looked over at Aurelia. "It's both, right?"

"Mm. It's both," she said, smiling playfully.

"Hey, aren't you both a little too in sync lately." Lesti gave me a mock glare. "You're supposed to be *my* familiar, you know."

I hopped down from her arms and walked over toward the door. "I'm your familiar, and as your familiar, I'm telling you to hurry up and finish packing up so we can go. You need to come up with a plan for this sparring match tomorrow."

"Fine, fine, I'm hurrying." Lesti quickly finished stowing all her materials in her bag, and we headed off to our first strategy meeting for the upcoming spring tournament.

Sparring Match

The next day, we found ourselves standing out on the training grounds. The entire space was filled to the brim with students. It was only the second time I had seen so many of them in one place, with the first being when they announced the practical test results. The only place that wasn't overflowing with students was the center of the training grounds, which was left open for some reason.

Looking around, it seemed like the various classes were roughly grouped by their years. Nearby, all the second year students congregated together, each listening to their teacher's instructions. I even recognized some of Lesti's former classmates in the crowd. Meanwhile, the first-year students had gathered not too far from us. Many of them kept glancing over at the third-year classes, which was understandable. After all, they stood out more than any of the others.

The third-years closed out the massive circle of people on the grounds a good distance from us. They took up the most space because they all had their familiars. All shapes and sizes of magical beasts stood next to their masters, making the area look like the world's strangest petting zoo. It was a sight to behold.

"Everyone, gather around. I know it's a bit crazy out here, but I hope you'll give me your full attention." Malkael struggled to get his class organized and to be heard over the throng of people on the grounds. It seemed a bit silly to do things this way. Realistically, it would have been more efficient for everyone to give their lectures inside before moving on to live demonstrations on the training grounds.

"Now, I'd like to go over the fundamentals behind the fireball spell today. It's one of the most common attack spells and is easy to use in almost any environment," Malkael continued his lecture somewhat awkwardly. It was clear he was used to working in a classroom. He seemed slightly lost without a blackboard behind him, often resorting to gesturing vaguely with his hands.

I also found the contents of his lecture to be far less engaging than usual. For one thing, it was just wrong. Malkael lectured on and on about how fire spells would work almost anywhere because they didn't require any raw materials outside of magical energy. However, I knew better than that. With the knowledge I had from my old world and my ability to see magic in action, I could tell how fire spells actually worked.

In my old world, fire needed three things to burn: fuel, heat, and oxygen. The last two were simple enough. Magic could be used to produce heat, and the air in almost any place had vast supplies of oxygen. It was the fuel that presented the greatest challenge. In most cases, it was quickly supplied from the air in the vicinity, using what I assumed to be some sort of flammable gas, such as hydrogen.

When I had told Lesti about all this, she had nearly exploded with excitement, rushing to implement the information in her Fireball spell. I was honestly a little scared to see the results. Her fireballs had already been relatively quick and powerful due to her efficient magical energy usage and specific instructions. What would she be able to do when armed with the science behind how spells like Fireball worked?

"So, in conclusion, fire magic is often one of the best sources of offensive magic for a mage." Malkael looked around, seemingly relieved to have gotten through his lecture. "Now, how about we have a demonstration. I'd like a volunteer. Who's interested?"

Without missing a beat, Lesti pushed her way to the front of the group and threw up her hand. "I'll volunteer, Instructor Malkael!"

Malkael grimaced slightly, but with no other volunteers, nodded anyway. "Alright, Ms. Vilia. If you'd please join me. First, I'll demonstrate the proper chant and form, then I'd like you to show me your best Fireball. Understood?"

Lesti hesitated before responding. "M-my best Fireball? Are you sure about that?"

"Yes, I'm quite sure." Malkael glared at Lesti. "There's no point in an exercise like this if you don't give it your best shot."

"O-okay. If you say so," Lesti hesitantly replied. Several of the students from her old class, who were nearby, seemed to have overheard the conversation, quickly moving further away. This earned them a perplexed look from Lani until she saw Lesti standing at the front of the class. At which point, she instructed her entire group to give us more space.

"Alright, then. Let's begin." Malkael launched into one of the usual long-winded chants that I had grown accustomed to seeing from mages using image-based magic. Each word and phrase was carefully constructed to help bring a sharp image to mind for the caster. Still, it was so incredibly slow compared to instruction magic that it was practically useless. Lesti could have cast ten fireballs in the same amount of time this chant took.

I carefully watched as the magic got to work around Malkael. It gathered different types of fuel from the air nearby and increased the heat directly in front of his hand. Slowly, a ball of burning gas formed in front of him. When his chant was finished, he sent it flying at the nearby dummy target.

Upon impact, it gave off a rather small explosion, catching parts of the target on fire briefly before fizzling out. Malkael's spell was definitely more powerful than most of the students', showing he had some skill. But I had the feeling he was in for a rude awakening soon.

Turning back to the class, Malkael launched into another lecture. "As you can see, the effectiveness of your magic is directly related to the clarity of your mental image and your understanding of how the spell is accomplished. For a spell such as Fireball, the former is far more important since the steps are so simple." He quickly turned back to Lesti and gestured toward the target. "Now, Ms. Vilia, if you could please give it your best shot."

"Alright, here goes." Lesti turned toward the target and snapped her fingers with her left hand. The gesture caused Malkael to furrow his brow, seemingly unsure of its purpose. Then Lesti raised her hand and, with a single word, cast her spell. "Fireball!"

In an instant, a ball of flame larger than her entire body formed in front of her. However, it didn't stay like that. Almost faster than the eye could see, her spell compressed the fireball down to the size of a basketball and launched it. In a heartbeat, the sphere collided with the target and erupted with such force that it blew the dummy apart. A shockwave rushed across the courtyard, and bits of burning wood flew into the air.

Looking over, I could see Lani rubbing her temples even as she threw a few spells out to deflect the debris. Meanwhile, Malkael stared wide-eyed at the demolished dummy. Even Lesti seemed to have realized she had messed up this time, as she was frozen in place, staring at the chaos she had caused.

That idiot. How many times do I have to tell her to only use experimental spell modifications when we're alone? However, I couldn't be too angry. This was partially my fault, after all. Lesti had been looking to improve the force of her Fireball spell based on the information I had told her. As she experimented with different balances of fuel, oxygen, and heat, I suggested compressing a large amount of everything down into a tighter space.

I wasn't exactly a physicist in my past life, but I knew that compressing all that gas and heat into a smaller area would result in a lot of pressure. In theory, that pressure had to go somewhere when the spell was released, and it looked like I was right. Although, at this point, it would probably be better off named Explosion instead of Fireball.

Even as I mentally kicked myself for not warning Lesti beforehand, the entire academy stared at both her and the now-exploded dummy in silence. A strange tension had filled the air as if the students were unsure of how to react to the destructive force they had just seen. Thankfully, Malkael broke the awkward silence.

"Y-yes, um, thank you, Ms. Vilia. That was certainly an excellent example of Fireball." He smiled awkwardly as he forced the words out of his mouth. "Now, who would like to go next?"

Not a single student volunteered. I couldn't blame them. After all, who would want to follow up on the massive display of power they had just seen? Still, the class had to keep moving forward, and in the end, it was Alex who stepped up. "Instructor Malkael. A suggestion, if I may?"

"Certainly, Mr. Bestroff. Go ahead."

"Since Lesti's magic has completely destroyed the target dummy, it seems like continuing with demonstrations would be difficult." Alex gestured toward the smoldering spot where the dummy used to exist.

"Ah, yes. That's a very good point." Malkael finally recovered from his shock and realized the problem with his plan. "I'll have to prepare a new target."

"Indeed. So, rather than waste our precious practice time, why don't we skip straight to sparring matches for now?" Alex smiled sympathetically at Malkael. "I believe almost everyone in the first class has a strong understanding of the concepts you explained due to your excellent lessons, so there shouldn't be any problems there."

"Ah, y-yes. An excellent idea. Very well," Malkael said, making to ask for volunteers. "Are there any—"

"Hahaha!" Lesti's loud, boisterous laugh cut Malkael off. "So, you're finally ready to face me, Alex?"

Alex let out a heavy sigh. "That's not what I was saying at all. Besides, haven't you caused enough trouble already today? I feel like you should sit this one out."

"Not a chance!" Lesti pointed her finger at Alex and shouted loudly enough for the entire field to hear. "Alexander Bestroff, I challenge you to a sparring match!"

Immediately, a wave of chatter spread through the crowded field. "Hey, someone challenged the Bestroff boy!"

"Alex? Are they crazy?"

"Crazy might be one word for it. It's that redhead who declared she'd take the first spot from him during the test results ceremony."

"Oh, man. I've gotta see this!"

In almost no time, a fervor had spread across the grounds. Lesti stared smugly over at Alex, clearly aware of what she had done. If Alex backed down now, it would look like he was running away. It would also be a huge letdown for all the students excited to see the two of them in action.

Alex glared at her before turning and heading for the center of the field.

"Fine, have it your way. Don't say I didn't warn you, though."

"Beat me first before you say stuff like that." Lesti turned toward Malkael. "Instructor, would you be so kind as to set up the proper protections for our match?"

"Yes, of course." He looked around as if searching for something before his eyes locked onto Lani. "Instructor Lania, I apologize for this, but would you mind assisting me? I believe we will need extra protection in place if those two are going to fight."

"No, please don't apologize. It's the least I can do." Lani, still rubbing her temple, headed for the center of the grounds to help prepare for the sparring match.

When all was said and done, nearly all the instructors decided to help with the preparations. I guess they figured that their classes wouldn't be paying them any attention anyway. Several of them cast spells to erect magical barriers around the area. Meanwhile, others prepared another one I had never heard of called Magic Armor to protect the combatants and Malkael, the judge.

Once everyone was in place and the instructors had finished casting all their spells, Malkael gave a brief rundown of the rules. "Just as in the tournament, the winner will be determined by who can break the Magic Armor spell protecting their opponent first. However, if your opponent surrenders or steps outside of the battle area, you will also be declared the winner."

Malkael turned his gaze to Lesti. "In the tournament, severely injuring or maiming your opponents is against the rules. Any such injuries here will result in consequences for the offender. Do you both understand?" Both Alex and Lesti nodded. "Very well, then. On my signal, you may begin."

Malkael walked back to the edge of the protected area and raised his hand over his head. The crowd grew tense as they waited for him to give the signal to start. Both combatants prepared in their own ways; Alex crouched low, while Lesti stood tall and pointed both hands at him with her feet firmly planted.

Malkael took one last glance at each of them, then swung his arm down.

"Begin!"

"Shattered Earth! Fireball!" To the naked eye, Lesti was the first one to make a move. In a heartbeat, she cast two spells, the first an earth spell that caused spikes to shoot up out of the ground between her and Alex. She knew she had to maintain her distance from him if she had any hope of winning. This spell was clearly meant to slow him down. At the same time, she started her attack with a simple Fireball spell, being sure not to compress it this time.

However, with my vision, I could see the flow of magical energy around Alex, which was why I noticed it. Without uttering a single word, he cast a spell that finished at lightning speed, far faster than any image-based magic possibly could. It was completed even before Lesti's were, and he launched himself at her.

Lesti had thrown quite a few obstacles in his way. Plus, even without compressing it, her fireball was enough to knock out his Magic Armor in one go. However, Alex was prepared. As the fireball closed in on him, he leapt into the air, clearing it with ease and sending himself hurtling toward Lesti with a stern expression on his face.

Lesti, on the other hand, smiled boldly, clearly enjoying the challenge that Alex posed to her. Even presented with her extreme attack power and obstacles to his mobility, he hadn't hesitated for a moment. She quickly raised her hands toward him and fired off another spell. "Air Blast!"

A ball of compressed air flew towards Alex. With no footing, I couldn't see how he would dodge the attack. It seemed unlikely that he knew how to use Air Walk. According to Skell, that was a specialty that Frederick had created. Yet, Alex managed to surprise me.

Without a word, Alex's absurd store of magical energy went to work. Reaching out, it pulled up a large amount of earth from below him, forming a massive wave of dirt and rock. It rose to meet Alex, allowing him to land on top while blocking Lesti's Air Blast at the same time. However, it didn't stop there.

The massive pile of dirt came crashing down toward Lesti, threatening to crush her under its weight. Reacting quickly, she threw up a solid wall of hardened earth between them using Earth Wall. Alex's spell slammed into hers. But due to the loose flowing nature of the earthen wave, Lesti's wall was able to hold as it flowed over and around it.

The entire attack caused a massive cloud of dust and dirt to kick up, preventing the others from seeing. I closed my eyes, quickly switching to my magic sense, and felt my heart drop. Standing behind Lesti as she huddled behind her Earth Wall was Alex. He had ridden the wave past her defenses and was now within striking distance.

Before I could warn Lesti, he was on her. Picking her up by her collar, he pulled his fist back and slammed it into the Magic Armor defending her. With his powerful enhancement magic, the barrier shattered like glass. The match was over before the dust could even clear.

Alex set Lesti back on her feet, and I opened my eyes. The dust finally cleared, and everyone could see that the magical barrier protecting her was gone.

Malkael raised his hand in the air once more. "The winner of this sparring match is Alexander Bestroff. Very well done, both of you. If you both perform at that level in the tournament, you'll do just fine."

Neither were listening to Malkael's praise. The two stared each other down as if probing one another's thoughts. The crowds of students had already started discussing the brief but explosive match. Most of them were unsurprised by the result. After all, Alex was the top-ranking second-year student. A few people from Lesti's previous class seemed to be enjoying her loss, calling her a disappointment.

After a moment, the teachers began breaking up the crowd and returning to their lessons. Alex and Lesti finally broke off their staring contest and walked over to join Malkael. Lesti's brow was furrowed in thought, and her gaze was distant as she reviewed their sparring match in her head. She had said she wanted to face Alex to learn precisely where she stood, and I thought their battle had done just that.

Malkael turned back to the rest of the class. "Now, since we can't continue our demonstrations properly, I'd like to take this opportunity to review the match you all just viewed. Can anyone tell me where they think each of the combatants did well, as well as where they could improve?"

Lesti returned and sat by me, seemingly ignoring the conversation as she worked through the match on her own. Seeing her state, I figured I should follow along so that I could update her on everyone else's thoughts later. Elliot ended up being the first one to speak, immediately attacking Lesti's weaknesses.

"Well, it's pretty obvious that Lesti simply lacked in two areas compared to Alex." He glanced over at her out of the corner of his eye before continuing. "First, the amount of magical energy she has really held her back. Compared to her opponent, the amount of raw power she can dump into her spells is pretty limited. She makes up for it to a degree by being incredibly efficient with the magic she does have. However, in this case, that wasn't enough to overcome the gap between the two."

Elliot then made a fist, staring down at it as he recalled the rest of the fight. "The second problem is that she lacks in close quarters combat. She's forced to maintain her distance because the match is decided as soon as she gets close. Still, I know from experience that a strategy like that won't work." Lesti finally looked up, pulled from her thoughts by what Elliot said. "Alex is just too fast with his body enhancement magic. You'll never hit him at range because it gives him enough time to dodge."

Malkael nodded with a pleased expression on his face. "Excellent analysis Mr. Gambriel. I think you bring up some good points." Turning his gaze toward Lesti, he continued, "Ms. Vilia, what are your thoughts? Is there anything else you think contributed to your defeat?"

Lesti took a deep breath and nodded. "Honestly, I had already expected the first two things to be an issue. That's why I came up with the plan that I did. By messing up the terrain and forcing Alex into the air, I had hoped to take away his mobility while keeping him at range."

The whole class stared at Lesti for a long moment, shocked. I could understand their reactions. Lesti usually came off as such a carefree, happy-go-lucky type that it was surprising that she would come up with a reasonable plan. But if you really knew her, this sort of thing was one of her biggest strengths.

Lesti had very sound reasoning skills. That was why she was so good with magic circles and why she always did so well at researching magic. Coming up with a well-thought-out plan like this was right up her alley. Yet, she had still lost, and we both knew the exact reason why.

"Still, I underestimated him." Lesti furrowed her brow as she looked over at Alex. "The speed he was able to cast his spells at was way faster than I expected. I've never seen anyone cast image-based spells that quickly. In fact, if I didn't know better, I would say you were using instruction-based magic."

"I could say the same thing to you." Alex shot a harsh glare back at Lesti. "The speed of your spells, their efficiency, everything about them screams that you're using instruction-based magic. No, something even beyond that." His accusation hung in the air a moment before he smiled as if it were all a joke. "Still, we both know that's impossible. Only third-year students are allowed to learn that after all."

Lesti forced a smile onto her own face and shrugged her shoulders. "I guess we'll leave it at that, then." However, her expression hardened once more. "But I won't be losing to you in the tournament, so make sure you're ready!"

Her declaration complete, Lesti finally walked away and sat by me. The other students continued their discussion and analysis of the fight. Some gave other tactics Lesti could have tried, but almost none of them seemed realistic. After a while, Lesti's voice echoed in my mind as she used our telepathic connection to communicate with me privately. *"What do you think? There's no way that was image-based magic, right?"*

I groomed myself peacefully as I replied, *"He was definitely lying. The way his magic worked was exactly the same as your magic, if less efficient. That was instruction-based magic."*

"I agree." Lesti wrapped her arms around her knees and buried her head between her legs. *"Still, if that's the case, then where did he learn it?"*

I stared up at the sky, pondering the possibilities. *"Maybe a teacher taught him in secret?"*

"No, I doubt that." Lesti was firm in her denial. *"The headmistress keeps close*

tabs on things around here. A student being taught instruction-based magic by the staff would be pretty dangerous. Especially if it was someone who was already super strong like Alex. She would probably shut them down."

"She didn't stop me from teaching you, though."

Leaning back, she stared up at the clear sky above with me. *"Isn't that just because we discovered a safer way to learn instruction-based magic? I imagine if we were using traditional means, then she would have shut you down."*

I turned my gaze to Alex, who was still listening to the class discussion. "That's a good point, but where do you think he learned it then?"

Lesti stood up and brushed herself off. "Well, I have a few ideas, but I'm not sure at the moment. In the end, it doesn't really matter anyway. What's important is that we know he can use it."

"Yeah, I suppose that's true." I looked over at Lesti. "Still, isn't that going to make it pretty hard for you to win? He's basically neutralized one of your biggest advantages."

"Well, it'll be a pain, but I'll come up with something." Lesti turned and shot me her typical fearless grin. I was filled with the usual sense of pride and happiness I felt when she pushed forward. However, there was also a tinge of anxiety mixed into those emotions.

Lesti was working hard to move forward after we had failed to save the magical beasts Thel'al had enslaved. Yet, at this moment, there was hardly anything I could do for her. All I was capable of was simply watching over her and making sure she didn't overwork herself.

Just as those feelings started to rear their ugly head, Malkael ended the group discussion. "Alright, I think that's enough discussion for today." Looking around at all the students, he smiled softly. "Please come prepared tomorrow for more hands-on training. Class dismissed!"

With that, the students began to go their separate ways. Several of the other classes had ended as well, but a few continued their lectures. It was quite a chaotic scene. Students went every which direction while instructors tried to lecture over the growing noise.

"Rarf!"

Fang ran over to join us, Aurelia hot on his trail. He stopped in front of me, lowered his front half to the ground, and looked up at me eagerly, ready to play. I guess the sparring match and masses of people had gotten him all worked up.

I looked back at Lesti. "Well, it looks like I might be occupied for a while. You didn't need me for anything, did you?"

She smiled wryly. "Nope. I'm just going to go get some dinner with Auri, and then we'll be heading to the usual practice spot. You can meet us there, okay?"

"Sounds good." With a nod, I turned my attention back to Fang. Quick as lightning, I reached out and bopped him gently on the head before dashing off. He gave chase, his tongue flopping out of his mouth as our game of tag began.

Gardens and Letters

I peeked out from my hiding place, looking to see how much time I had. Fang had been chasing me around for some time, and my stamina had finally given out. Using a little misdirection, I had managed to slip away by darting around the corner and using Air Walk to go over the top of the girl's dorm. After that, I climbed a tree, hiding among the branches. I knew it was only a matter of time before Fang came and found me. I could already see him tracking my scent off in the distance.

I looked around the area through the foliage around me. The sun was already starting to drop, even though the sky was still a clear blue color. Students hurried across the grounds as they went about their day. Everything was as ordinary as it could be. The peaceful nature of the scenery and the warm sun peeking through the leaves left me wanting to take a nap.

Just as I was considering that option, I heard the rhythmic sound of dirt being tilled nearby. Gazing between the branches, I spotted a small garden being worked by a young girl I had never seen before. She wasn't dressed in the usual uniform of the academy. Instead, she wore a simple beige tunic and brown trousers with sturdy leather boots. A straw hat topped off the outfit, protecting her face from the sun.

I hadn't noticed a garden behind the dorm when I was summoned to this world in the fall. The girl must have started it on her own once spring had rolled around. There wasn't much growing at the moment as it was still early in the season. Yet, she hummed happily as she tilled the land and prepared it for the first seeds of spring.

I watched as she continued to work the field until the rhythm of her tilling started to lull me to sleep. I closed my eyes as I began to drift off. However, before I could relax entirely, I had to check on where Fang was. The last thing I needed was him sneaking up on me while I was napping. So, I activated my magic sense causing the darkness around me to fill with color.

I extended my senses out in the direction I had last seen Fang and saw his distinctive signature still sniffing around. As far away as he was, his magic was oddly bright, but thanks to that, I could probably get in a short cat nap with no issues. But before I could do that, something else caught my attention. It was the girl and the field that she had been tilling.

On the edge of my senses, I could see that the glow of magic was far more spread out than I would have expected from a single girl. When I turned my attention that way, my jaw nearly fell to the ground. The entire field that the girl had tilled up until this point was aglow with magical energy. This wasn't the tiny glow of simple life, such as bugs and weeds, either. No, this was the glow that I would have expected from a larger creature.

The only problem was that there was no such creature in the area. The glow came from the tilled earth itself. Even more shocking was where it was all coming from. As the girl continued to till the soil, her own magic flowed down through her hoe and into the dirt, infusing it with a golden light.

I stared in awe as I watched the girl infuse her tools and, by proxy, the very earth around her with magic. As simple as breathing, she was doing something that I had been trying to figure out for over a month. Since we had first seen Thela'al's bracelets from the slums, we had been trying to figure out how to infuse objects with magical energy in the same way. I tried to use my vision to figure out how she was doing it, but the girl froze as I started to focus.

Unsure of what was happening, I opened my eyes and found her staring at the base of my tree. Looking down, I saw Fang standing at the bottom, looking up at me with his tail wagging happily. Realizing that my relaxation time was up, I hopped down from the tree using Air Walk. Fang made to chase me but paused, looking confused when I didn't run.

"Sorry, Fang." I rubbed up against him and turned my gaze over toward the mysterious girl. "There's something I need to look into, so playtime is over for now."

With a slight whine, Fang laid down and looked up at me with puppy dog eyes. He had learned to do that from Lesti, since she would pet him or play with him every time he did it. Still, I had to ignore him this time around. I began walking toward the nearby field.

As I drew closer, I was able to see the girl's face for the first time. Bright blue eyes peered out from under her hat, looking at me nervously. She appeared to be even younger than Lesti, albeit slightly taller, probably a first-year student. Poking out from under her hat were strands of light pink hair, cut far shorter than I would have expected for a girl in this world.

I continued to approach with my heart set on asking the girl how she had managed to infuse the ground with magic, but tears started to form in her eyes as I drew near. I paused, unsure of what to do. I had no idea what was bothering her or why she looked so scared.

Taking one more step forward, I called out to her. "Hello. Sorry to bother you, I-"

"..." The girl muttered something under her breath and started shaking slightly.

Suddenly worried about the girl, I decided to ask what was wrong. "A-are you okay? You're shaking rather hard."

This time she managed to sputter out a response that I could hear. "S-stay away from me."

I paused for a moment, considering my options. For some odd reason, this girl seemed really scared of me. But I needed to know her secret, so I took one tiny, cautious step toward her. That appeared to be her breaking point.

"No! Stay away from me!" Dropping her hoe, the girl took off running in the opposite direction at full speed.

"Hey! Wait! I just want to talk!" I tried to call out to her, but before I could stop her, she had disappeared around the corner of the building. Even worse, Fang was giving chase, misinterpreting her fear as playfulness. I let out a heavy sigh as I heard Fang's barking and the girl's screams echo in the distance.

***

A couple of hours later, I finally managed to wear Fang out. So, we both headed back to the unused classroom that Lesti and Aurelia used for our evening study sessions. As for the girl, Fang chased her around until she finally ran into the girls' dorm and locked herself in her room. Even after that, he had stood outside, barking until I scolded him.

Based on her reaction to Fang and me, I concluded she must be scared of animals. There was really no other reason that she would run away from us like that. That was going to make talking to her rather difficult, but I had a plan. If she was scared of me, then I'd just get Lesti to speak to her. It was a good opportunity for her to make a new friend anyway.

Unfortunately, when we entered the classroom, I found Lesti was in an unusually foul mood. She stared out the window with an anxious look on her face that was tinged with anger. It wasn't like her to let something get under her skin like that. Realizing something big must have happened, I went over and jumped up on the desk to join her.

"What's with the scary face?" I brushed against her arm to get her attention as she glared out the window. "Did something happen?"

Suddenly realizing I was there, Lesti blinked rapidly and smiled gently as she reached over to scratch behind my ears. "Oh, Astria. Sorry. I didn't see you come in." She picked up a couple of pieces of parchment off the table. "It's just the contents of these letters has me a little worried. It's nothing big, but…"

As her voice trailed off, the tension returned to her expression. She read the letter once more before letting out a heavy sigh. "I really don't want to deal with that jerk."

"That jerk?" I tilted my head in confusion. "Is the letter from Frederick?"

Lesti let out a little chuckle. "I wish. Frederick may be a bit of a spartan teacher, but he's a good person under all that. No, these letters are from my uncle and Elliot."

"What's so bad about them? You've said before that your uncle is a good man, and Elliot seems like an alright guy himself, so what's the problem?"

"It's not the people sending the letters that are the problem. It's the contents. First, Elliot shows up at dinner and gives me this invitation to celebrate his birthday," she said as she held up one of the letters for me to see.

"Oh, that's not so bad." I felt some of the tension drain from my body. I had thought something awful was going on based on her reaction, but it was just a birthday party.

"Well, that's true, but I hate these sorts of events. I have to get all dressed up in a fancy dress and act all ladylike. It's a giant pain, but I'm somewhat used to it, so I can get through it. Still, the real problem is in the contents of the second letter." Lesti set the previous letter down and picked up the other one. "It's a warning from my uncle. My betrothed will be visiting to check up on me and attend Elliot's party."

All at once, everything clicked into place in my head. Not only was Lesti going to have to attend a stuffy party that ran counter to her nature, but the person she despised most in the world was going to be there.

"I'm guessing there's no way you can get out of going, huh?"

She shook her head. "No. If I skipped, it would be a huge insult to Elliot. Plus, it would probably send Augustine, my betrothed, on a rather nasty tirade. Got any other ideas?"

"Well." My tail swished across the floor as I tried to come up with some way to make this whole thing less miserable for Lesti. Nothing really came to mind. She couldn't skip, and I couldn't think of a good way to keep her fiance away from her. "I think you're just going to have to deal with it. Sorry. Don't worry, though. I'll be there with you, so I doubt this Augustine guy tries any funny business."

Lesti smiled at me. "Yeah. That's true. Although, even if he did try anything, I would just blow him away at this point. He's not much of a mage after all."

"Mm. You could easily beat him, I'd say." Aurelia walked over to join us, having finally given Fang enough attention for him to stop pestering her.

"What about you, Aurelia? Are you going to the party?"

Aurelia grimaced slightly at my question before replying, "I'm not sure."

"What!? You're not going?" Before she could even explain her reasoning, Lesti was looking up at her with a pitiful look. "Come on, Auri! You have to go. It'll be so boring without you!"

Seeing that she looked troubled by Lesti's outburst, I decided to probe deeper. "Is there some reason you don't want to go?"

"Mm. I'd like to go, but I'm worried about my current position. By now, the news that I sold out the smuggling operation will have gotten back to Lord Dawster." She turned to gaze out the window as the last rays of the sun faded into the horizon. "It's likely that one of his sons, or a lesser lord from his territory, will be there. What if they cause a scene?"

Lesti shook her head. "I doubt they'd do something like that in such a public place. It's more likely that they'll just try and revoke your sponsorship here at the school. As far as they know, you're more valuable to them alive. They need you as a bargaining chip with your tribe."

"Yeah, that's true." I nodded in agreement. "If something happened to her, then her entire family would probably fight like they were possessed to drive Dawster's men from the forest."

"But if I lose my sponsorship, you won't be able to train me anymore." Aurelia looked at me, eyes full of worry.

However, without any hesitation, Lesti blew those fears away with a smug grin on her face. "Oh, even if they revoke your sponsorship, you're not going anywhere. After all, I was planning on becoming your sponsor either way."

"My sponsor?!" Aurelia looked at Lesti wide-eyed. "But, how? I'm not a citizen of your territory."

"That's true, but you're not a citizen of the Dawster territory either." Lesti's smile grew more devilish. "In fact, you're not even part of the alliance, technically. So, you're like a foreign exchange student, of sorts."

I tilted my head to the side. "Wait, if what you're saying is true, then does the alliance allow foreign students to enroll in the academy? I thought this place was to train mages to bolster the military. Isn't allowing Aurelia to enter counterproductive to that?"

Lesti nodded. "That's right. Normally, a foreigner would never be allowed to study here, but there is one exception. Students from a foreign territory that have a mutual defense agreement with their sponsor."

"Ah!"

Aurelia and I both shouted at the same time as we realized the meaning behind Lesti's words. As part of the beast smuggling incident, Lesti had gotten Aurelia to agree to work with us. Part of that agreement was that her clan would enter into a mutual defense agreement with her territory. Apparently, the process was already underway behind the scenes, thanks to her uncle. But there was one thing I didn't understand.

"Wait, then how did Lord Dawster get her enrolled here?"

Lesti shrugged. "He lied, of course. According to the headmistress, the school was presented with a copy of the defense treaty. It was supposedly signed by the chief of the Mori clan and the Lord Dawster. I'm guessing they bribed whoever was sent to inspect the claim as well because they confirmed it."

"Of course they did." My tail swished about wildly as I tried to suppress my agitation. "Well, I guess it works out for us in the end, so it's fine."

Lesti nodded in agreement. "Yeah, it should be fine until they realize that the Mori clan has set up an agreement with us. Once word gets around about that, they might try some shady tricks." Standing up, she looked at Aurelia and me with her usual enthusiastic smile. "With that in mind, as well as the upcoming spring tournament, I'd like to speed up our training a bit."

I tilted my head to the side. "What did you have in mind?"

Lesti put both her hands behind her head, looking at me as if the answer should be obvious. "Well, I was thinking that we should start skipping Malkael's special training sessions and hold our own private training sessions instead."

"You want to do what!?" As a former teacher, I was slightly offended that she wanted to skip Malkael's class. At the same time, I kind of understood where she was coming from. Still, I wasn't going to let her off without a proper explanation. "Tell me your reasoning. Depending on the answer, there may be a lecture in store for you."

"Mm. I'm curious too. Why do you want to skip?" Aurelia chimed in with a quick nod.

"Alright. Let me explain." Lesti took a deep breath before continuing. "I honestly think that there's nothing that Malkael can teach us at this point.

You saw his Fireball today, right? I've noticed it before, but I don't think that he can use instruction-based magic."

I kept my gaze firmly fixed on Lesti. "Yeah, I noticed the same thing. It's a bit strange to me. Even Lani seems to be able to use it, and she never trained at the school."

Lesti pointed at me. "Exactly! I talked to Lani about where she had learned it, and it seems that Frederick trained her as part of her being hired here. So, why wasn't the same thing done for Malkael?"

"Isn't that just because Frederick is busy hunting down Thel'al?" Aurelia asked.

"I don't think so. All the teachers here can use instruction-based magic, as far as I can tell. Malkael seems to be the only exception."

"Alright," I decided to cut her off before we got too far off-topic. "So, what does this have to do with you wanting to skip class?"

"Right." Lesti cleared her throat and continued, "The main reason is that Malkael's lessons don't have any value to me. I can't really use image-based magic. Plus, he's mostly teaching the basics, so students will be able to transition to instruction-based magic if they're chosen. Since I'm already using instruction-based magic, there's no point."

"What about Aurelia? You said you wanted her to skip as well, right?"

"Yeah." Lesti nodded and looked over at Aurelia. "I think you should focus on your coordination with Fang as well as the training that Astria has been giving you. Both of those will help keep you safe if Lord Dawster tries anything. Being able to sense magic, even vaguely, should help protect you from surprise attacks. With the element of surprise gone, the two of you should be able to defeat any assassins."

Aurelia looked at Fang for a moment, then shifted her gaze to me. "What do you think, Instructor?"

Closing my eyes for a moment, I considered everything Lesti had said. Once I had come to my decision, I opened my eyes once more. "I agree with Lesti. I think our time would best be spent on our own training." I turned to glare at her. "You're still going to get permission from Malkael, though. It would be rude to just stop showing up to class. Got it?"

"Yes, ma'am."

"Good. With that settled, there's just one more thing that we need to discuss."

Lesti looked at me, seemingly confused. "There's more?"

"Yeah—while I was out running around with Fang today, I saw this girl working a small garden behind the girls' dorm."

"Working a garden?" Lesti furrowed her brow and looked over toward Aurelia. "Was there a garden behind the dorm?"

"Rarf!" Fang looked up at Aurelia as he barked, his tail wagging excitedly. He must have been saying something to her because it took her a minute to reply.

"Well, I wasn't aware of one." Aurelia broke eye contact with Fang and turned to look at us. "Fang says there's a nice girl with short hair who started one a few days ago. She apparently plays tag with him."

I was about to ask when he had played tag with her, then remembered how he had chased her back to her dorm. The silly little pup had mistaken her running away in fear as a game of tag. It would probably be better to let him know, but whenever I looked at his goofy face, he seemed so happy I couldn't bring myself to tell him the truth.

"R-right. Tag." Shaking my whole body to recover my focus, I steered the conversation back towards its original purpose. "Anyway, as this girl was working the garden, I noticed something strange. The land she had tilled was infused with her magical energy, just like the collars and bracelets!"

Lesti suddenly swooped me up in her hands and held me at her eye level. "Are you sure? The magic wasn't dissipating like it did for us?"

"Well, it wasn't perfect, but it was a lot closer than we ever got." My tail flicked through the air as I recalled the girl's magic imbuing the earth around her. "It was dissipating very slowly, but at that rate, it would probably take days to clear out entirely. That and I don't think she was doing it on purpose."

A worried frown started to form on Lesti's face. "You think it was just a fluke?"

I shook my head. "I don't think it was a fluke, but I can't be sure, if I'm honest." I turned my gaze over toward Fang and sent a private message to

Lesti. *"Don't tell Fang this, but I think that girl is scared of animals. When I approached her, she froze up and ran away. Fang chased her all the way back to the dorm screaming in terror. I never got the chance to ask her about it."*

"I see. That's a problem." Lesti furrowed her brow in thought for a moment before her usual cheerful smile returned. "Still, if that's the case, then Auri and I will just have to approach her. We'll go see her tomorrow after classes and ask her about this technique of hers."

"Mm. Count me in," Aurelia nodded with a smile. "Meeting someone who can communicate with nature like that sounds fun."

"Alright, then it's settled." Lesti finally sat me down as she laid out our plans for tomorrow. "First thing tomorrow, we'll ask Malkael about skipping out on his special training classes. Then, we'll start our new training regimen. Finally, when classes finish, we'll go see Astria's mystery girl. Sound good?"

"Mm. No objections here."

"Ruff!"

"Sounds good to me."

"Alright, then let's turn in early tonight. Tomorrow's going to be a big day, after all."

With no objections, everyone started to pack up their stuff. Despite Lesti taking forever to get her things packed, we still left the classroom far earlier than we normally would. I knew that taking a break like this was a good idea every once in a while, but at the same time, I felt restless after not putting in our usual hours. With those conflicting emotions running through my head, I followed the group back to the dorm.

* * *

Later that evening, I lay curled up next to Lesti, enjoying the warmth of her body even as I failed to drift off to sleep. In my head, the fight between Alex and Lesti kept replaying over and over again. Each time, I used my imagination to slightly tweak the battle, but she still lost no matter what I changed. There was a simple wall that I just couldn't see her overcoming, and that was Alex's raw magic output.

The speed and strength of his spells were simply astounding. Having finally seen him in action, I could see why he hadn't been impressed by Lesti's improvements. The efficiency that I had so proudly bragged about over a month ago meant nothing to him. Even if Lesti increased the performance of her spells tenfold, she wouldn't get anywhere near what Alex could accomplish through raw power.

Nevertheless, I couldn't give up on it. I knew there had to be a way, so I started to play the battle over in my mind once more. However, just as I did, I heard Lesti whisper in the darkness, "Astria? You awake?"

Looking over, I could see her staring at the ceiling, wide awake. "Yeah, I'm awake," I said. "Is something wrong?"

"I just can't sleep, is all." She rolled over on her side and looked down at me. After lying like that for a while, she started talking again. "I just keep thinking about Elliot's party."

"That's what you're worried about?" I was surprised. I had expected Lesti to be more worried about her battle with Alex than Elliot's party. After all, she said she didn't care much for formal events like that. Wondering what was going on, I repositioned myself so that I was curled up just under Lesti's chin. "So, what's eating at you? You're not the type to normally worry about something like this."

She snuggled up against me and ran her fingers through my fur. "It's just that I can't figure out why Augustine is coming. He's never shown any interest in me before now. He viewed me as a tool for claiming territory of his own and nothing more. For him to suddenly decide to show up like this, it makes me think he's up to something."

I laid there for a moment, thinking about what Lesti had said. However, I could only come up with one possible reason Augustine would show an interest in her now. "I think it's because you're part of the first class now, right? He's probably worried that someone else is going to swoop in and try and steal you. I can imagine there are more than a few nobles who would be interested after all. I mean, you're second in your class, and marrying you guarantees them some territory."

Lesti's hand froze. "So, that's why, huh? It's pretty frustrating that I couldn't come up with that myself."

"Frustrating?" I glanced up at her, curious as to what she meant.

"Yeah." She began running her fingers through my fur again as she explained. "Even though I plan on defying the will of the council and claiming my parents' territory as my own, I just assumed that others would follow their decisions blindly. I never even considered the possibility that someone else would try and take me as their bride. It just shows how much I've been underestimating my rivals."

Rubbing the top of my head against her chin, I tried to comfort her. "I think that's pretty normal. The council has been the greatest authority in the alliance for your entire life, right? Most people wouldn't be thinking about defying them at such a young age. Especially since your family wasn't particularly influential. It's just a matter of perspective, and yours is just now changing, I think."

"Perspective, huh?"

"Yep. Besides, isn't this a good thing?" I decided to try and lift the solemn mood that had fallen over our conversation by changing the subject a little, "After all, not all the guys who come to marry you will be like that Augustine creep. Maybe one of them will sweep you off your feet, and you won't have to go through all the trouble of defying the council."

Lesti grabbed my ear and tugged on it playfully, replying in a mocking tone, "As if! If anything, my new rank as second in my year just means that the list of people I'm willing to accept has grown even smaller. After all, I can't go handing the future of my people over to someone who isn't at least as great as I am."

"Is that so?" I batted away the hand that was tugging at my ear and looked up at her. "Then, I guess we'll just have to make sure that they all understand how great you are to filter out all the bad apples, huh?"

Lesti looked down at me and smiled. "Yeah. We'll show them all what we're made of. Once we're done, nobody will dare mess with us!"

"That's the spirit." With the strange mood finally gone and my own excess energy burned, I curled up and let sleep start to take hold of me. However, just as I was drifting off, I heard Lesti's faint whisper.

"Thanks, Astria."

A gentle purr rippled through my body in response as I finally drifted off to sleep.

Malkael's Magic

The next morning, we found ourselves in the teacher's quarters, standing before the door to Malkael's room. All four of us had gotten up extra early, and the girls had quickly eaten their breakfast before coming here. The halls were still mostly empty except for a few students and teachers, who were always up this early.

With a deep breath, Lesti reached out and knocked on Malkael's door. "Instructor Malkael. It's Lesti and Aurelia. There's something we wish to discuss with you."

The sound of footsteps echoed from inside, and a moment later, the door swung open. Standing there, staring at us with a perplexed expression, was Malkael. Even though we had shown up unannounced, he was still well put together. His long hair was pulled up into its usual neat ponytail, and he was already dressed, seemingly ready for the day. For a moment, I wondered why he was always showing up to class at the last minute since he seemed so prepared, then I looked past him into the room.

The space behind him was a chaotic mess of scrolls, books, and ink. The desk and bookshelves that lined the walls were overflowing to the point that only a single path existed through the room. Even the bed had scrolls and books tossed on top of it. The chaos was in such hard contrast with Malkael's appearance that it was hard to believe he lived here.

"Wow." Seeing the mess sprawled out behind Malkael, Lesti let out her own sigh of disbelief. "Instructor Malkael, you have so many books."

"W-well, yes. You see…" Malkael began to stutter out an excuse, but before he could, Lesti cut him off.

"It's amazing! Are any of them on magic runes? If they are, can I borrow them?!" With eyes that practically sparkled, she stared at the sea of books and scrolls. Her reaction caught me off guard, causing me to look up at her in shock. Apparently, her sigh hadn't been one of disbelief, but of wonder. Seeing the look on her face, I got the sneaking suspicion that I would have to be careful, or else our room would end up like this in the future.

Malkael also stared at her with a surprised look on his face for a moment before recovering. "N-no. I'm afraid that the contents of my personal collection aren't suitable for second-year students."

Lesti looked at him with a blank stare for a moment before asking another question. "You mean they have to do with instruction-based magic?"

"Yes, that's correct."

At hearing his response, her face lit up, and she took a step forward. "Then it's no problem! I'm sure you noticed in my sparring match with Alex, but I already use instruction-based magic, so it's totally fine. Come on. Please? I've already read through all the books that the library and Lani have on the subject, and it's really slowing down my research."

Malkael took a step back as Lesti continued to press forward, trying to convince him to lend her his books. Seeing that he didn't know how to handle the situation, I decided to step in and save him. I transformed into my tiger form and picked Lesti up by her collar like a kitten. "Knock it off. We didn't come here for this. Besides, no one is supposed to know you can use instruction-based magic, remember?"

Lesti looked back at me with her cheeks puffed out. "Oh, give me a break. There's no way he hasn't figured it out after that sparring match." She turned her attention back to Malkael, who was still in recovery mode. "Right, Instructor?"

Realizing that she wasn't going to let the subject go, he let out a heavy sigh. "It's true. I had my suspicions before based on your magic circle research, but the sparring match pretty much confirmed them." A dark expression came over his face. "Yet, even with all my evidence, the headmistress refuses to act. Just how did you manage to pull that off?"

"Well, that's a secret, but if you let me borrow some of your books, I might give you a hint. Still, it actually works out that you know about it. We want to skip your tournament preparation classes and do our own self-training."

I sat Lesti down, and Malkael gazed at her as if he were trying to see through some sort of facade. "What's your reason for wanting to skip? Do you find my lessons lacking in some way?"

Lesti quickly waved both hands in the air in front of her. "No, no. It's not that your lessons are bad or anything. It's just..." She paused for a moment, trying to choose her words carefully. "You can't use instruction-based magic, can you, Instructor?"

Malkael's eyes went wide at her expression. "How did you know that?"

"Sorry. That would be my fault." I transformed back into my normal form and stepped around Lesti, so I could look Malkael in the eye. "My ability is that I can see the flow of magical energy when people cast spells. Just watching that is enough for me to tell that you use image-based magic."

"I see." Malkael frowned, clearly not happy that his secret was out, and turned back to Lesti. "It's true that I can't use instruction-based magic, so most of what I can teach you won't be applicable in the tournament. Fine, I'll grant you permission. What about you, Ms. Aurelia?"

"Mm. I would like to skip as well." Aurelia turned her gaze to me. "I'm training with Astria to learn a unique skill. I think that's what's best for me."

Malkael brought his hand to his chin as he considered her request. Seeing he wasn't entirely convinced, I decided to give him one last push. "Instructor Malkael, I would like to request that you allow Aurelia to focus on our special training as well. This isn't just important for the tournament, but given her situation, for her future as well."

"Her future." Malkael closed his eyes for a moment before opening them. "Very well. I heard about some of Ms. Aurelia's circumstances from the headmistress after the attack on the academy. If you believe this training will be valuable to her, then I will trust your judgment. However, I do have one condition for both of you."

"Sure. We're asking a lot of you here, so as long as it's not too unreasonable, we can play along." Lesti smiled brightly.

I could only stare at her in disbelief. The way she had agreed to his conditions without even hearing what they were was just plain reckless, even for her. I understood that she probably felt bad for putting Malkael out like this, but still.

Fortunately, Malkael dismissed my worries a moment later. "I'd like you both to show me the results of your training before the tournament. I need to judge if whatever you have learned is safe to use."

"Makes sense to me."

"Mm. I'm fine with that."

The conditions were reasonable, and both girls readily agreed to them without any hesitation. I could only imagine that this resulted from seeing Lesti's compressed Fireball spell out in the field. No doubt Malkael was worried she would come up with some other crazy variation of a spell that could seriously injure someone who wasn't prepared.

"Alright." Lesti pumped her fists excitedly. "Let's go get started right away, then. Thanks for your time, Instructor!"

Lesti turned and started down the hall toward our usual study spot, and the rest of us made to follow her. However, after a few steps, I came to a stop. Something was bothering me, something that I wanted to ask Malkael about. Lesti noticed my hesitation and shot me a questioning glance. "Is something the matter, Astria?"

"No, it's nothing." I turned back toward Malkael, looking at the group over my shoulder. "There's just something I'd like to ask Instructor Malkael. Go on without me. I'll catch up."

"Alright. Try not to take too long, though. Aurelia can only do so much of her training without you." With that quick comment and a wave, Lesti and the others set off down the hall, leaving Malkael and myself alone.

"Well, then." I turned my gaze to Malkael, looking him in the eye. "Why don't we step inside your room, Instructor? I think this is a conversation that's best kept private."

Malkael narrowed his eyes at me as if trying to probe my intentions. "Very well, come in."

Stepping aside, he allowed me to walk past him into the room. I had noticed it slightly before, but the musty smells of ink and paper filled the space, making it feel a bit like a library. Well, if that library had been hit by a tornado anyway. At my size, the entire room almost felt like a labyrinth with books and scrolls stacked all over the place.

I carefully followed the only walking path back through the room and jumped up onto one of the few clear spaces on the bed. Malkael made his way over as well and joined me, sitting in the chair at his desk. Looking at me sitting amongst the piles of books and scrolls hastily tossed on his bed, he seemed to realize just how messy the place was.

"My apologies for the mess. I rarely have guests in my chambers," he said as he fidgeted slightly, almost as if he had the sudden compulsion to clean the place.

I started grooming myself, trying to act as casual as possible. "Not a problem. Although you really should look at cleaning this place up. It'll leave a bad impression on your students."

"I'll keep that in mind. At any rate, what was it you wanted to discuss?"

I stopped my grooming and looked around at the piles and books strewn about the room. "There was something you said that caught my attention. Your books aren't suitable for second-year students because they have to do with instruction-based magic, right?" I turned my gaze back to Malkael so I could see his response. "That doesn't make any sense to me. Why would someone who can't use it have so many books on the subject?"

Malkael averted his gaze, staring down at one of the nearby books. With a distant smile on his face, he reached out and ran his fingers over the cover. "So, you noticed that. The answer isn't anything special, though. I hope to one day be able to use instruction-based magic again."

I felt my ears perk up at his choice of words. "Again? So you're saying that you used to be able to use it, but you can't anymore?"

"That's right. Not since I lost my family." He turned his gaze back to me, a sudden determination in his eyes. "Do you remember the night I found you and your master in that old classroom with that magic circle?"

"Yeah." I thought back to that night. "You mentioned something about the magic she was using being demon worshiper magic, and tried to stop us. What was that about, anyway?"

Malkael nodded. "I've since confirmed this with the headmistress, but your master took those runes from an artifact produced by the archdemon Thel'al, correct?"

"That's right, but I don't see why that makes them evil. They're just a tool and like any tool, whether they're good or bad will depend on how you use them."

"A fair enough opinion. However, I think there are some things that mortal men shouldn't meddle in, and those runes lead directly down that path."

I furrowed my brow at Malkael's declaration. I vaguely remembered that similar debates had been had back in my old world. However, instead of magic, the worry had been that technology would lead to mankind playing god. Still, I hadn't seen anything yet that would lead me to believe such a problem existed in this world, so I decided to press Malkael. "What makes you so certain? I haven't seen anything that makes me believe what you're saying so far."

"I doubt you have. At first glance, the runes seem harmless. After all, they don't allow you to do anything a well-constructed spell written out in long-form couldn't do." Malkael got up and started pacing back and forth in the small space. "You're aware of the ancient runes scattered about our world?"

I shook my head. "No, I'm not."

"I see. Allow me to give a brief explanation, then." Without even realizing it, Malkael had shifted into instructor mode and began giving me a lecture. "Our world is filled with ruins from what many believe was a civilization far more advanced than our own. This theory mostly comes from the many powerful magic artifacts we have recovered from them. Their capabilities far exceed what any mage or nation can currently accomplish, and they're treated as national treasures due to their power."

"Wait, so every country is basically stockpiling superweapons from these ruins?" I felt my fur stand on end a little at the idea. "That sounds like a recipe for disaster."

"Yes. There have certainly been issues with this in the past." Malkael walked over to the wall and tapped on a map he had hanging there. His finger landed on a large nation just to the northwest of the alliance. "In fact, that's how the empire came about. A single small country came to possess enough artifacts that their neighbors couldn't resist them. It wasn't until the alliance was formed that their campaign could be stopped. That's not really important, though. What's important is that I've actually had a chance to inspect some artifacts in the alliance's possession over the years. Can you guess what I found?"

Malkael turned and sifted through the piles of paper on his desk and pulled out two drawings. One was of the staff that the headmistress had used the night the beasts had attacked the academy. Meanwhile, the other was a sketch of the collar we had recovered from Fang and the runes on it. As my eyes flitted between the two, they went wide as I realized what Malkael was getting at.

"These runes, a bunch of them are the same."

Malkael nodded. "That's right. It's not just these two items in particular either." He paused, his face becoming strained as if what he was about to say physically pained him. "Every artifact that I have ever studied has had some of the runes that can be attributed to demons and their followers carved onto them. In particular, the runes for combining smaller processes are quite common."

I felt my tail twitch about as Malkael continued his explanation. There were a few things that weren't adding up to me. "Wait—if the runes are carved onto these artifacts, why aren't they used more commonly in magic?"

Malkael shrugged. "As I'm sure you know, most people consider runes and magic circles to be useless. They require the caster to provide magic energy, which makes them less than ideal for use in combat."

"If that's the case, then why are these artifacts so valued?"

"That's because almost every single one can somehow store magic." He pointed to the picture of the staff. "The crystal here on the top stores an absolutely absurd amount of magical energy, which can then be used to power the artifact and enhance the wielder's spells."

"So, they're just like the artifacts Thel'al made." Thanks to Malkael's explanation and having watched Lesti analyze Fang's collar, I knew why no one was bothering to study the runes on these artifacts. People felt you needed a magic energy source in order for them to be useful, but they couldn't create anything like the crystal. Despite all the research Lesti had done into Thel'al's runes, not a single one of them had been related to storing the magical energy inside the collar. There was some other piece of the puzzle that was missing there.

"Based on your expression, I take it you've realized the issue?" Malkael placed the drawing he was holding on top of a nearby stack of books. "No one has been able to discover the secret to storing magical energy inside an object; without that, these runes are useless. In fact, I find it quite strange that your master is so fascinated with them. It seems like she could find more productive things to do with her time."

Ah, that's right. He doesn't know that you can use magic circles as a stand-in for instruction-magic chants. Of course, it seems like a waste of time to him, but if that's the case...

"Then, let me ask you this, Malkael." I looked him right in the eye as I addressed him. "Why are you studying the artifacts?"

At my question, the pained expression returned to his face, and his tone became self-deprecating. "Maybe it's because I'm a fool who can't let go of the past. You heard my exchange with my brother on the night of the attack, yes?"

"I did." I furrowed my brow as I tried to recall what exactly Ulrich had said. "You said he killed your family, but he claimed you had your own part in that. What exactly did he mean by that?"

"I would advise you don't listen to anything a filthy demon worshiper like my brother says." Malkael's response was calm, but I could feel the rage and anger that were bubbling under the surface as he spoke. "My brother was a talented mage who had graduated near the top of his class here at the academy. He was even selected to be one of the students who learned instruction-based magic, the first in my family's history. My parents were so proud of him, and I was, too.

"Then everything fell apart." Malkael looked down at the drawing of the artifact he had set nearby. "One day, he was hired to join a research expedition to look for artifacts in one of the many ruins scattered about our territory. When he came back, he was a changed man. He had always strived to be the best at his studies before. However, after that expedition, he threw himself into studying everything he could about magic runes. At first, it was fine. Researching magical runes was odd, but there was nothing sinister about it. Then the rumors started."

Malkael paused, his gaze distant as he recalled what seemed to be a rather dark period in his past. "At first, it was nothing but small animals, things like snakes and birds. The maids found their corpses, cut open and disfigured. However, reports soon came in about my brother trying to buy livestock. My parents confronted him on why he needed such things, but when asked, he would only tell them that he needed it for his research. They forbid him from making any such purchases, of course."

"I'm guessing that didn't stop him, though." I felt my own gaze grow stern as I listened to Malkael's story. Based on what he had said so far, I could guess where this was going.

"That's right. When he was forbidden from purchasing them, he simply stole them, took them out into the woods, and performed his heinous experiments there." Malkael began to shake, his knuckles going white as he clenched his fists. "Finally, one day, my parents had had enough. They went to confront him in his lab that he had set up in the cellar. When they didn't return immediately, I began to worry, so I went after them. What I found there was madness."

Malkael gritted his teeth, his eyes wild as he recalled what he had seen. "When I went into the cellar, I found my parents bound and gagged. Meanwhile, my brother was bartering away their lives to a greater demon to form a pact with it. He had constructed some sick, twisted form of the summoning ritual.

"When I saw what he had done, what he had become, I flew into a fury and attacked him and his greater demon. However, the demon was far stronger than I had realized. Only being a third year at the academy at the time, I had barely begun to use instruction-based magic myself." Malkael's voice began to tremble. "I-I knew it was risky, but I had to do it. Otherwise, none of us would have survived, and that thing would have gone free."

He stopped, breathing ragged, eyes hollow. I could tell how much this was tearing him up inside. "Malkael, that's enough. You don't have to tell me if you don't want to."

Malkael's eyes lost their distant look as she stared at me for a long moment. Taking a deep breath, he spoke once more. "No, you need to hear this so that you can protect your master. Keep her from making the same mistake I did. I-I hastily constructed a flame spell using instruction-based magic, one strong enough to destroy the greater demon. However, I made it too strong."

Malkael pulled up the sleeve on his right arm. Up to his elbow, everything was normal. However, past that, his skin was disfigured and scarred, as though it had been burned many years ago. "The spell reduced the greater demon to ash along with my parents. My brother and I were the only survivors. He was able to escape by using the demon as a shield. Meanwhile, I was severely injured by the blowback from the spell."

I stared at Malkael's arm for a long moment, unsure what I should say. But I couldn't sit there all day and say nothing, so I steeled my resolve. "I-I'm sorry. To lose your family in such a manner. That's horrible."

Malkael ran his fingers over his scars. "I was never able to forgive myself for my mistake that night. If I hadn't messed up my spell, my parents wouldn't have died, and my brother wouldn't have escaped. Don't let your master make the same mistake I did, Astria."

It broke my heart to see Malkael blame himself for everything like that. He was nothing more than a child when this had happened. I doubted that facing off against a greater demon was something most people could survive, not to mention defeating the thing. Most likely, if he hadn't taken the gamble that he had, both he and his parents would have died, and the greater demon would have gone free.

Still, I knew that nothing I could say to him at this point would help him. If anything, it would only make him resent me. So, I said the only thing I could. "Don't worry. I'll protect her. After all, that's my job as her familiar."

Malkael closed his eyes and took a deep breath. When he opened them again, his gaze was steady, and a gentle smile played across his lips. "Thank you. I'm sure you'll do an excellent job. Now, if you'll excuse me, I need to prepare for class."

"Yes, of course. I'm sorry for taking up so much of your time, Instructor."

When Malkael didn't move, I made my way to the door and let myself out using magic. I had gotten the answers I wanted. It wasn't that Malkael didn't know how to use instruction-based magic, but rather that his regret stopped him from doing so. With a heavy heart, I closed the door behind me and made my way down the hall to join Lesti, wishing I hadn't let my curiosity get the better of me.

A Lonely Nightmare

A young girl stood in the kitchen, helping her mother prepare dinner. Everything was peaceful in their small home as the family chatted happily about nothing in particular. Yet, for some reason, the girl couldn't shake the anxiety welling up from deep inside her. Perhaps it was because she already knew what came next.

As she struggled to ignore her impending sense of doom, a knock came at the door. Her mother set her knife down and headed over to answer it, mumbling about the late hour. Inside, the girl screamed at her not to answer it, begging and pleading for her not to open the door. However, no matter how much she wished for it, her body wouldn't move. She simply stood there, cutting vegetables.

A few moments later, there was a loud shout and a thud. The girl turned to find her mother knocked to the ground, several dark figures pushing into their home. She tried to flee to her father's side, but they reached her first and pulled her toward the door. She struggled with everything she had to break free, but they forced her outside and began to drag her down the street.

Her father rushed out after her but was quickly grabbed by several of the shadowy figures. Pulling as hard as she could, the girl managed to slip free from her assailant and raced down the street toward her father. Before she could reach him, another large, shadowy figure dashed in front of her, filling her vision.

Unlike the others, this one wasn't human, but some form of beast. Large, piercing yellow eyes that seemed to stare into her soul were accompanied by a mouth full of razor-sharp fangs. Again, she tried to run, tried to fight back, but her body wouldn't move. She could only stand there frozen with fear as those piercing yellow eyes drew closer and closer, filling her vision.

Then, just as suddenly as it had all begun, it ended. Rose jolted awake in a cold sweat, breathing heavily. The first light of dawn peaked in through her window as she stared at the ceiling of her barren room in the girls' dormitory. It took her several minutes to get her emotions under control enough to get out of bed and begin preparing for the day. Even then, the piercing yellow eyes stuck in the back of her head, refusing to fade away.

She let out a heavy sigh as she finished dressing. The nightmare had haunted her for years, but it had grown more frequent recently. If she had to give a reason, it would probably be them. The image of a cheery red-headed girl and her much more mellow friend with unusually green hair flashed through her mind, along with their two familiars. Every day for the previous week, they had tried to approach her, going so far as to chase her around campus.

She had told them she wasn't interested in talking, that she simply wanted to be left alone, but the girl named Lesti had insisted on getting to know her. At first, she had just assumed that they would give up after a few days, but each day the group had become more aggressive, and Rose was beginning to reach her wit's end. The baron had gone to great lengths to ensure she was alone, and she had done everything she could to keep it that way. She had to. Yet, those four were wrecking everything.

As she headed out to the field to do her work for the morning, she swore to herself that she would properly chase them off today. No matter how much they insisted, she was going to get them to leave her alone. She slowly built up her confidence as she circled the dorm, repeating the same thing over and over in her head. *I'll make them give up for sure today.*

Finally, with an emphatic nod, she picked up her gardening hoe with a determined look on her face. But in her determination, she failed to realize one thing. The piercing yellow eyes that so frequently haunted her even after she had awoken from her dreams were nowhere to be seen, replaced by the image of a cheerful girl with fiery red hair and bright green eyes.

***

Later that afternoon, Rose once again headed out to her little garden behind the girls' dorm. But this time, she was constantly glancing around, keeping an eye out for any signs of the second-year girls and their familiars. A few other nearby students looked at her with perplexed expressions, but she hardly noticed them with how focused she was. To her surprise, she managed to make it to the garden without ever spotting said second-years.

That's unusual. Normally, they come running over the moment classes end. It really is such a pain. The pair of girls were rather famous. Not only were they both near the top of their year, but they both had familiars, despite only being second years. Having them run up and try to talk to her in front of so many other students drew a lot of unwanted attention.

As she picked up her garden hoe, she scanned the area one last time. All around her, students moved about in small groups, chatting with each other, laughing, and talking about the tournament preparation classes. For a long moment, Rose just stood there watching them, emotions that she had long forgotten beginning to well up within her.

Since starting at the academy, she had accepted she wouldn't be a typical student. The baron had only enrolled her here in the hopes she would be able to use the academy's resources and knowledge to figure out how to use her ability better. Nothing else mattered to him—not her classes, nor her relationships with her fellow students. Until now, she had been fine with that, going so far as to start this garden and sacrificing the time she could be spending studying or making friends to instead try and learn just a bit more about her ability.

It wasn't that she didn't feel lonely or that she didn't want to study magic. Rather, it was that she knew there was no point in trying. She had to follow the baron's orders, or she would lose everything. Knowing that, she had taken her true feelings and pushed them deep down inside her, locking them away.

Yet as she stood there watching her fellow students, she felt the pangs of loneliness surfacing, forcing themselves out of the prison she had locked them in. Shaking her head to try and ward off the feelings she couldn't acknowledge, she took her hoe and began to till the field. With each swing, she slammed the tool into the ground with far more force than necessary, desperate to shake off the emotions continuing to plague her.

Eventually, she managed to push her feelings back inside their prison. But as she continued to work, she found herself occasionally glancing up, looking for any sign of the group. The sun drifted lower and lower in the sky as more time passed, but no matter how often she looked for them, they were never there.

"I guess they finally gave up. Looks like I won't have to chase them off myself," Rose muttered to herself. Rather than feeling relieved, the same emotions that she had been pushing down before came floating to the surface once more. This time, they overwhelmed her.

"I guess nothing's going to change after all." As the words left her mouth, an intense sense of despair swept over her, threatening to completely crush her spirit. Her limbs suddenly felt heavy, and the world around her seemed far darker than before. Then, just as it felt like that despair would swallow her up entirely, she heard hushed voices from nearby.

Rose's head snapped up, and she scanned the area looking for the source. Then she saw it—the briefest flash of bright red hair and green eyes ducked behind the corner of the dorm as she looked in that direction. Suddenly, the heaviness left her limbs, and the world grew just a bit brighter.

Rose

After parting ways with Malkael, I met up with the others and tried to help Aurelia with her training. But my mind wasn't in the right state after hearing his story, and I couldn't focus. After about an hour, Lesti got mad at me and suggested that we go outside so Aurelia and Fang could do some combat training.

We went over to the training grounds since they would be empty until the afternoon. Lesti read one of the tomes she had borrowed from the library while I watched Aurelia and Fang, letting my mind wander. Despite my messed up mental state, I still observed quite a bit of their training.

It seemed like the focus was to help Fang learn how to move around Aurelia as they fought without tripping her up. The technique reminded me of shadowboxing. Aurelia exchanged blows with an invisible enemy, her daggers flitting through the air with impressive agility. Meanwhile, she used her mental connection with Fang to direct him on how to move.

The pup had taken to it almost instantly, darting around her, growling and snapping at the invisible target they fought. The way they moved about the field together was almost like an intricate dance. One mistake and they would be stumbling over each other. Yet that never happened, which was impressive to see, since learning this kind of coordination usually took years to develop.

The pair were just finishing up their latest mock battle when a familiar voice called out to Lesti and me from behind. "That's some impressive coordination those two have going on, huh?" Turning, I found Elliot approaching us with a wooden spear on his shoulder. He watched the pair, and they continued to flit about the training ground. "Still, don't you think you two should be helping them out? This sort of training will only get them so far when it comes to a real battle."

Lesti pulled her nose out of her book and turned to face Elliot. "Astria isn't feeling well, and I'm not much help when it comes to combat training, so this is all they can do for now. Anyway, what brings you here, Elliot? Skipping lunch?"

"Yeah, I thought I would come get some practice in. Your fight with Alex yesterday has me all worked up." Elliot narrowed his eyes as he recalled yesterday's battle. "I knew his enhancement magic was strong from our previous fights, but I'd never seen him use magic like that Earth Wave spell before. Made me feel like he had been holding back on me, you know?"

"I doubt that's the case. He probably just thought that melee combat was the best way to beat you." Lesti shrugged her shoulders. "He doesn't seem like the type to hold back on anyone, after all."

Elliot, rather than being encouraged, slumped his shoulders. "Yeah. That's true. Still, that just means he can beat me at my own specialty and doesn't need anything else." His disappointment didn't last long. He quickly recovered, shooting Lesti a teasing grin. "I guess it's still better than getting trounced like you did, huh?"

Lesti snapped her book shut and stood. Wheeling around, she glared up at Elliot, who was quite a bit taller than her. "He didn't trounce me! I just underestimated him a little bit. Next time, I'm going to win, just you wait!"

"Oh, and how are you going to do that?" Elliot crossed his arms as he looked down at her. "You're terrible at melee combat, and your magic isn't good enough to hold him at bay."

"I know all that!" Lesti took a swing at Elliot with the book in her hand. He easily stepped back, avoiding the blow. "I'm doing all the research I can to come up with countermeasures, but it's hard. He just has so much magical energy that it's absurd."

The teasing look fell off of Elliot's face, and he stared at Lesti as she continued to fume. "Wait, you're serious? You haven't come up with any ideas?"

"What's that supposed to mean?" Lesti took another swing with the book, but this time Elliot caught it with his free hand instead of dodging. "It's only been a day, you know!"

"Isn't the answer obvious, though?" Elliot continued to stare at Lesti as though she were missing the point entirely. "The best way for you to be able to beat him is to get better at melee combat."

Lesti's face formed a scowl so fierce it might have made Fang whimper. "That's absurd! I'll never get anywhere as strong as Alex by the tournament. Why would I waste my time on that?"

"Actually, I think it's a good idea." I looked up at Lesti, who was now staring at me dumbfounded. "It's not like you have to be as good as Alex at melee combat. You don't need to learn how to use a sword or anything like that either. All that you need to do is be able to avoid getting defeated long enough to regain your distance, right, Elliot?"

I turned and looked at Elliot, who nodded at me with a smile. "As expected, you catch on quick. She's right." He turned his gaze back to Lesti, his expression growing serious once more. "You need to focus on learning and perfecting spells that you can use in close range combat. When I heard that you were skipping class, I thought that must be what you were doing, but here I find out that you're just wasting time shoving your nose in a book. I'm a bit upset that I lost my number two spot to you."

"Oh, is that so?" Lesti took a step back and pointed her finger at Elliot. "You act all high and mighty, but you've never beaten Alex either, have you?"

"Alright, you've got me there." Elliot held his hands up in defeat. "Anyway, that's actually what I wanted to talk to you both about. I was thinking about skipping Malkael's classes as well and having Astria train me instead." He turned his gaze to me. "What do you say?"

I cocked my head to the side. "Why me? I'm no combat expert, you know."

"Well, I heard from Aurelia the other day that she was doing special training with you." He scratched the back of his head and looked over at the pair still going through their training routine. "So, I thought you might be able to do something like that for me. You know, teach me some secret skill that would let me get an edge on him."

I sat, pondering the idea for a moment. I was only able to give Aurelia special training because of how unique her magic flow was. On the other hand, Elliot was perfectly normal, so I didn't have anything to work off of. In fact, I would usually have dismissed his request on the spot, but I thought he might be able to help me with Lesti's combat training.

"Alright, I'll do it, but there are two conditions. First, I don't have anything I can train you on just yet. So, you'll have to wait until I can figure something out."

Elliot nodded. "That seems reasonable enough. I kind of sprung this on you after all. What's the second condition?"

My tail flicked about wildly. "You have to help all of us with our combat training until it's time for the tournament."

"All of you?!" He stared at me, mouth agape. Clearly, he hadn't expected me to ask for him to train all four of us. "When am I going to have time for my own training then?"

I shrugged. "We'll figure out the details later. It's not as though we'll be doing combat training all the time, anyway. Lesti has her research, and Aurelia has her special training with me, so I'm sure you'll have time."

"Alright." Elliot let out a heavy sigh. "I still think you're asking for a bit much, but you've got yourself a deal."

"Great. Then, we'll start tomorrow, after you get permission to skip class from Malkael."

"Sounds good."

"Looking forward to working with you, Elliot." Lesti smiled up at him with her usual bright cheer. Despite her complaints, she seemed rather excited about having someone to teach her close-quarters combat. It was good to see her smiling again. Between my sour mood and her frustration at not finding any leads on beating Alex, she had been grumpy all morning.

With everything settled, Elliot decided to go and get some lunch after all. It seemed our negotiations had made him hungry. Meanwhile, Aurelia and Fang finished their combat training, so we decided to grab some food and head to our usual study spot. Thankfully, the dark cloud that had been looming over me was finally gone. I didn't have time to worry about that now that I had two students to train.

***

"There she is." I peeked around the corner of the girls' dorm along with Lesti, Aurelia, and Fang. It had been a week since we had initially made our plans to contact the pink-haired girl, and nothing had gone to plan. At first, Lesti had tried approaching her normally, but she had quickly brushed us off and made her escape. After that, Lesti had gotten more and more aggressive in trying to chase her down.

However, that seemed to have the opposite effect as she had just tried even harder to get us to leave her alone. So, today, we were going with a different plan. I had told Lesti and Aurelia that the girl appeared to be afraid of Fang and me. She also seemed to be very sensitive about what her classmates thought of her, always getting flustered whenever we tried talking to her in front of them. Based on that, Lesti and Aurelia were going to approach her without us here at her garden and see if that made any difference.

"I-is she really infusing the earth with magical energy?" Lesti watched the girl with a skeptical look on her face. "It looks like she's just gardening like any normal person would."

I closed my eyes and checked once more to make sure last time hadn't been a fluke. "Yeah. I can still see her magic flowing into the ground, just like last time."

"Alright." Lesti looked over at Aurelia. "It looks like we're up, then. Let's go, Auri."

Aurelia gave her a quick nod before looking down at Fang with a stern expression. "Mm. Fang, you stay with Astria and guard her, okay?"

The pup laid down and looked up at her with big, sad eyes, but she simply ignored him. Lesti was the only one that trick would work on. Seeing that he wasn't going to get his way, he let out a slight whimper. But even though he was being a brat about it, Fang never once made to move from my side as the pair walked toward the girl.

As they approached, she looked up from her work, eyeing them cautiously.

Lesti waved at the girl with her usual bright cheerfulness and called out to her. Unfortunately, I couldn't hear what they were saying at that distance, but it wasn't like I was unprepared. I had thought that this exact problem might come up and had a plan.

"Come on, Fang. We're going to get closer."

Hearing that we weren't going to be stuck watching from afar, Fang's tail started wagging wildly. He just looked at me, confused, however, when I walked off in the opposite direction. Even so, his master had told him to stay with me, so he did just that.

Walking around to the front of the building, I quickly transformed into my tiger form and picked Fang up by his scruff, causing him to let out a startled yip. I felt a little bad for surprising him, but time was of the essence. Every second we wasted here was a second where we couldn't hear their conversation.

With Fang secured, I leapt onto the roof of the building and set him down before transforming back into my usual form. "Alright, let's-"

I started to head toward the peak of the roof but suddenly found myself being crowded by Fang. I looked back at him, getting ready to scold him, only to find him shaking like a leaf as he glanced nervously down at the ground. "Wait, are you scared of heights?"

The only response I got was a slight whimper and Fang scooting even closer to me. "I'm sorry, but we can't turn back now." I felt bad for the little guy, but getting over this fear would be good for him in the long run. You never knew where a fight could break out, after all. "Just stay close to me and don't look down. It'll be fine, I promise."

While he clearly wasn't happy about it, Fang gave a quick nod. I turned and made my way up to the peak of the roof. Looking over, I could see Aurelia and Lesti talking to the girl below, but I still couldn't hear them. So, I flattened my body out and crawled on my belly as quietly as I could down toward them. Fang, seeing what I was doing, followed suit. As we slowly made our way down the slope of the roof, the girls' conversation started to become clearer.

"So, you're a first-year, Rose?"

"Y-yes, that's right, Ms. Vilia."

"Oh, just call me Lesti. Ms. Vilia is way too stiff."

"Oh, no. I could never…"

Due to how close they were standing to the building and how low I was keeping myself, I couldn't see the girls, but at least I could hear their conversation. I decided this was close enough. However, as soon as I relaxed, I realized that something was wrong. Fang, who had been sticking to me like glue, wasn't behind me. Turning, I found him frozen in place about halfway up the slope with shaky legs.

"Fang, what are you doing? Come on, it's okay." Seeing how stressed he was, I tried my best to calm the pup down. "You can do it. Just make your way down toward me. One step at a time."

Fang let out a little whimper as he shuffled back and forth, seemingly unsure where to place his feet. Then, finally coaxed forward by my encouragement, he took a hesitant step forward, followed by another. "That's it. Good boy. See? You can do it."

Growing bolder, he began to take larger strides. Then, it all went wrong as his foot slipped, and he tumbled down the roof toward me. I had twisted my own body into an awkward position to try and help Fang while keeping my own balance, leaving me unable to react properly. A ball of fluff plowed into me, sending us both flying over the edge of the roof toward the ground below.

The drop wasn't lethal, but it could result in broken bones, so I tried my best to break our fall. Grabbing hold of Fang's body and pulling him close, I cast Air Blast. Rather than shooting the air toward the ground, I reversed the direction by specifying Fang as the target. I also adjusted the power, reducing it to just be enough to slow us down.

Just before we hit the ground, the blast of air exploded upward, sending dirt and dust flying everywhere. It collided with Fang and me as we fell from above and killed most of our momentum, causing us to land gently in the small garden with a little puff of dirt. I immediately checked Fang to make sure he was okay, and thankfully he was just fine, if a little shaken. The garden we had landed in wasn't quite as lucky.

The earth was loose from being tilled recently, and my spell had contained enough force that it had blown the soil everywhere, undoing much of Rose's hard work. The girls were standing right by where we had fallen covered in dirt, staring at us with confused looks. Lesti's confused look turned to one of exasperation as soon as she realized it was Fang and me that had crash-landed in the garden. Meanwhile, Rose let out a squeak and hid behind Aurelia, who seemed unsure of what to do with the younger girl clinging to her.

"Astria, just what are you doing?" Lesti motioned to the garden around her. "You were supposed to wait for us back at the corner, so why are you crashing down from the sky and ruining Rose's garden?"

"A-Astria?" Rose peeked out from behind Aurelia to look at Fang and me. "Oh, it's just your familiars?"

Oddly, she seemed to be a little relieved upon seeing that it was us. Then again, I guess I would have been worried too if something had just come crashing down on me from above without warning.

"Ah, yeah. I'm really sorry they messed up your garden, Rose. I promise we'll help you get it put back in order."

"Mm. Yeah." Aurelia looked over at Fang and me with the commanding presence she usually reserved for Fang's training. "Isn't that right, you two?"

"Y-yes, of course." I swallowed at the sheer weight of Aurelia's presence. It was the first time she had ever used that tone with me, and it was surprisingly effective, despite me being a former human. "I'm really sorry about this. We just didn't want to scare you, so we tried to stay out of sight, but we couldn't hear. So, I figured if we got up on the roof, then it wouldn't be a problem, you know?"

Rose stared at me from behind Aurelia for a long moment, her eyes wide. "She really can talk. That's amazing."

Her reaction was one that I had gotten quite a bit since I had arrived in this world. It was odd to be called amazing just for having the ability to talk. Thankfully, it seemed like that might prove to be useful in this case. Apparently, hearing me talk had caused Rose to become slightly less fearful of me—though that also seemed rather odd.

"Yes. Allow me to introduce myself. I'm Astria, Lesti's familiar." I raised my paw as if waving at her, quickly lowering it again as soon as I realized how awkward it felt. "Anyway, I'm really sorry about your garden. I promise I'll help you fix it, but I'm curious. Why did you run away from me the other day when I tried to talk to you?"

"Well, that's because…" She looked over at me, but as soon as her eyes met mine, she winced and turned her gaze away. "I'm sorry. It's just a bit much for me."

"No, it's alright. I'm sorry. I made you uncomfortable." Seeing just how much she struggled to maintain eye contact with me, I decided to drop the subject. "I hope that you can learn to trust me in due time, but for now, let's get this mess cleaned up."

We spent the rest of the afternoon getting the garden back in order. Honestly, it wouldn't have taken that long, but Lesti refused to let us use magic. She reasoned that if Rose did all of the work without magic, then using magic to fix it wouldn't be fair. I couldn't say that I agreed with her logic there, but I didn't complain. After all, it was the perfect chance to observe Rose's ability up close.

In the end, she never ended up using that ability. No matter how often I checked, no magic flowed into the earth that she worked. I considered the possibility that she was hiding it from us but quickly realized that that didn't make sense. She didn't know that I could see magical energy, and had no reason to hide it from us. It seemed far more likely that she was just nervous being around Fang and me. The entire time we were working, she intentionally kept her distance and barely let us out of her sight, glancing over every few minutes.

We finished up our work just as the sun was beginning to set on the horizon, casting a warm orange glow across the garden. Lesti invited Rose to join us for dinner, but she declined, saying she was tired. So, the group decided to grab some food from the dining hall and then head to our usual classroom for evening training.

* * *

"Found you!" Elliot's voice rang out from the doorway as he stood there, grinning at us like he had won some sort of game. It was later that evening, and we had all just begun our personal training sessions. I was working with Aurelia on sensing her magical energy. Meanwhile, Lesti was pouring over her books and scrolls, studying magical runes, and Fang was doing what Aurelia called tracking training.

She had spread some hidden objects around the room with a particular scent on them, along with some treats. Fang was supposed to use that scent to find them. So, he was currently wandering around the room with his nose to the ground, sniffing about. He didn't even react when Elliot walked into the room, other than to briefly glance up at him. Honestly, the power of treats was terrifying.

"Elliot, what are you doing here?" Lesti asked, looking up from her book.

"I went to ask Malkael for his permission to join your training session, and while I was there, he mentioned that you usually trained in this unused classroom late into the night." Elliot paused to look at us skeptically, "Although, besides Lesti, it doesn't look like the rest of you are doing any real training."

I glared at him, my tail swishing back and forth in irritation. "Just because we're not bashing each other's heads in doesn't mean we're not training."

He shrugged. "That's true, I suppose. Anyway, did you give any thought to what special training I could do?"

I shook my head. "Sorry. I haven't had time. We spent all afternoon helping a first-year named Rose fix up her garden."

"Rose?" Elliot's brow furrowed, "You mean the first year with pink hair? That Rose?"

"Yeah. That's the one," I replied, cocking my head to the side. "Do you know her or something?"

"You could say that. She's sponsored by one of the lesser nobles in my father's territory. He apparently discovered her when he made an order at her family's apothecary business." Elliot furrowed his brow. "Says she has a hidden talent or something. Though he won't tell us what it is."

Hidden talent? Could they be talking about her ability to infuse things with magical energy? If that's the case then it would mean that they have some way to see magic, like me. Still, I shouldn't jump to conclusions. The ability they're talking about could be something else.

"A lesser noble is hiding something like that from your father?" Lesti looked at Elliot with a puzzled expression on her face. "What's Lord Gambriel thinking, allowing such a thing?"

Elliot shrugged his shoulders, "At the time, we had more important things to worry about. The last intrusion by the kingdom took a pretty heavy toll on our territory. My father was still dealing with the political fallout." He paused for a moment, his expression growing more serious. "Still, a word of warning. Be careful about getting too involved with that girl. Something about her situation doesn't feel right."

"Sorry, but that's not going to happen." Lesti smiled fearlessly back at him. "I've taken quite an interest in her myself."

"Haha. I figured you would say that. Still, don't say that I didn't warn you." Elliot turned his gaze to me. "At any rate, if you don't have any training figured out for me, can I just join in whatever Aurelia is doing for now?"

"I'm not sure if it'll do you any good. Even Aurelia hasn't made any major progress on it yet, but I don't mind." I looked over at Aurelia, who was still sitting on the floor. "Do you mind?"

"Mmm. It's fine." She stood and brushed herself off, looking around the room. "I just need to check on Fang first. Give me a second."

"Sure, I'll fill Elliot in on what we're doing in the meantime." I shifted my attention back to the young man as Aurelia went to the back of the classroom looking for Fang. I started to explain my own power, as well as what I was having Aurelia do. But just as I was getting into it, a shout came from the back of the classroom.

"Fang?! What's wrong?"

I turned and saw Aurelia pick up Fang from the ground. Even from here, I could tell his breathing was labored and his eyes were screwed shut as if he were in intense pain. Everyone quickly abandoned what we were doing and rushed over to check on the situation.

I was the first to arrive, leaping onto the desk nearby. "Aurelia, what's wrong? What happened to Fang?"

"I don't know. When I found him, he was just lying on the floor like this. He's burning up."

I stepped closer and brushed up against the pup. Just like she had said, it felt like he had an extreme fever. Still, what could have happened while we weren't watching? Just a few minutes ago, he had been happily doing his training like nothing was wrong.

"At any rate, we're not going to figure anything out while standing around here. We should take him to the infirmary." While the rest of us were trying to figure out what had happened, Elliot made a sound suggestion. "I'll go and find the headmistress. The usual staff members aren't here this late, but I'm sure she can find someone to help."

Lesti took a deep breath to calm herself and nodded. "That's a good idea. We'll meet you there. In the meantime, we'll see if we can figure out what's happening."

With a plan decided on, we all rushed out of the room, trying our best to suppress our fears.

Fever and Progress

Aurelia sat on a bed in the infirmary, dipping a rag into a basin of water that Lesti had filled with magic. We still had no idea what was happening with Fang, so we were trying our best to cool him off. Lesti and I were discussing ideas, but neither of us knew enough about familiars to guess at what was happening. I was kicking myself for not asking Skell more questions when I had the chance.

Just as I was thinking about the massive black dragon, Elliot burst into the room with the headmistress hot on his heels. "I've brought Headmistress Rena with me. How's he doing?"

Aurelia looked up at the headmistress, panic written on her face. "We've managed to cool him down a bit, but he still isn't responding to anything I say."

"May I see him?" The headmistress stepped around Elliot. Aurelia nodded and moved aside so that she could reach Fang, who was lying on the bed. Reaching out, she gently placed the back of her hand on his forehead. "Strange."

"Do you have any idea what's wrong with him?" Lesti hesitantly asked as the headmistress stared at Fang with a furrowed brow. "I wish I could say that I did, but I've never seen anything like this before. Still, I think we can eliminate normal illness."

"What makes you say that?" I asked from my spot at the end of the bed.

"In all my years, I've never once heard of a familiar getting sick." The headmistress looked over at me, meeting my gaze squarely. "No one is sure why, but it seems like you're all resistant to disease for some reason. I can't rule out the possibility entirely, but I think it's the last thing we should look at. Have you checked his magical energy flow, Astria?"

"No, I haven't, but why?"

"It's just a theory, but this might have something to do with him absorbing Thel'al's magic." The headmistress reached over and gently stroked the purple fur on Fang's flank. "According to what you've told me, an elemental hound would normally absorb its magic from nature. If that's the case, then our friend here is quite different, and we don't know how that might be affecting him."

She was right. My tail twitched about in agitation as I berated myself mentally for not considering that possibility. I had been so caught up in the idea that Fang must be sick that I hadn't considered that magic might be the cause. Still, now wasn't the time to be getting down on myself. Setting my irritation aside, I closed my eyes and let the world of magic expand around me.

I could see the others' magical energy flowing through their bodies and dissipating into the air around us, but one member of our group stood out far more than the others. Fang's little body was filled to the brim with magical energy, and he was generating more at an accelerated rate. In a way, it reminded me of Alex.

However, there was one massive difference between the two. Alex's magic dissipated far more quickly than Fang's. That's what always gave him that overwhelming aura. On the other hand, Fang didn't seem to release his magic nearly as fast as he could produce it. He was like a magical balloon in danger of bursting, the energy inside him roiling about as it searched for release.

Opening my eyes, I found the others staring at me anxiously. "It looks like Fang has somehow started to produce more magical energy than he can release naturally. Since he doesn't know how to use his magic yet, he can't drain it on his own." I turned my gaze to Aurelia. "As his master, you're going to have to drain the magic from him and use it to cast a spell."

Aurelia nodded with a determined look on her face. "Okay. Just tell me what to do, and I'll do it."

I paused for a moment before looking over at Lesti. "Well, actually. I don't know how to do it either, do you?"

Lesti shook her head briefly before turning her gaze toward the headmistress. "I'm not sure how it works either. I've never had a reason to use Astria's energy before, so I never learned how."

"I suppose that makes sense. This is normally something that you wouldn't be taught until you're third years, so I guess I'll explain." The headmistress took a deep breath and straightened her posture before beginning her lecture. "You'll have to forgive me if I'm a bit rusty. I haven't given a lecture in nearly a decade."

"First, we don't fully understand how drawing the magical energy from a familiar works." She gestured toward me. "Although, after learning about Astria's ability to sense magical energy, I suspect that it requires a lower-level version of that."

"You mean, you have to be able to sense magical energy to draw it out from your familiar?" I asked.

"Correct. However, most students can't do that. Actively sensing and manipulating your own magical energy is a skill that has to be built up over many, many years. Only someone like you who can see and feel magical energy could master it so quickly."

"Wait, so what are we supposed to do then?" Lesti practically jumped out of her seat. "We don't have years for Auri to learn how to do this. She has to do it now!"

"Calm yourself, Ms. Vilia." The headmistress held up her hand, signaling for Lesti to stop her rant. "There is a shortcut that we use to bypass this limitation and allow anyone to use their familiar's energy. It's rather simple, too. Although it comes with its own set of limitations."

Aurelia continued to stare straight at the headmistress, clearly growing impatient. "It doesn't matter. As long as it'll save Fang, I don't care if it's limited."

"Right, I suppose we are short on time, so let me get to the point. All you need to do is use an image-based spell and include a visual of the power for the spell coming from Fang instead of you."

A long moment of silence stretched out after the headmistress's statement until I finally broke it. "Wait, that's all?"

"Yes. That's it. Simple, isn't it?"

"It's super simple, so why didn't you just tell us that in the first place?!" I stared at the headmistress, dumbfounded. Fang was lying on the bed in critical condition, and we had no idea how much time we had to save him. Yet, here she was, giving us a bunch of information we didn't need. What was she thinking?

"Now, calm down. I didn't tell you all of that for nothing." She turned her gaze back to Aurelia, her expression growing serious. "Aurelia, when you cast your spell, I want you to remember what I told you about sensing and manipulating magical energy. The more you understand the principles behind the magic you're trying to cast, the better you can communicate that in your vision. Make sure to clearly show what you want to be accomplished and how you want it done in your mind's eye."

Aurelia gave a quick nod before turning around to face Fang. "Mm. I'll try my best."

With one last deep breath, she closed her eyes and I saw her magical energy begin to take shape—but instead of forming her spell, it reached out towards Fang. The tendrils of golden light reached out and gently made contact with him. When they did, his magical energy exploded into life, and Aurelia began her chant.

"Oh, spirits of the forest, offer me your power, so I might hunt my enemies unseen. Blind my foes with your gentle embrace. Secret Mist!"

As her brief chant ended, more and more of Fang's magical energy poured out of his body, reaching about the room and even beyond. Not only was the reach impressive, but so was the speed at which the spell was completed. If I hadn't seen this before, I might have panicked based on the massive amount of magic dumped into it. However, I knew this spell was harmless as long as you didn't try to run around inside its effect.

The spell finished casting a moment later. A massive wave of fog exploded out from where Aurelia was standing, filling the room and the hallway beyond. Lesti and Elliot let out surprised yells while the headmistress warned them not to move. Meanwhile, I closed my eyes and got to work inspecting Fang.

Thankfully, it looked like Aurelia's spell had done the trick. The amount of magical energy inside his body had been significantly reduced, though there was still quite a bit left. With some of it gone now, I could easily see just how much magical energy he was generating. It was nearly on par with what Alex produced. Even so, it wasn't so bad that he'd have to have it continuously drained. As long as he used some spells regularly or Aurelia used his excess magical energy for him, he'd be fine.

What I was nervous about was his physical condition. His fever had been extremely high. I could only hope that it hadn't caused any lasting damage. Despite the fog still obscuring the room, I used my magic sense to carefully edge my way across the bed toward Fang. Meanwhile, I could see Aurelia, who had been standing the closest to him, reach out and run her hand across his flank.

Her movements were surprisingly smooth despite the fog. She might have been close enough to see Fang through it, or perhaps she had simply reached out to where he had been before. Either way, I decided to check with her and see how he was doing, rather than interrupt. "Has his fever gone down?"

"Mm. His breathing is more relaxed too. With some rest, I think he should be fine."

From within the fog, I heard a sigh of relief followed by Lesti's voice. "That's great news, but can you do something about this fog, Auri? I can't see a thing."

"Oh, right. Sorry."

I felt Aurelia's magic begin to gather and pull energy from Fang's body once again. Watching it the second time, I began to realize some of the flaws that the headmistress had mentioned. Mainly, you wouldn't be able to use this technique if you were low on magical energy yourself. Since you were essentially casting a spell to tap into your familiar's magic, it required some power to fuel it until the connection was established. If you didn't have enough magical energy left for that, then you'd be out of luck.

Soon, her spell finished, and a gentle wind began to slowly guide the fog out of the building. After a few moments, the room was clear except for the lingering dampness that seemed to cling to everything. Lesti and the others, finally free to move around without worrying about running into each other, came over to check on Fang.

The pup's breathing had returned to normal, just as Aurelia had said. Seeing him sleeping peacefully, I felt all of the tension drain from my body as the fear and anxiety that had been weighing me down were lifted. "Thank goodness he's alright. That nearly gave me a heart attack."

"Gave you a heart attack?" The headmistress glared over at Elliot. "Imagine my dismay when Mr. Gambriel came bursting into my office, yelling that something terrible had happened."

We all turned to stare at Elliot, who scratched his cheek awkwardly. "Sorry. I guess I got a little too worked up."

"It's fine." Lesti let out an exhausted sigh before smiling up at him. "Thanks for going to get help, Elliot."

Elliot puffed out his chest and grinned ear to ear. "No problem. It's what anyone would do."

Aurelia then turned to the headmistress. "Thank you so much as well, headmistress. Without your guidance, I wouldn't have been able to save Fang."

"No need to thank me. Guiding students through their growth and studies is the whole reason I'm here." The headmistress smiled softly for a moment before returning to her usual stern expression. "At any rate, you should all be getting to bed, should you not? It's rather late, and you've already had quite an exciting evening."

I let out a yawn of my own as the adrenaline faded. My exhaustion had started to catch up with me. "I agree. Let's all get to bed."

No one seemed to have any complaints, so we all agreed to meet out on the training field the next morning before returning to the dorms. Aurelia carried Fang in her arms the whole way back, her brow furrowed in thought.

* * *

The next morning Lesti and I woke up at our usual time and went to get breakfast before heading out to the training grounds. Usually, we would run into Aurelia there and eat breakfast together, but she seemed to be missing today. Lesti scanned the room while waiting for her soup to be served with a worried look on her face. "It's unusual for Aurelia to miss breakfast. I hope nothing happened with Fang last night."

The lady serving the soup seemed to notice her concern and spoke up as she handed Lesti her bowl. "Oh if you're looking for your friend, little miss, her and that hound of hers already had their breakfast and left a bit ago."

"Oh, really? That's a relief. Thank you for letting me know." Lesti smiled brightly at the kind woman before turning and finding a table to eat her breakfast.

I hopped up next to her as she started to cram food into her mouth at an alarming rate. "What are you in such a hurry for all of a sudden?"

Lesti started to try and respond but realized her mouth was full and spent several seconds trying to swallow before finally succeeding. "I mean, aren't you curious? Aurelia never leaves without us anymore. There must be some reason, right?"

"I guess that's true..."

Thinking back on it, she was right. Since the pair started eating breakfast together after the beast attack, Aurelia waited for Lesti in the dining hall, even if she was done eating. My mind began to wander through the possibilities, and soon I found my tail flicking about impatiently as I waited for her to finish.

After a few minutes, she drained the rest of her soup and slammed the bowl down onto the table. "Done! Let's get going!"

She hurriedly returned her dishes, and we made our way to the training grounds. Lesti shivered slightly as we walked across the lawn. The mornings were still quite chilly, and the thin mist that still hung in the air didn't make things any better. As we approached our destination, I began to pick up on a strange sequence of sounds.

A loud thud echoed through the morning air from somewhere in the mists. It was shortly followed by the rustling of leaves. Then there would be a long pause before the cycle would repeat itself. After we walked a bit further, Lesti noticed it as well. Knowing no one besides Aurelia would be on the field this early, we headed toward the noise.

Eventually, a large tree near the edge of the training grounds came into view through the mist. Aurelia stood just about an arm's length from the tree. She had a low, wide stance and her eyes were screwed shut with focus. After taking a deep breath, she pivoted at the hips, and her right arm exploded forward toward the tree with incredible speed. Just before she made contact, her fist stopped, hovering in the air just a few inches from the trunk of the tree.

Thud.

My eyes went wide as a dull thud echoed from the tree. The branches swayed back and forth as the tree shook slightly from the impact, causing a few loose leaves to flutter to the ground. Nearby, Fang began to dart around, trying to catch them all before they hit the ground. Aurelia watched him with a faint smile before noticing us and waving.

"Good morning, Auri! It looks like Fang is doing better today?" Lesti called out as she waved to her friend.

Aurelia nodded. "Mm. He's back to his usual self this morning, thanks to everyone's help."

I closed my eyes and checked Fang's magical energy. Just as I had suspected, it had already started to fill back up. It would still be a while before he was in danger again, but I wanted to make sure it didn't get to that point. "It looks like his magic is filling up really fast still. Make sure you draw some of it out every once in a while. Otherwise, it's going to build up again. Okay, Aurelia?"

"Mm. I will." Despite saying she would take care of it, Aurelia looked at Fang with a worried expression. "Still, I would like for him to learn to use his magic on his own. That way, he'll be safe even if I'm not around."

I highly doubted that a situation like that would ever occur, but it wouldn't hurt to be prepared, just in case. Besides, having some extra magic at his disposal would only help Fang out in the future. But I wasn't sure how to teach him. From what I understood, most magical beasts could just use some form of magic naturally. For elemental hounds, this was based on the type of magic they absorbed. Unfortunately, I had no idea what sort of abilities would come from having absorbed Thel'al's magic.

As I was mulling over the problem in my mind, Lesti pointed at Aurelia. "We can worry about that later! More importantly, how did you do that thing with the tree? You didn't touch it, right?"

"Oh, right. You couldn't see it, could you?" I turned my attention back to Aurelia. "It looks like you figured out how to manipulate your magical energy a bit after last night, huh?"

When Aurelia punched at the tree, my eyes had seen the wave of magical energy that had extended from her hand to hit it. That energy had condensed into something like a magical barrier and had struck the tree before dissipating. She had punched the tree with her magic—but it didn't seem like she had perfected it yet.

"Mm. When I drew out Fang's magical energy, there was so much of it that I could sort of feel it." Aurelia stared down at her hands as she continued. "After I understood what it was like, I was finally able to pinpoint the energy in my own body as well. Although, I still can't manipulate it very well without a spell."

Her explanation lined up with what I had seen as well. During her punch, Aurelia had been casting a relatively quick and simple spell. I could see her magical energy doing something to her body at that time, and now I knew what it was. She was using it to help propel and harden her magic. Even if she had to rely on a spell, for now, it was fantastic progress after over a month of no breakthroughs.

"Alright. For now, I want you to continue to focus on perfecting this technique. However, rather than trying to use your energy outside of your body, I want you to work on changing the way it flows inside your body. Think you can do that?"

"Mm. I can, but"—Aurelia nodded, then looked at her hands with a confused expression before turning her gaze back to me—"why wouldn't I just focus on using the magic in my hands?"

I sat and thought for a moment, trying to think of the best way to explain my reasoning to her before responding. "Let me ask you this. Do you think you could beat Elliot in a one on one fight if you mastered that punching technique?"

Aurelia shook her head without even a moment of hesitation. "Mmm. Even if I mastered this, Elliot is incredibly skilled at close-quarters combat. He would easily negate such a straightforward attack."

I felt a gentle thrumming in my chest as Aurelia noticed the exact problem. She had a good sense of her abilities and what their limits were. Unlike Lesti, she could recognize when she was outclassed and understand why without even needing to fight the person. "Now, what if you had more angles of attack? For example, if you could use the same technique with kicks or even your daggers?"

"Mm. It would be harder to defend against." Aurelia furrowed her brow in thought. "Okay. I'll work on moving my magical energy around. Will you help me, Instructor?"

"Sorry, but I have something else I need to work on." I turned my gaze over to Fang, who was sniffing around the base of the tree. "Now that his abilities are starting to manifest, I want to figure out what they are as soon as possible. I'll check in with you when I can, though."

"Mm. I'll be fine." Aurelia followed my gaze. "I'll leave Fang to you. Take care of him for me."

"Now, as for you." I turned and faced Lesti.

"M-me?" She looked down at me with a slightly fearful expression on her face. "I was just planning on reading through my books."

"You'll be doing no such thing." I glared up at her, my tail twitching about. "Starting today, you're going to use the morning to practice sparring with Elliot."

"You really think doing that's going to help me? I'm not suddenly going to turn into a master of close-quarters combat overnight, you know."

"I wouldn't be recommending it if I didn't think it would help." I gazed past her at the figure of Elliot walking towards us through the morning mist, my tail twitching about in excitement. "Besides, I'm not expecting you to fight normally. I want you to do what you usually do."

"What I normally do?" She looked at me with a confused look on her face.

"That's right. I want you to blow his and everyone else's expectations out of the water in your own crazy way. You can think of a way to do that, right?"

Lesti grinned with her usual fearlessness and puffed out her chest. "Ha! Of course, I can do that! After this tournament, I'm going to be taking that number one spot after all."

"Well, sounds like you're rearing to go. Did I miss something?" Elliot called out as he finally finished crossing the field and joined us. He was carrying a wooden practice spear today as well, clearly ready to spar.

"Actually, Elliot, I was just telling Lesti that she would be sparring with you in the mornings from now on. You don't mind, right?"

"I mean, I don't mind, but I'd like to get some training of my own in, too." Elliot grimaced as he threw a sidelong glance at Lesti.

"You're still saying that?! Alright, let's go, then!" Lesti snapped at him, pointing out toward the field. "I'll show you exactly why I'm the number two in our year now!"

"Oh, is that right?" A dark expression came over Elliot's face as the two began glaring at each other. "Let's see what you can do, you cocky brat."

With that, Elliot turned and marched off toward the center of the training grounds, Lesti hot on his heels. The pair badgered each other the whole way with an intensity that I'd never seen from either of them before. *I wonder if I got Lesti a little too worked up there? I'll do Fang's training nearby just in case.*

Getting Closer

Later that day, we were all packing up our things to visit Rose again. It was about time for classes to finish, and we figured she would be working on her garden after that. We hadn't gotten the chance to ask her about her ability yet, thanks to Fang and me falling from the roof last time, so we planned to try again today.

"Everything still hurts," Lesti whined as she packed up her things. She was covered in bruises from her morning training with Elliot. Despite both their attitudes earlier today, neither had gone overboard—but that also meant Elliot had come out on top in every bout. Lesti wasn't used to having to hold back her magic in combat, and her inexperience showed.

Until now, she either fought alongside me or was able to use her spells at full strength. She had never needed to be particularly clever about how she used her magic. That was why I had asked Elliot to spar with her. Lesti was a bright girl, and she wasn't afraid of hard work either. It was a bit harsh, but throwing her to the wolves like this would be the fastest way for her to improve.

"Oh, quit your whining," Elliot called from the doorway with a playful smirk on his face. "My brothers gave me bruises ten times worse than that during our training sessions. You'll be fine."

Lesti glared back at him as she shoved her last book into her bag. "You're lucky we're going to meet up with Rose, or I'd give you a piece of my mind."

Elliot's smile faded at the mention of Rose. "You're still planning on trying to befriend her, huh?"

"That's right, and nothing is going to stop me, so don't even think about trying." Lesti pushed past Elliot and walked out of the classroom with Aurelia. Typically, this is where Elliot would have parted ways with us, but he followed the pair down the hall for some reason.

Confused, I trotted to catch up with him. "You're coming with us, Elliot?"

"Yeah." He kept his gaze fixed on the back of Lesti's head as he spoke to me. "If she's going to get involved with Rose, then I need to be aware of what's going on. Otherwise, it could become an issue."

"What's the big deal? We're just getting to know her."

Elliot glanced down at me. "You expect me to believe that one of the most famous students here at the school took an interest in a first-year girl, a commoner no less, completely at random?"

So, he knows more than he let on last time after all. I wonder why he's so secretive about it?

"Well, I guess it doesn't matter either way." I turned my gaze back to Lesti. "At this point, she'd still talk to her even if you told her it would make her the enemy of your family."

Elliot's eyes went wide at my statement. "She really thinks Rose's ability is that valuable?"

I let out a short laugh at just how off the mark he was. "Of course not. Lesti would never put her own people's future at risk over something like that."

"Then, why?" Elliot asked, looking down at me as if I were some sort of alien.

"It's simple." I broke out into a trot and glanced back over my shoulder at him. "She wants to be friends with her."

Without waiting to see Elliot's reaction, I turned and caught up with Lesti and Aurelia. Still, thanks to my sharp hearing, I heard the words he muttered under his breath as he chuckled. "What a stupid reason."

* * *

As expected, we found Rose working her garden behind the girls' dormitory. Upon seeing our approach, she waved nervously, keeping a close eye on

Fang and me. Apparently, our previous meeting hadn't been enough to get rid of her fear of us. At least she wasn't running away screaming this time.

But just as she started to relax a little, her eyes went wide, and she froze. "M-Master Elliot, what are you doing here? Is there some sort of problem?"

Elliot smiled gently at the flustered girl and waved his hand. "No, nothing of the sort. I'm just here as a member of their training group today. Also, there's no need to refer to me by my title here, Rose. We're all equals according to the rules of the academy."

Rose let out a sigh of relief. "I see. Then, is there something I can help you all with?"

"Well, we were wondering if we could help you with your garden." Lesti grabbed Rose's hand and pushed her face quite close, causing her to lean back. "Can we?"

"My garden? Well—" Rose glanced nervously over at Elliot, who just nodded with a defeated smile on his face. "I-I guess it will be alright. Honestly, it will help me out as well. This is more work than I expected."

"Great! Just tell us what to do, and we'll get to work."

"Okay. I was planning to plant the seeds today." Rose walked over to a large sack lying near the edge of the field and returned with a handful of seeds. "I'll show you how to do it. Then, each of us can work on a different part of the garden."

"Mm. Please show us." Aurelia took off her cloak and handed it to Fang, who clumsily carried it over to the edge of the field. Rose began to show the girls how to properly plant the seeds, including the correct depth and spacing for each one. Meanwhile, I sat off to the side and pretended to take a nap, while actually watching Rose's magic.

She didn't inject any of her magic into the seeds as she had done with the soil. She was just planting them like any average person would. As they went to work, I kept a close eye on her, but she didn't change anything, no matter how long I watched.

After about an hour, Rose finished up her portion of the field and moved on to help the others, but she was turned away by a rather indignant Lesti, who insisted that Rose take a break while they finished. Faced with Lesti's unusually strong will, Rose couldn't argue with her, so she went and sat down in the shade of a nearby tree, waiting for the pair to finish.

Seeing my chance, I got up and stealthily moved to sit over by her, making sure to keep enough distance so she wouldn't freak out. "Can I ask you a question, Rose?"

She jumped a little upon hearing my voice, her head swiveling about until her gaze finally locked onto me. Her expression told me that she was nervous, but she didn't look outright scared this time. She stared at me for a long moment, her gaze darting over toward Elliot once or twice before responding. "Sure. If it's something that I can answer, then I don't mind."

"Thank you." I sat upright and wrapped my tail around my feet, trying to look as unimposing as possible. "I'm just curious why you didn't infuse the seeds with your magic like you did with the soil. Is there some difference between the two?"

Rose's eyes went wide when she heard my question. "How do you know about that? Don't tell me you're some sort of spy sent to make sure that my secret doesn't leak to the world, and that you'll kill me if it does?!"

Rose's expression grew frantic as she clearly spiraled off into some delusion of her own creation. I was so caught off guard that I couldn't respond immediately. However, I soon saw that she was about to continue, and decided it best if I nipped her misconceptions in the bud.

"S-sorry. I wasn't trying to spy on you or anything like that. It's just that one of my abilities is that I can see magical energy." I looked toward the tree on the other side of the field. "The other day when I was napping in that tree, I noticed that the parts of the field you had tilled were filled with magic. I was planning to ask you about it when you suddenly ran away."

"Oh, is that all? Thank goodness. I'm sorry. It's just that I'm not very good with animals." Rose looked at me apologetically before turning her gaze toward Lesti and Aurelia working the field. "Did you tell them about my ability?"

I hesitated for a minute, thinking it might be better if she thought I was the only one who knew. In the end, I couldn't bring myself to lie to her. "I did. I told them about it later that evening."

"So, that's why she came up and talked to me so suddenly." Rose turned her gaze downward, staring at her dusty boots. "I thought it was strange that someone so famous would bother with me."

I felt an uneasiness growing inside me as she echoed Elliot's words from earlier. From her perspective, it probably looked like we were only interested in her for her power, and in my case, I think that was true. Seeing her looking so depressed, I felt disgusted with myself.

"This may sound like I'm making excuses since I'm the one who told them about your ability."—I looked over at Lesti and Aurelia—"but I don't think the reason they approached you really matters. Whether it's your looks, power, or some talent you have, people take an interest in others for all sorts of reasons. What's really important is how they treat you and what kind of relationship they want with you."

Rose looked out at Lesti and Aurelia in the field, a conflicted expression on her face. Lesti noticed her watching and waved as she called out to her. "Rose! We're finished, so come check our work already."

Rose stood up, dusted herself off, and started walking over toward the pair. However, she came to a stop after just a few feet and turned around to look at me. "I don't infuse the seeds with magical energy because I can't. No matter how hard I try, it never takes." A strangely pained looking expression crossed her face at that moment. "I guess it's just a limitation of mine."

Without waiting for my response, she turned and jogged over to join Lesti and Aurelia. Thankfully, it seemed like my words had gotten through to her just a little bit.

Internally, I let out a sigh of relief and turned my thoughts to what she had said. I had learned a little bit about magical infusion, but Rose's words seemed to imply that it wasn't impossible to infuse living matter with magical energy. Rather, it seemed like she simply wasn't capable of it herself. But even if that was true, why did it look like it pained her so much?

* * *

A few days later, we once again found ourselves heading to the usual classroom for our evening training session, but Rose was with us this time around. We had spent the last several days helping her work her field in the evening. Afterward, Lesti always invited her to join us for dinner. The first several times, she refused, but today she had finally accepted. The three had hit it off pretty well, chatting up a storm as they ate. It was the first time I had seen Rose smile so much since we had met her.

She was joining us for training because, during their chat, Rose had mentioned to Lesti that she felt nervous about the tournament. Lesti, being who she was, immediately promised I could make Rose the top of her class. I did my best to deny any such claims, but I couldn't keep up with Lesti's endless praise for me. So, now I found myself with not one but two students that I didn't have any idea of how to train.

"This is it." Lesti walked into the room ahead of Rose, spun around on her heel, and grinned at me mischievously. "This is where we spend our evenings, slaving away under the harsh tutelage of Instructor Astria."

Rose eyed me warily after hearing Lesti's declaration. It was bad enough she was nervous around me because I was an Astral Cat, but now Lesti was going to make her think I was some sort of demon teacher. I wasn't going to be able to teach her anything at this rate, so despite my irritation at Lesti, I did my best to respond calmly. "Relax. She's just joking. My training methods aren't anything too crazy."

"How can you say that when I have bruises like these thanks to your training?" Lesti pointed to a rather nasty looking bruise that she had gotten from her training with Elliot, pouting all the while.

"Th-that wasn't my fault!" My eyes darted about as I tried to come up with an excuse. "You're the one who got Elliot all worked up before sparring with him. You only have yourself to blame!"

"What kind of instructor doesn't accept responsibility for her student's injuries?" Lesti looked at me with mock shock. "I should report you to the headmistress!"

"For the last time, I'm not an instructor!" I finally lost my cool at Lesti's teasing and snapped back at her.

"Mmm. That's not true. You're a great instructor," Aurelia chimed in at the worst possible time. I turned, ready to give her a piece of my mind, but unlike Lesti, she was gazing at me with an expression so earnest and sincere that I couldn't possibly refute her.

Seeing my anger disarmed by Aurelia, Rose let out a little chuckle. "This seems like a fun environment to learn in. I'll be looking forward to your lessons, Instructor Astria."

Rose curtsied rather skillfully, catching me off guard. I hadn't expected such a gesture from a commoner girl. It made me wonder where she learned that from. Was her sponsor training her to enter noble society or something?

As my thoughts wandered off, Rose looked at me expectantly. Realizing that she was waiting for my response, I let out a heavy sigh. "Fine. You win. I'll figure out something to help you in the tournament. What's one more at this point anyway."

"Yes!" Lesti pumped her fist and ran over to Rose, embracing her in a swift hug. "This is gonna be great. I'm looking forward to working with you, Rose."

"Mm. I am too." Aurelia smiled at her gently. "Let's all work hard together."

Rose, clearly surprised by Lesti's enthusiastic embrace, stared at the two for a moment before smiling brightly. "Yeah. Let's all do our best!"

"Alright, let's get to work then. Aurelia, how is your training going? Making any progress?" I hopped up on a nearby desk and started to get each of my charges in order. Unlike a standard classroom, each of my students had their own unique training, so I would have to be organized about this.

"Mm. It's still pretty hard, but I'm starting to get the hang of it."

"Alright, keep working at it then." I nodded briefly before turning my gaze to my next target. "Lesti, were you able to get any ideas from your training with Elliot this morning?"

Lesti grinned at me. "Yeah, I have a few ideas." Her expression then grew more serious. "Still, I don't think they're going to be enough to beat Alex. I'll keep working at it, though."

"Good. Then, the last one would be Fang." I paused for a moment as I looked down at the pup, whose tail was wagging excitedly at being mentioned. "Sorry. We can't work on your ability here in the classroom.

There isn't enough space."

Fang lowered his head and whined slightly when I mentioned that he would be left out. I was excited to keep working on his abilities. We made some excellent progress earlier in the day, but there was no way we could spar and use magic here in the classroom.

"Don't whine. Practice your tracking instead. There are treats in it for you if you do a good job."

"Rarf!"

At the mention of treats, Fang perked up instantly. No matter how many times I saw it, it was scary how well that worked. With him taken care of, I turned my attention to my newest student. "That just leaves you, Rose. If it's fine with you, I'd like to ask a few questions before we get started."

"Of course."

Rose's reply was a bit stiff as the others moved off to do their training, leaving her alone with me. I felt my tail start to swish about in irritation, but suppressed the urge. It was going to be frustrating trying to teach someone who was always on edge around me, but showing that frustration would only make things worse. Besides, I'm sure Rose had her reasons for being scared of animals.

"Perfect. Then why don't we start with your ability to infuse magic into objects? I'll need to know more about how it works in order to come up with ways you can use it in the tournament."

"Well, I don't mind since you already know about my ability, but..." Rose paused, glancing over toward the doorway. "I don't think I'll be able to use it in the tournament. My sponsor has ordered me to keep it a secret."

"I see." I lowered my gaze for a moment as I thought through my options. "Well, I certainly don't want to cause issues with your sponsor. However, I think you should work on cultivating that ability of yours either way."

Rose turned her gaze away from the doorway and back to me, a surprised look written on her face. "What makes you think that?"

"Sorry if I'm being too forward here, but I don't think the tournament results are going to be that important to your future, right?" I glanced over at Lesti and Aurelia as they both threw themselves into their studies. "For those two, the tournament is an important chance to show off their abilities. They need to get good results to help secure the future that they want. Since your sponsor already knows about your ability, I'm assuming they plan to hire you after you graduate, so you'll do quite nicely for yourself, no?"

"I suppose that's true. Regardless of my results in the tournament, my future is already set in stone thanks to my ability."

Rose smiled softly as she confirmed my reasoning, but for some reason, the smile didn't seem to reach her eyes. First, Elliot was acting strange, and now this. I was beginning to wonder what was going on behind the scenes here. But it wasn't my business to meddle in. Rose had asked me to teach her, and that's what I was going to do.

"If that's the case, then we should take a longer-term approach to your training. You have three years that you'll be spending here at the academy. If you can start to find ways to use your ability now, then it will only help you out once you graduate. Whether you decide to use what you learn publicly, I'll leave up to you."

"Very well." Rose took a deep breath and sat upright. "What is it you wanted to know?"

"First, how does your ability work exactly? Lesti and I have tried to put our magic into objects more times than we can count, but every time it just drains away."

"Well, I'm honestly not one hundred percent sure how it works myself, but…" Rose tilted her head and looked up toward the ceiling. "If I had to give you an answer, I'd say that I don't put magic into objects. I put feelings into them."

"Feelings?" I cocked my head to the side, trying to decipher her strange statement. "Sorry, I don't understand."

"Alright, let's use the field as an example, then. When I'm tilling the field, watering the plants, or anything else related to farming, I don't think about infusing the soil with magic." Rose pulled both hands close to her chest and gazed down at them before slowly opening them as she continued to speak. "Instead, I think about how I want the plant to grow well. I pour those feelings into my work, and apparently, that causes my magic to flow into the soil."

"I see, so you think about the result that you want. Wait, doesn't that sound just like image-based magic?" I looked up at Rose, confused. Something about what she was saying didn't add up. "I just don't see how that's different from what Lesti and I were trying. Sure, the end goals were different. No, wait. Rather than being different, it was like we didn't have an end goal in mind at all."

Rose furrowed her brow as she processed what I was saying. "No end goal in mind, huh?" Then, all of a sudden, her eyes went wide. "It's the same."

"What do you mean?" I asked.

"My sponsor would try and have me create artifacts, but he never gave me a clear direction on what they should do. I had no end goal in mind. It never worked, not even once. Maybe, you can't just put magic inside an object with no purpose. You have to give it a reason for being there. When I would help my parents create medicines, I would always think that I wanted the medicine to be super effective and make whoever was using it recover quickly. Was that the key this whole time?"

"I can't believe it was so simple." I stared at Rose, dumbfounded. Thinking back on it, it all made sense. All of the items that Thel'al had created that held magic had some other purpose. The bracelets and Fang's collar tried to corrupt the wearer's soul. Meanwhile, Fang's anklets transformed the wearer, enhancing their physical abilities. Lesti and I had never even thought to try anything like that.

Just as this revelation hit both of us, a clunk came from just outside the door. Our gazes snapped over to see who was there. A moment later, Elliot stepped around the corner, carrying a small bag with him. Rather than relaxing when she saw it was Elliot, Rose only grew tenser.

"I'm sorry, but I have to go." Standing up quickly, she power-walked out of the room, pushing past Elliot. "Excuse me."

"Rose, where are you going? What's wrong?" Lesti stood up and made to follow after her, but Elliot blocked her path.

"Leave her be for now. We need to talk." Elliot's expression wasn't his usual casual, joking one. It was clear he didn't have any intention of letting

Lesti follow after Rose.

"Elliot, what's going on?" I glared at him from my spot on the desk, fur bristling. "Why is Rose acting so scared of you?"

Elliot, seeing my body language, threw up his hands. "Hold on, I plan on explaining everything, so just calm down, okay?"

I took a deep breath, trying to compose myself. "Fine, I'll hear you out."

He let out a sigh of relief before looking at Lesti and Aurelia in turn. " You two should take a seat as well. I think you both need to hear about this too." They both sat at the front of the classroom while Elliot stood there, gathering his thoughts.

Rose's Situation

"So, let's begin with some basic facts." Elliot looked at the three of us as we sat in front of him. "First, I want you all to know that I'm just now learning about Rose's ability, same as you."

I had just finished giving Elliot a rundown of Rose's ability. After my conversation with her, I felt like something was off, but it didn't seem like she would open up to us anytime soon. Besides that, Elliot had pretty much figured it out already after overhearing our conversation. There wasn't much point in hiding it from him, and he didn't seem the type to try and take advantage of Rose, either.

Lesti sat up straight at his statement, fully focused. "Right. We covered this before. Rose's sponsor didn't tell your father what her special ability was when he asked for permission to send her to the academy. Plus, your father, being busy with the fallout from the war, didn't push him for answers."

"That's right. As you know, when a lower-ranked noble within a territory wants to sponsor someone, he has to give his reasoning to the lord of the territory. In this case, Rose's sponsor used the political situation in our territory to hide her ability from my father."

"Isn't that kind of dangerous for him?" I asked. "Why would he take that kind of risk?"

"Before I answer that, I need to ask you one last time—are you sure you want to continue to be involved with Rose? If we go any further, then you'll become involved in the internal affairs of the Gambriel family, and there won't be any going back."

Lesti stood up, a surprisingly serious expression on her face. "As if I would let something as small as the internal affairs of another family stop me! Rose is our friend, and if she's in trouble, we intend to help her out, right, Auri?"

Aurelia smiled up at Lesti before turning to Elliot, her gaze full of conviction. "Mm. We'll definitely help her out."

Elliot, for his part, looked utterly baffled. "Friend? Didn't you two meet her just the other day? Aren't you rushing things a bit?"

"E-even if we haven't spent that much time with her, we can still be friends, you know!" Lesti slammed her hands on the desk. Her argument was pretty weak overall, but Elliot only smiled.

"Well, I can't say I hate that sort of attitude. Alright then, if your minds are made up, who am I to stop you?" He paused, taking a deep breath before continuing. "For some time now, we have suspected Baron Arvis, Rose's sponsor, of planning a coup."

"A coup?!" Lesti's eyes narrowed at Elliot. "How is Rose involved in this?"

"Calm down. I'm getting to that." Elliot glared back at Lesti, clearly irritated at the interruption. "My father has had his spies investigating Arvis. Until recently, we weren't able to find any evidence of his plans. Then, a little over a year ago, he brought Rose to us and asked for my father's permission to enroll her in the academy. But he never once mentioned the abilities that I just heard about. Instead, he just implied that Rose had some sort of hidden talent."

Elliot turned and began pacing back and forth in front of us, brow furrowed in thought. "My father found this strange. Rose had been mentioned in our spy's reports, but the spy had never once seen Rose using magic."

"What's so strange about that?" I tilted my head to the side. "Isn't it possible that the spy just happened to never be around when Rose used magic?"

"You might think that, but the castle that Baron Arvis holds is rather small. Plus, both the spy and Rose had been there for over a year at this point." Elliot stopped pacing and turned to meet my gaze. "If Rose's abilities were normal, then she would have been practicing them out in the open. The spy's reports and Arvis's request tipped my father off that something else was going on. He agreed to allow Rose to attend the academy and contacted me to keep an eye on her."

"So, you've been spying on her for your father." I stood and took a step toward Elliot. "Does that mean that you're planning on reporting what you just found to him?"

I braced myself for Elliot's response. If he was going to tell his father about Rose's ability, then I might have to stop him. Just like they had a spy in the Arvis household, it was likely that Baron Arvis had a spy in their home. If that was the case and they heard the news, then Rose could find herself in danger of some sort. I had to assume she was being threatened in some way, based on her reaction to Elliot showing up.

Elliot looked over toward the door, a frustrated look on his face. "I wish I could, but it seems like that might be dangerous at this point. Based on Rose's reaction, I think Baron Arvis may be threatening her in some way." I felt the tension drain from my muscles. Thankfully, Elliot had reached the same conclusion as me.

Elliot turned his gaze back toward us. "That's where you all come in. If I'm around, then Rose will be on her guard, so I'd like you to see if you can find out what Baron Arvis is using to threaten her. Can I ask for your help with this?"

Lesti stood up and puffed out her chest proudly, hands on her hips. "Leave it to us. We'll find out whatever Baron Arvis is plotting. No problem." She paused for a moment, her expression turning more serious. "Still, we're going to need some sort of hard evidence, right? That might be a little bit harder to get."

Elliot grinned and thumped his chest. "Leave that to me. I've got some ideas on that front." He reached into his bag and pulled out a small coin pouch, which jingled a little as he moved it about. "I want you to take this as payment. It should be enough to cover your expenses."

Lesti's face grew suspicious. "Expenses? Why would I have expenses?"

Elliot pushed the coins into her hand. "As part of my plan, I'd like you to convince Rose to come to my birthday party. She'll probably come up with some excuse like not having a dress, so use this money to buy her one. You can use whatever is leftover to line any pockets as you see necessary."

"Oh, right. The party." Lesti's shoulders slumped as she remembered the event that she was dreading. "I guess I have one more reason I can't skip now."

Elliot furrowed his brow. "Is there something about my party that's causing you trouble?"

"Ah, sorry." She waved her hands in front of her as if trying to clear the air. "I'm not trying to be rude. It's just that my future husband is going to be there, and I'm not looking forward to dealing with him."

"Ah, right. You're engaged to Augustine Vanderbolt, aren't you?" Elliot's gaze turned to one of pity. "I certainly don't envy anyone who has to deal with that foul man. Let me know if I can help in any way."

"Thanks. I will." Lesti stood up and started packing up her stuff. "In the meantime, let's get to bed a bit early tonight. We're going to have a long day tomorrow."

"Long day?" Aurelia finally spoke up for the first time in a while. "Aren't we just training?"

Lesti turned and looked at her with a smile. "We're taking the day off from training tomorrow." Her smile turned into a mischievous grin. "We've got some shopping to do."

* * *

"Are you sure we should be doing this?" I looked up at Lesti, feeling extremely nervous. It was early morning, and we were crouched behind the corner of the girls' dormitory, looking out at Rose's garden. Aurelia and Fang were with us, waiting for Rose to show up.

"What's the problem?" Lesti looked down at me with a smile so innocent, it was clearly fake. "We're just going to invite her to go shopping with us."

"The problem is with the part of your plan where we kidnap her if she refuses!" I swatted Lesti on the leg. "How is doing something like that okay in your book?"

"It's not kidnapping." Lesti's voice trailed off for a moment, and her gaze drifted off to the side. "It's invoking my noble privilege."

Next to us, Aurelia giggled slightly, causing me to turn and glare at her. "I can't believe you're on board with this plan, Aurelia. I would think you'd be against a noble abusing her privilege like this."

"Mmm. This is for a good cause, so it's okay." She smiled gently at me. "Besides, after yesterday, I think this is the only way that will work."

"Only way what will work?" a familiar voice whispered behind us. Hearing it caused all of us to freeze and stop our bickering. Slowly turning around, I found Rose standing there with her watering can in hand, staring at us with a perplexed look on her face. I couldn't blame her for that, either. There the four of us were, crouched down beside the dorm, whispering to each other.

"Oh, Rose, what are you doing here?" Lesti looked down at the full watering can in her hands. "Wouldn't it have been faster to go around the building the other way if you're coming from the well?"

Rose held the watering can up. "Oh, this? Yeah. I normally go the other way, but I forgot my hat in my room, so I stopped by to get it. After that, I kind of just came this way on a whim. What about you guys? What are you all doing here?"

I decided to jump in before the other two said something crazy. "We were just waiting for you. We were wondering if you wanted to take a break from classes today and go shopping with us in town instead. You know, a girls' day out."

"That sounds like a lot of fun." For a moment, I believed that we had avoided the worst-case scenario. But Rose dashed those hopes only a second later. "We shouldn't be skipping classes, though. It's rude to the instructors. They spend a lot of time preparing for their lessons, you know."

What a good kid! Why can't these two be more appreciative of their instructors like she is? I turned to glare at Lesti and Aurelia, but just as I did, they suddenly backed down.

"Yeah, I guess you're right." Lesti stepped aside to let Rose pass. "We'll just have to go some other time."

Aurelia grabbed the watering can out of her hands. "Mm. Come on. We'll help you water the garden."

The three of them headed off toward the garden with Fang in tow while I

ROSE'S SITUATION

stared at them in utter disbelief. *Was that entire thing about kidnapping her a joke? No, no, no. If that's the case, then I was the only one who was taking it seriously?!* I was so embarrassed I wanted to go hide, but it was unlikely that they realized that I had thought they were serious. Wandering off would only make them suspicious, so I quietly followed them and waited nearby while they tended to the garden.

"So, if during classes won't work, then how about after class today?" Lesti suddenly made her suggestion as she tugged at a few weeds cropping up in the garden alongside Rose.

"Well, that should be fine, but I have to take care of the garden." Rose looked at the field around her. "I'm not sure there will be time to do everything that's needed if we go shopping."

"Why don't we take care of the garden work for you?" Aurelia called out from the other side of the garden where she was watering the plants. "We have free study all day, so we can stop a little early to take care of it."

"Yeah, just tell us what needs to be done," Lesti said.

"Oh, That would be perfect!" Rose smiled innocently at Lesti as she tossed aside the last of the weeds. "Let me just go over what needs to be done, then."

She started to list off a series of tasks longer than I think the other girls had expected. It included watering the plants again, checking for pests, and recording the growth of the crops. Lesti grabbed some parchment from her bag and jotted everything down so that we wouldn't forget. After that, Rose headed for her class while we went to the training grounds.

As soon as Rose was out of earshot, Lesti let out a relieved sigh. "Thank goodness we didn't have to kidnap her. That would have been a real pain to explain to the headmistress."

"Wait, you were serious about that?!" I looked up at Lesti, suddenly more confused than I had been earlier. "After you let her refuse earlier, I thought that you must have been joking!"

"Of course not!" Lesti looked at me like I was the crazy one. "It's one thing if she just doesn't want to skip class, but if she had turned us down completely, then we would have kidnapped her for sure. Right, Auri?"

"Mm. I'm glad we didn't have to. Rose is nice, and I wouldn't want to upset her."

I threw a deadpan stare the way of both girls, finally giving in to my irritation with the pair. "I'm definitely upping the intensity of both of your training regimens, starting today."

* * *

Later that afternoon, the four of us were waiting by the school gate for Rose. Aurelia had been hesitant to bring Fang with us, worried that his presence would make people nervous. Lesti had managed to convince her it would be fine since they were both wearing their academy uniforms. According to her, students and instructors at the academy could go wherever they wanted with their familiars, so the townsfolk were used to seeing them.

I could tell Aurelia was nervous. We hadn't even left yet, and she was already keeping Fang on a short leash, having him sit beside her calmly. He didn't seem to mind. He simply watched the various students as they passed through the gate, tail wagging all the while.

As I sat there marveling at his ability to enjoy even the simplest things in life, I heard Rose's familiar voice call out to us. "I'm sorry I'm late. Our instructor ran over with his end of lesson speech."

Lesti smiled brightly as Rose came jogging up, slightly out of breath. "No worries. Are you ready to go? Not forgetting anything?"

"Yeah, I'm all set."

"Great! Then let's go." Lesti turned and walked out the gate, making a quick left. It was the same direction we had taken when heading to the commoner district before. However, this time, rather than taking a right at the end of the road, Lesti took a left. As I looked up the street, I could see that the shops were getting fancier the further along one walked. Rose must have noticed the same thing because she began to fidget nervously.

"Um, are you sure we're going the right way, Lesti?" After a few minutes of walking up the street, Rose finally broke the silence, eyes nervously darting from one store window to the next.

Each one was filled with expensive-looking clothes, decorations, and other luxury goods. Despite the buildings being the same basic layout as the other parts of the merchant district, with stone walls and blue tile roofs, the area had a completely different vibe thanks to the quality of the products being sold. Even the people shopping were dressed far more nicely than average.

Lesti grabbed Rose by the arm with a big smile. "It's fine! There's a great shop up ahead here that I thought we could check out."

At first glance, Lesti's actions seemed innocent enough. But to anyone who knew her well enough, it was plain to see that she was hanging onto Rose to make it harder for her to run away. Aurelia wasn't sitting by idly, either. As soon as Rose started to act nervous, she gave Fang a subtle hand signal, and the pup began carefully trailing behind Rose, cutting off her escape route. It was utterly ridiculous how much effort and coordination they had put into this.

"Won't a shop in this part of town be rather pricey, though?" Rose's gaze fell to the ground. "I'm just a commoner, so I don't have much money."

"Oh, is that all you're worried about? Don't sweat it. Elliot's footing the bill this time."

At Lesti's mention of Elliot, Rose stopped dead in her tracks and stared at her, eyes wide. "What do you mean Master Elliot is paying for this? Why would he do that?"

Lesti stopped and looked over at Rose meekly. "Well, to be honest, Elliot asked us to convince you to attend his birthday party with us. He gave us money to buy you a dress, saying you'd use not having one as an excuse not to attend."

"So, what you're saying is that you didn't invite me out for a fun day of shopping, but rather to fulfill some promise you made to Master Elliot?" Rose looked back and forth between Lesti and Aurelia before turning on her heel and shrugging off Lesti's arm. "I'm going back to the academy."

Unfortunately for her, all she saw when she turned around was Fang, who growled playfully at another hand signal from Aurelia. Rose froze on the spot again, pure terror written all over her face. Aurelia, now sure that she wasn't going to make a run for it, finally spoke up. "Can't it be both?"

Rose blinked rapidly, seemingly surprised by Aurelia's question. "What do you mean?"

"Of course, we made a promise to Elliot, but I was looking forward to going shopping with you today." Aurelia glanced over at Lesti. "Right?"

"Yep! Even if Elliot hadn't asked us to do this, we still would have invited you." Lesti averted her gaze slightly and scratched her cheek. "Although, we might have picked a cheaper place to go."

Seeing Rose still had doubts, I decided to give her one last push. "Rose, we may be doing this at Elliot's request, but that's only because we think it's what's best for you. If Elliot was just after your abilities, we would have turned him down."

"Mm. Astria's right." Aurelia walked over and grabbed Rose's hand. "We all want to help you out in whatever way we can, so I hope you'll trust us."

"It's not that I don't trust you. It's just, there's so much at stake. If they find out I'm involved with Master Elliot..." Rose bit her lip, her body trembling slightly. It was clear from her reaction that Baron Arvis had threatened her in a pretty severe manner.

"At any rate, let's not worry about that right now." Lesti, seeing her reaction, grabbed back onto Rose's arm. "The only tasks we were given were to get you a dress and make sure you go to the party. There's no harm in that, right? So, let's get shopping!"

With that, she took off down the street at a quick walk, practically dragging Rose behind her, causing the younger girl to cry out. "Lesti?! Hold on, you're going too fast!"

"That's because we've wasted too much time. If we don't hurry, the shop will close."

Aurelia shot me a concerned look, and we both followed after Lesti. Something about her behavior was off. I knew that we still had plenty of time to get to the shop. After all, no store in the entire city would close this early.

Just as I was starting to worry, Lesti sent me a message privately. *"Astria, don't look behind us, but we're being followed. I'm going to duck into an alley nearby. Can you cut off the exit for whoever follows us?"*

"Yeah, I'll take care of it." I switched the target of my thoughts over to Fang,

who was walking along beside me. *"Okay, buddy. It's time to put your new skill that we worked on to the test. You up for it?"*

"Rarf!" Fang let out an excited bark and licked me right along the side of my face. Apparently, he was ready to go.

A few seconds later, Lesti called out to the other girls and suddenly pulled Rose toward a nearby alley. "Come on. I know a shortcut. We'll have plenty of time if we go this way."

Rose started to hesitate as Lesti led her off the street. However, Aurelia's gentle hand on her back and calm gaze kept her moving forward. We all ducked into the alleyway, which was still infinitely cleaner than the alleys in the commoner district. I thought about hiding near the entrance, but there was no trash or crates for me to duck behind. So, instead, I followed everyone else to the far end.

Whoever was tailing us was doing a pretty good job of keeping their distance. Based on the fact that they had only just entered the alley as we were about to exit, it seemed that their main objective was just to keep an eye on us. This would have been the perfect place to spring an ambush, after all.

Unfortunately for him, he wasn't aware of Fang's new ability. *"Alright Fang, use your shadow step to get behind him and cut off his escape route."*

Fang let out a low growl as he leapt into action. In an instant, he disappeared from his spot beside me. Not wanting to get left behind, I turned and charged toward our pursuer myself, transforming into my leopard form as I went. I would have preferred my tiger form, but the alley was a little too narrow for that.

Seeing me turn and start charging his way, the man tried to make a break for it. But he was immediately met with Fang, who had appeared behind him. This was Fang's new ability, which I was calling Shadow Step. It was honestly a bit of a misnomer, but I thought it was a good fit with his black and purple fur.

Rather than jumping to someone's shadow like you would expect, Fang used the massive amounts of magical energy building up inside him to briefly boost his speed to an absurd level. Honestly, even I had trouble following his movement when he used it. Right now, the main drawback was that he could only use it in short bursts, but for a situation like this, it was perfect.

Suddenly pinned between two magical familiars, the man put his hands up as if surrendering. Now that I was close enough to get a good look at him, I could see that he was a bit out of place here. Most people in this part of town were relatively clean by this world's standards and wore fancy clothes. This man wasn't quite up to the same level.

His beard was ragged, and his brown hair was dirty. On top of that, while nice, his clothes were clearly dated and didn't match the style that others were wearing. It wasn't so bad that he would immediately draw suspicion. But once you noticed him, he definitely felt out of place.

"So, care to explain what you're doing following a bunch of girls into a dark alley like this, mister?" Lesti asked as she came walking up behind me.

"I wasn't following nobody." The man turned and faced me, maybe deciding I was the more significant threat. "I was just going about my day and decided to take a shortcut."

"Oh, is that right?" Lesti smiled at the man innocently. "Then, if you don't mind me asking, what's the name of the shop you were headed to?"

"Th-the shop I was headed to?" The man faltered a moment before recovering and putting on his air of indignation once more. "Well, if you must know, I was headed to the tailor."

He smiled smugly down at Lesti, but she only stared back at him with a stone-faced expression. "Alright, which one?"

"W-which one?"

"Yes, you see, unlike in the commoner district, shops in this part of town have their own names." Lesti grinned at the man who was growing more flustered by the second. "Surely you must know that if you're enough of a regular in this area to be taking a shortcut through an alley like this."

The man gritted his teeth. He knew he was caught, but apparently, he hadn't completely given up yet. "That's enough! I won't be patronized by a bunch of little brats like you!" Turning on his heel, he made his way toward Fang. "I'm a busy man, so I'll be on my way now."

As he made to move past Fang, Aurelia snapped her fingers, her signal for Fang to attack. I helped her with training it enough times that I almost reflexively dodged at the noise. This time, though, I wasn't the target. Fang leapt toward the man's face, front paws slamming into his chest. He didn't weigh enough yet to knock down a fully grown man, but his target panicked at the sight of a small elemental hound lunging at his face and stumbled backward, losing his balance.

He landed flat on his back with Fang on his chest, still growling and trying to act fierce while his little tail wagged like crazy, completely breaking the illusion. Rather than let the pup's hard work go to waste, I decided to give him a hand with his intimidation. I slammed one paw down on the ground next to the man's head and brought my face close to his, snarling the whole while.

"I'm going to give you one last chance. Tell us why you were following us, or else you may not be walking home."

The threats themselves were completely empty. It was pretty obvious that this man was just a commoner who had gotten in way over his head. Maiming him for no good reason wouldn't have sat right with me. But he didn't know that, and he didn't need to.

The man's face turned pale, and his eyes went wide. "Alright, I'll talk. Ain't no amount of money worth this. Some noble hired me to follow the pink-haired girl if she left the campus."

"Which noble?" I snarled at the man. "Do you have a name?"

"I-I don't know. I've never met them in person. They sent a servant, and their name was never mentioned. I needed the money, so I didn't ask questions."

Lesti walked up to stand beside me and looked down at the man. "He must have given you more orders than just to follow her. What else did he order you to do?"

"Just report back on what I saw, nothing else." The man's gaze grew stern. "Following a little girl around town was already a pretty sketchy job, but I figured there wouldn't be no harm in it, so I went ahead and took it. Anything more than that and I would have been out."

Lesti crouched down near the man's face. "What's your name?"

"I-it's Gregory."

"Alright, Gregory. How much is this noble paying you?"

"One half silver a day for the next week."

"Not even a whole gold, huh?" Lesti reached into her bag and pulled out a small gold coin. "Tell you what, if you'll pass on some bad information to your employer, this is yours. What do you say?"

The man looked at the gold with a stunned expression for a moment before a broad grin spread across his face. "As long as it's nothing that'll get me caught, you've got yourself a deal."

A mischievous grin spread across Lesti's face. "Perfect. Then here's what you're going to tell him."

Gathering Info

"Ah, that was so much fun!" Lesti smiled broadly as we walked down the street towards the academy. We had just finished purchasing dresses for Rose and Aurelia, and it was getting rather late. The orange glow of the setting sun cast long shadows on the street, bathing the buildings on the opposite side in a warm light.

"Mm. We should do it again sometime." Aurelia watched Lesti with a soft smile as she walked ahead of the rest of the group.

"Yeah. Although, we'll have to cut back on the budget next time," Lesti replied. "How about you, Rose? Did you have fun?"

Rose didn't respond. She just continued to stare at the sunset, gaze distant. Lesti fell back a few paces and waved her hand in front of Rose's face. "Hello? Rose? Anybody home?"

Rose's attention suddenly snapped back to the present moment. "Oh, um, yes. Sorry. Did you need something?"

Lesti puffed out her cheeks as she stared at her distracted friend. "I was asking if you had fun shopping with us, but you weren't responding. Is everything okay?"

"Yes. I did have fun." Rose paused for a moment, wringing her hands together. "It's just that I'm worried about that man that was following us. What if he was lying, or if he decides to tell Baron Arvis what happened for some reason?"

"Oh, is that all? I wouldn't worry about that. It doesn't matter what that man does." Lesti shrugged.

Rose stared at Lesti, a confused expression on her face. "What do you mean it doesn't matter?"

"The whole point of telling him that lie was to get the baron to make a move," Lesti replied as she smiled in return. "Even if he finds out that his spy was caught and that we were actively working against him, he'll be forced to take some sort of action."

"Ah, so that's why you had the messenger tell him something about you two being close friends." My tail began to swish about as I realized what Lesti was up to. "I was wondering why you would want the baron to know you were getting closer to Rose."

"Yeah. I'm guessing the baron is trying to keep Rose isolated so that others don't discover her ability. If that's the case, he'll see us becoming friends as a threat." Lesti's gaze grew more serious. "He may likely send you a messenger here in the coming days, Rose. He'll probably threaten you in some way. When that happens, I want you to consult us before doing anything, got it?"

Rose nodded hesitantly. "O-okay. I'll do my best."

Lesti grabbed on to Rose's arm, pulling her close. "Perfect. Don't worry. Everything is going to be fine. I promise."

We reached the fork in the road where we needed to turn to head back to the academy. However, Lesti kept walking forward in the direction of the commoner district. Turning on her heel, she addressed the two girls who were looking at her with confused expressions. "Alright, you guys, this is where we part ways. Astria and I have some business down in the commoner district. Make sure Rose gets back safely. Okay, Auri?"

"Mm. Leave it to me." Aurelia waved to Lesti without the slightest hint of concern on her face.

"Let's go, Astria." Lesti turned on her heel and headed toward the gate to the commoner district.

I trotted along quickly to catch up with her. I was a bit concerned that we were walking to that part of town this late. I didn't think there were many ordinary people who would be a threat to us, but Thel'al still hadn't been found, and I wasn't sure how active those under his influence might be in the city.

"So, what are we going to the commoner district for?" I looked up at Lesti as we strode along.

"We're going to see Dag," Lesti replied privately. *"I need to get any information I can on Baron Arvis. Normally, I'd ask Lani to look into it, but time is of the essence in this case."*

"Fair enough, but how are we going to find him?" I looked around as many of the stores in the area had already started to close up for the evening. *"Won't the market be shut down by the time we get there?"*

Lesti stuck her nose up in the air a little. *"Just who do you think I am? Dag told me how to get in touch with him after the market closes. He said I was a valued client."*

I ignored Lesti's mock haughtiness, rolling my eyes. *"I think it's your money that he values. He'd probably give special treatment to anyone who had coin to throw around."*

"Yeah. That's probably true." Lesti went back to her normal, serious tone. *"Still, it works out for us in this case, so there's no point in complaining. Now, let's focus on the task at hand."*

As she said that, we approached the gate, and Theo's familiar face came into view. At first, I almost didn't recognize him. He looked far worse for wear than when I had last seen him. There were bags under his eyes, and he looked as though he had lost a bit of weight. Even so, he dealt with each person as they passed through the gate with a smile.

Seeing our approach, he raised his hand and waved to us. "Well, if it isn't little Lesti. What are you doing heading down to the commoner district so late?"

Lesti returned the gesture, looking Theo up and down worriedly. "We're just going to visit an acquaintance of ours; we won't be long. Never mind us, though. What's going on with you? You look terrible!"

"Is it that obvious?" Theo smiled wryly. "They've been working us like dogs lately. Unfortunately, I can't say too much more than that. Just know that the whole guard unit is overworked right now and downright irritable because of it."

Looking at the other guards operating the gate, it was pretty clear he wasn't exaggerating. They all looked just as exhausted as Theo. "Did something happen to bring this on?"

Theo glanced about quickly, making sure no one else was paying attention, then whispered, "You didn't hear this from me, but apparently the fights and murders down in the slum were caused by demon worshipers, peddling some weird artifacts that make people go mad."

He let out a heavy sigh. "Thanks to that, they've had us all working overtime while they search for the culprits. Whoever was responsible seems to have gone into hiding. We haven't been able to find anything, so things have calmed down here lately—but keep your wits about you, alright?"

"We will. Thanks for the warning, Theo." Lesti patted him on the shoulder and started to head through the gate. "We need to get a move on, don't want to be out too late. Take care of yourself, alright?"

"I will. Stay out of trouble, you two." With a final wave, Theo turned back to his duties and started checking the next person passing through the gate.

Lesti and I continued down into the maze-like streets and back alleys of the commoner district. We walked along in silence, ducking through a series of passages that I had never been through before. It was still disorienting, but I could at least tell we were headed in the opposite direction of the slums.

I looked around at the unfamiliar scenery, trying my best to memorize as much as I could. "So, care to tell me where we're going exactly?"

"Well, I haven't been there before, but apparently the building is down near the east gate." She paused for a moment, glancing down at me nervously as she walked. "Just try not to freak out when we get down there, okay?"

I suddenly felt alarm bells going off in the back of my head. "Why exactly would I freak out?"

Lesti grimaced slightly before increasing her pace. "It'll be easier to just show you. Come on."

We wandered through the back alleys for a while longer. As we went, I once again noticed that the atmosphere of the town started to shift, though it wasn't quite the same as when we went to the slums. While the slums had been filthy and falling apart, this area just felt seedy. Men wandered the back alleys completely drunk, despite how early it was in the evening. The soft glow of lanterns filtered in from the main street ahead as the sun finally set.

GATHERING INFO

We finally stepped out of the alleyways, and I froze. Looking down the street, I could see any number of bars and brothels. Each one had a lantern placed outside, lighting their entrance and making this perhaps the most well-lit area of the city. Despite that, this was clearly not a place for a thirteen-year-old girl to be. Women of the night actively wandered the street looking for their next customer. Meanwhile, any number of drunkards called out to them as they staggered from one tavern to the next, despite the early hour.

"Come on, don't stop," Lesti chastised me, snapping me out of my shock. "We're looking for a tavern called The Black Dragon."

"Are you crazy?!" Despite my complaints, I quickly followed after Lesti. "We shouldn't be wandering around here at night. What if the headmistress finds out, or even worse, Lani?"

"How are they ever going to find out? It's not like either of them would be down here."

She had a good point, but I was still feeling anxious. We stood out like a sore thumb here. As we walked along, almost everyone we passed stared at us, and a few of the drunks even catcalled Lesti. That alone was enough to nearly make my stomach turn. What kind of monsters would catcall a thirteen-year-old girl? Even Lesti was obviously affected by it, grimacing as she turned a slight shade of pink at some of the obscenities shouted at her.

Thankfully, it wasn't long before we found where we were going, a relatively small tavern in a two-story building. The windows were shuttered, and no one lingered outside. In fact, it appeared that most people were giving the place a rather wide berth. Despite that, I could hear the sounds of drinking and merriment coming from inside as we approached.

Looking up, I noticed the signboard. However, rather than having the name written on it, it merely featured the distinct image of a black dragon's face. For some odd reason, the drawing looked somewhat familiar, though I couldn't place why. It wasn't very realistic or detailed; I couldn't say that it reminded me of Skell.

"Come on. Let's go inside." Before I had time to dig into the sign, Lesti pushed open the door, and I followed her in. At first, the sounds of rowdy conversation and clinking glasses washed over us but were quickly replaced by dead silence as the patrons noticed us. The tavern wasn't very full, but every person inside stared at us.

Lesti walked toward the bar, and I followed her, keeping an eye out for any threatening movements. The tavern was just as tiny as it had looked on the outside. Four long tables, two on each side, filled the space. Each one had bench seating to maximize the number of people that could be crammed into the small room. On the back wall sat the bar. Behind that was the entrance to the kitchen from which the scent of grilled meats wafted out. The only thing I didn't see was a staircase to get to the second floor.

As we approached the bar, the bartender glared down at us. "You lost, little girl? We don't serve kids here. If you're looking to get back to the academy, then it's that way."

The bartender flicked his head back in the direction we had come from. He was a rather large, muscular man, with a bald, clean-shaven head. Honestly, he looked just as much like a bouncer as he did a barkeep. I guess in this world there wasn't much difference in most cases.

"We're here to see Dag." Lesti somehow managed to hold a steady voice, despite how out of place we obviously were. "He told me I could find him here after the market closed."

"I don't know who you're talking about, little lady. Now get out of my tavern before I throw you out myself. This is no place for children."

"I'm not going anywhere until I see Dag." Lesti pulled two small silver coins out of her bag and placed them on the counter. "Perhaps this could change your mind?"

"No can do, little lady." The man narrowed his eyes at her and gestured to several of the men sitting at the tables behind us. "I won't be bought and paid for by some rich, spoiled noble. Now, this is your last chance. Get out of here."

Glancing over my shoulder, I could see several men drinking at the long tables rise and move toward us. From what I could see, none of them were armed. "Lesti. It looks like they don't plan on talking this out."

Lesti looked back as well. "Well, I guess this is as good of a time as any to try it out." She turned her back on the men, facing the barkeep once more

GATHERING INFO

before quickly snapping her fingers. "Prepare Fireball, repeat five."

At Lesti's words, five fireballs sprang to life in the air around her, one for each of the four men behind us and an additional one for the barkeep. But rather than immediately flying toward their targets, the fireballs hung in the air, causing the area to become quite hot. The men approaching us from behind stopped on the spot, looking back and forth at each other with surprised expressions.

The barkeep seemed equally surprised. His eyes widened a bit before returning to a full-on scowl. "Who are you, girl, and where did you learn to do that?"

Lesti puffed out her chest in pride. "My name is Lesti Vilia, soon to be the greatest mage the academy has ever seen. As for where I learned this"—Lesti looked around at the fireballs hovering around her before grinning at the barkeep—"I figured it out myself. Amazing, right?"

The barkeep let out a heavy sigh. "I see. The commander did mention a redhead that was too big for her britches."

While his words piqued my curiosity, I didn't have much time to think about it. The moment he stopped talking, the barkeep began to cast a spell. I stared at him for a moment, stunned. From what I knew, most commoners couldn't use magic. Yet, this man was casting a rather challenging water-based spell in poor conditions—and silently, no less. Lesti's fireballs had already taken a lot of the moisture out of the nearby air, meaning his magic had to reach pretty far to gather the water needed.

After recovering from my initial shock, I quickly moved to stop whatever he was planning. Reaching out with my own magic, I carefully undid the part of the spell that held the gathered water together, causing it to fall to the floor in a puddle. Rather than being shocked, the barkeep just glanced at it like he had expected that to happen before turning his gaze back to me.

"I guess you're Astria, then?"

"How do you know who I am?" I glared at the man and prepared to shift into tiger form, just in case.

"I don't know of anyone else who could counter a completely silent spell like that." He grinned at me. "That and you being able to talk pretty much seals the deal."

The barkeep raised his hand, and the men behind us all relaxed, tense expressions turning to relaxed smiles as they each plopped back down on the bench. Lesti let out a relieved sigh and canceled her spell. "So, are you going to let us see Dag now?"

"Aye, I can do that." He walked over to the entrance to the back and looked over his shoulder at us. "Follow me. Oh, and try not to be too surprised, okay?"

Lesti and I both glanced at each other, unsure of what he meant. She shrugged, and we followed after the man. Just like the front, the back wasn't much to look at either. A long counter ran along the wall. In the right corner, there was a small hearth where the food was being cooked. In the back left corner, a fairly narrow staircase led up to the second floor.

We followed the barkeep up the stairs, where we found a single hallway running the building's length, with only two doors. We passed the first and headed to the second about three-quarters of the way down the hall. Stopping in front of it, the barkeep knocked three times. "Boss, you have some guests! The redhead girl and her cat familiar."

"Let 'em in," Dag's familiar voice called back from the other side of the door. Upon hearing his response, the barkeep winced.

"Not this crap again." Muttering softly enough that only my cat ears picked up on it, he pushed the door open.

Stepping inside, I was surprised to find that the room was extravagantly furnished. Expensive-looking curtains hung in front of the windows. Sitting in front of the ornately carved desk were two chairs, whose seats were covered in what appeared to be dyed leather. They almost looked like they might be comfortable to sit in. In addition to that, several fancy looking bookshelves, neatly stacked, lined the walls.

All in all, it was ultimately the opposite of Dag's chaotic and messy looking stall that he ran down in the market. Even his apparel was completely different. Rather than a dirty cloak, Dag wore a clean, black cloak with no hood, his face covered by a black masquerade mask. Under the cloak, his outfit was a simple but elegant tunic and trousers, similar to something a middle-grade merchant might wear.

Lesti eyed him suspiciously. "You know, that accent of yours really doesn't match your outfit or the decor. Would you mind dropping it?"

"Tch," Dag clicked his tongue at her. "What do you have to be such a stick-in-the-mud for? I put a lot of work into that accent, I'll have you know."

"Boss, I understand using the accent down in the market." The barkeep stared at Dag with an exasperated expression. "But the girl's right. It doesn't make any sense to use it here. Besides, it's kind of annoying."

"You too, Gladius?" Dag looked at his subordinate with a disappointed expression. "Fine. I'll keep your opinion in mind for the future. Now, hurry up and get out of here. If she's here, then we have important business to discuss."

"Yes, sir." Gladius made to head for the door but stopped glancing back over his shoulder. "If he gives you any trouble, just yell, and I'll come put him in his place."

Dag watched as he closed the door behind him before turning his attention back to us. "So, what can I help you two with? It must be pretty important if you're coming to see me this late."

Lesti walked over and took a seat in one of the comfy-looking chairs. "I need any information you can give me on Baron Arvis of the Gambriel territory."

Dag narrowed his eyes at her. "Well, that's not what I expected to hear. What are you doing getting involved in another territory's business?"

I hopped up on Lesti's lap. "It involves a friend of ours, and besides, we were requested to help with the matter by a member of the family, so it's not really interfering."

"A friend? You must mean the pink-haired girl, then. Rose, was it?"

"That's right." Lesti adjusted her posture, sitting up straight. "Still, what gives? You're awfully loose-lipped tonight. Normally, you would have been milking me for all I was worth."

Dag grinned mischievously. "That's all part of the act that I use when I'm out and about. Although, I will say it does bring in a nice bit of coin on the side. But the commander would have my hide if he found out that I tried to get money out of you when I wasn't undercover."

I was starting to get a little curious about who this commander figure might be, but Lesti didn't seem to care. "Well, that's a big help for me," she said. "I still think it was worth it, but your information was quite a drain on my expenses. So, are you going to tell me what you know about Arvis or not?"

"First, let's start with what you know."

Lesti gave Dag a brief rundown of everything we knew, leaving out the bits about Rose's abilities. Apparently, she didn't trust him completely. Dag listened calmly the entire time, although once or twice I noticed his expression shift slightly, perhaps getting some new insights into the situation.

When Lesti was done, he let out a heavy sigh and leaned back in his chair. "Well, it sounds like things are progressing more quickly than I thought. What a pain."

After a moment of collecting his thoughts, he leaned forward again. "Based on what you've told me, you know just about everything about the situation. However, there are two pieces that you're missing."

"What would those be?" Lesti asked.

"First, that girl has been in the baron's custody for years now. Based on reports I've received, she's been there since she was around eight years old."

"That long?" I felt Lesti tense up underneath me. "What about her family? I'm surprised they haven't said anything."

"That's the second thing. The family supposedly died in a fire years ago. That's why the baron brought her into his household." Dag paused for a moment, his expression growing dark, before continuing. "Sadly, the bodies were never found. Burned to ash, they said."

Lesti rolled her eyes. "There's no way that's true. Only a few things in this entire world can burn hot enough to reduce even a person's bones to ash. I doubt a random commoner family was dealing with something that would cause that."

"Yeah. It's pretty obviously a lie, but they managed to come up with a

GATHERING INFO

plausible enough excuse. Plus, even when we searched all of the baron's estates, the family was never found."

"Couldn't he have just been holding them somewhere else?" I chimed in with my own theory. "If I were trying to hide them, then I'd keep them someplace that's seemingly unassociated with me."

Dag began to rhythmically tap the table with his pointer finger. "Trust me, Lord Gambriel thought of that as well. For a while, he was digging into any hidden estates or connections that the baron might have, but he wasn't able to turn up anything."

"You say that he wasn't able to find anything, but does that mean you have?" Lesti jumped in and asked the question just a moment before me. Dag's tone implied that he knew something.

"That's right. Recently, we were able to find a few especially fancy estates here in the city that belonged to merchants who shouldn't be able to afford them. When we looked into the ledgers, we found that the numbers didn't add up. So, we started looking into where the extra money came from, and low and behold—it all traced right back to some minor noble in the baron's region."

"Not to the baron himself?" I asked.

"We have yet to find any direct link between the baron and the noble besides the obvious, but that's in part because our investigation was put on hold, due to a more pressing matter."

"I'm honestly surprised that you looked into the situation at all." Lesti locked her gaze onto Dag, staring daggers at him. "There's nothing in it for you that I can see, especially since you're just giving us this information for free."

Dag smiled wryly at her. "Let's just say that the baron's coup doesn't align with my organization's interests, and leave it at that. Besides, I'm not giving you this information for free. I'm using you as an informant."

"An informant?" Lesti asked.

"That's right. As I said before, we have more pressing matters to attend to now, so I really couldn't spare anyone to send word to the Gambriel family. However, if you and the Elliot boy are involved, then that changes things.

Do me a favor and pass on what I've told you to him."

"That's fine with me." Lesti stood up, holding me in her arms. "But I can't guarantee that he'll trust the information."

Dag leaned back in his chair and closed his eyes for a moment, as if considering something, before opening them once more. "If he gives you any trouble, just tell him the information comes from the Shadow Dragon Brigade. That should take care of any objections he has."

"Alright, I'll take care of it." Lesti turned on her heel and started out of the room, pausing as she reached for the door. "One last thing. If I find out that any of the information you gave me here today is bad or that you used me for some ill purpose, I'll have Astria beat the crap out of you and take back all of the money I paid you before."

Without waiting for his response, she opened the door and stepped into the hall. I hopped out of her arms and walked alongside her as we made our way back to the first floor. "Are you sure threatening him was a good idea?"

"I'm not too worried about it." Lesti grimaced slightly, "I doubt he gave us bad information, but I didn't like him using us for his own benefit like that. If you show somebody like that an ounce of weakness, they'll take advantage of you every chance they get."

I couldn't say that I disagreed with her logic, but I was concerned about making an enemy out of Dag. Before, he had just been some creep who sold information down in the market. Sure, he had been suspiciously well informed, but he didn't seem to hold any power that I could tell. That was all completely out the window now.

As we exited the kitchen and entered the bar area, I was surprised to find it empty except for Gladius. We hadn't been upstairs all that long, so it shouldn't have been late enough for the place to be closing down. More likely, the men that we had seen were all part of Dag's brigade and had left on assignments while we were talking.

Gladius gave us a brief nod as his only acknowledgment before we walked wordlessly out into lantern-lit streets of the red light district. As we made our way back toward the academy, I took one last glance behind me, burning the image of the place into my memory. There was a good chance I'd need to come back here again someday, much as I loathed the idea.

Secret Summons

The next morning, I found myself sitting in the same tree that I had used to hide from Fang the day I met Rose. After yesterday's events, Lesti asked me to keep an eye out and make sure no suspicious characters were hanging around. I highly doubted it would be an issue while she was on campus, but it was better safe than sorry.

So, I lazily napped in the tree, using my magic sense to keep an eye out for anyone approaching the little garden as Rose toiled away. *It looks like this morning is going to be pretty uneventful. Classes should be starting soon.* I let out a content purr, thinking I would be released from my watch duty after a few more minutes. However, as if the world were trying to spite me, I noticed someone approaching Rose just as she started to put away her tools.

Opening my eyes, I could see it was a younger male student, black hair pulled back into a long ponytail. It was a style popular among the noble boys. That, combined with the way he carried himself, pretty much confirmed his status in society. Although, looking closely, he seemed quite nervous for someone just out for a stroll.

As he approached Rose, he stuck a hand into his pocket and glanced around, making sure no one was watching. I felt the muscles in my body tense up, and I made my way to the ground, stalking after the boy just in case. Rose didn't seem to notice his approach as she lined up her hoe with the other tools along the dormitory's back wall.

The boy slowly pulled something out of his pocket, carefully hiding it in his palm in such a way that no one was likely to see it. Even with my keen feline vision, I couldn't make out what it was. Assuming the worst, I increased my pace, closing the gap between us. Just as the boy got close to Rose, I came up behind him and transformed.

Then he called out, "Is your name Rose?"

Turning around to face the boy, Rose froze with a look of pure terror on her face. Her eyes were wide, and her face went pale. For a moment, it seemed like she might have even forgotten to breathe. The boy held out his hand, but to my relief, it wasn't a weapon, but rather a small, rolled-up piece of parchment that he held. Feeling a sense of relief, I released my tiger transformation, which also seemed to cause Rose to start breathing again as well. Apparently, I had been the one who had scared her, and not the boy.

"Y-yes, that's me. Can I help you with something?"

"I was asked to deliver this note to you." He glanced around nervously, still not noticing me crouched down in his shadow. "It's apparently top-secret, so make sure you don't share it with anyone."

He quickly shoved the note into Rose's hand, not waiting for her to respond. Then he hastily walked off and headed for the main building without ever looking back.

As soon as he rounded the corner, I looked up at Rose. "Sorry about that. I didn't mean to scare you. I thought he might have had a weapon."

"It's fine," She paused and took a deep breath, some of the color finally returning to her face. "I was just startled, is all."

I felt bad, but there were more important things to worry about. "So, what's in the note? Based on the way he was acting, I can't imagine it's anything good."

Rose's expression grew troubled as she undid the wax seal on the note, unfurling it. Upon reading it, the color slowly drained from her face once again, and her hands started to shake. "I'm sorry. I have to go."

Rose turned and started to hurry off, but I darted into her path and stopped her. Something was clearly wrong, and I needed to find out what. "Sorry, but I can't let you go wandering off by yourself after what happened yesterday. I'm coming with you."

"Astria, please. I know you're just looking out for me, but you can't come with me. I need to be alone. Otherwise, who knows what they'll do…" Rose's voice trailed off, and she clutched the paper tightly to her chest.

It was a risky move, but I decided to try and use the information we had gotten from Dag the night before. "What they'll do to who? Your family?"

Rose's body went rigid, and she stared at me, frozen like a statue until a whisper finally escaped her lips. "How do you know about that?"

"Lesti and I did a little digging last night. I still don't know the details, but they're alive right?"

"I-I can't. If they find out that you know—" Rose stammered as she struggled to find a response. The fear and uncertainty she was feeling was something I had never had to deal with, coming from a mostly peaceful world. The closest experience I had was our fight with Thel'al, but that would have to do.

"Don't worry. Nothing is going to happen to them." I rubbed against Rose's leg, then looked up at her, mustering as much confidence as I could. "We'll rescue them and put an end to Baron Arvis's plans, no matter what. So, will you let us help you?"

She stood there for a long moment staring at the note in her hands, clutching it tightly. This was one of those moments where I wished that Lesti was around. She was a lot better at handling situations like this than I was. Seeing her hesitation, I started to think of some way to give her one more push.

Before I could, she finally responded, "Okay. I'll trust you. Please help me save my family."

Her voice was unsteady, and her hands shook, but the look in her eyes was resolute. Seeing her courage, I felt a gentle thrumming rise up in my chest. "Yeah. Leave it to us. Now, let's get moving, you can fill me in on the way, and I'll stay out of sight so that they think you're alone."

With that, I darted off and headed toward the front gate of the school via a separate route from Rose's. Getting there first, I waited for her to get into the street before following cautiously behind her. Along the way, she filled me in on the state of her family. It matched up with the information we had gotten from Dag. Unfortunately, she wasn't allowed to see them and didn't know where they were being held.

She also filled me in on how the baron was planning to use her ability. It seemed that he wanted Rose to make artifacts he could use to overpower Lord Gambriel and his forces. However, Rose didn't understand how her ability worked and wasn't capable of creating artifacts. So, he had sent her to the academy, hoping that she could find something there to break through her limitations. That play hadn't managed to pay off, though, as Rose still hadn't made any progress toward his goal.

As I mulled over these revelations, we made our way through the merchant district, heading to where I had previously followed Aurelia. However, before we could get to the area with the large manors owned by lesser nobles, we turned down a side street. The buildings here were still rather grand, but couldn't quite be called mansions. Even so, they were larger than anything an ordinary merchant could afford.

After walking down this street for a while, Rose checked her surroundings and knocked on one home's door. A moment later, a maid answered and showed her in, quickly closing the door behind her. *Well, this is going to be a problem. How am I going to get in there?*

I looked around for some other way to get into the estate, but all of the windows were shut tight. I quickly circled around back; the door there was locked as well, and the windows were still sealed. Just as I was about to give up and pry one of the windows open with brute force, I heard someone fiddling with the back door. A maid carrying a basket of clothes quickly stepped out and made to close the door behind her. However, she lost the grip on her basket and paused to prevent herself from dropping it.

During that brief moment where she was distracted, I boosted my speed to the max with magic and darted inside. A moment later, the door closed, and I heard the scraping of the key as she locked it from the outside. *That's rather paranoid. They must not want anyone to get in here.*

Looking around, I found myself alone in the hallway, though I was able to hear some muffled noise coming from the floor above me. I started slinking my way along the halls of the manor, looking for a way up to the second floor. Unlike the noble mansion I had snuck into, this place was fairly average on the inside. It lacked the glamorous decorations, relying instead on size to convey the wealth of the owner.

My search eventually led me to the front door, where I found a large parlor with a single staircase leading to the second floor. I could hear the voices above a little more clearly. I crawled up the stairs, keeping my body as low as I could. Upon reaching the top, I saw a door about halfway down the hall that was barely cracked open.

Creeping closer to the door, I peeked through the crack, finding Rose, along with one other man. He was rather fit looking and wore a simple yet elegant tunic and trousers, reminding me quite a bit of the outfit Dag had been wearing. He stood facing away from the door, looking at a map of the alliance hung on the wall behind him.

"My sources inform me that you've been spending more time with the Gambriel brat at the academy." He paused for a moment, letting his words hang in the air before continuing. "I believe I warned you what would happen if you got involved with him, didn't I?"

"Y-yes, Master Arvis." Rose was clearly flustered as she struggled to squeeze out her response, making me wonder what they had been talking about before. "I've been doing my best to avoid him, but he's classmates with some of my friends."

The baron turned and sauntered toward Rose until he was face-to-face with her, "It's Lord Arvis to you, commoner filth."

"M-my apologies, Lord Arvis. I didn't mean any disrespect."

Reaching up, he grabbed her under the chin, pinching her cheeks between his fingers. "Better. Still, I thought I had set up things rather nicely so that no one at the academy would get involved with you. Who are these supposed friends of yours?"

"Ish no one of importansh."

"Tch." Rose's slurred response seemed to irritate the baron, despite him being the cause of it. He shoved Rose back slightly before releasing her. "Speak normally, girl. I can't understand a word you're saying."

For a long moment, Rose paused, trembling. Based on her reaction, I assumed that the baron didn't usually get this aggressive with her. Sensing things might get out of hand, I decided to give Rose some support. *"Rose, I'm here. If you want me to step in, just call out my name, and I'll get you out of here."*

"Well, spit it out, girl. I haven't got all day!" Baron Arvis yelled at her, a snarl forming on his face.

This time, Rose didn't falter. Taking a deep breath to calm herself before replying, she said, "My apologies, Lord Arvis. I was saying that they're no one you need concern yourself with."

"I'll be the judge of that." He glared at Rose. "Give me their names now."

"Yes. Their names are Lesti Vilia and Aurelia from the first class, second-year."

"Vilia?" The baron paused, his brow furrowed. "Isn't that the girl who's been at the center of all ruckus going on at the academy lately? That could be trouble."

"My lord, if I may." From somewhere outside my range of vision, a third voice joined the conversation. "I don't believe the girl poses any threat to our plans. Her territory is a poor one with little in the way of resources and influence. It would be a simple matter to deny any claims that she would bring against you."

"I see. You make a rather good point." The baron paused for a moment, contemplating the other man's words. "Still, it's better safe than sorry. Have one of yours keep an eye on her just in case."

"As you wish, my lord."

"Now, getting down to business." The baron turned his gaze back on Rose, his expression growing stern. "As I was saying before, I'll be withdrawing your entry at the academy once the academic year is over."

"Could I ask for your reason, Lord Arvis?" Rose's voice was slightly shaky as she responded to the news. "I was under the impression that you wanted me to use the academy's resources to learn how to create artifacts."

"Our friend here has offered his services and will be giving me everything I need to overthrow those wretched fools in the Gambriel family," he replied with a smug grin on his face. "Fear not. I'll allow you to continue your studies in my manor as a backup plan. To that end, I'll need you to fail your remaining lessons so we don't draw any suspicion."

Rose's gaze turned toward the third man whom I couldn't see. "Are you quite certain about this? This man's claims seem dubious at best."

Just as she finished her thought, the baron's hand struck out like a whip, smacking her across the cheek with enough force to knock her to her knees. "Don't you ever question my judgment! Our new associate here has already provided results, unlike you. Maybe if you hadn't taken so long, I wouldn't have had to resort to relying on a third party!"

Rose brought a hand to her cheek, which was rapidly swelling, wincing as she touched it. "Forgive my rudeness, Lord Arvis. I was foolish to think that you would fall for the tricks of a simple con artist."

"Just be glad that I value your ability's potential." He sneered as he looked down at Rose. "Otherwise, I'd have you and that pathetic family of yours disposed of like the filth you are. At any rate, that's all I have to say on this matter. Get out of my sight."

"Yes, my lord." Pulling herself to her feet, Rose gave a brief curtsy and fled the room. I backed up as she opened the door so I wouldn't be seen. Quickly closing the door behind her, she made her way down the hallway.

I started to follow after, but just as I did, I heard the baron start speaking once more. "So, you said you had an idea for that Gambriel brat's birthday party, yes? Spit it out. I haven't got all day, you know."

"Yes." The other man's voice sounded almost gleeful as he replied. "You see, my employer has offered to stage an attack on the party. You and your men will subdue and capture the attackers, regaining you some of the trust of Lord Gambriel until you are ready to make your move."

"And what does this mysterious employer of yours get out of this? I doubt he's doing this out of the kindness of his heart."

Ker-thunk.

In the distance, I heard the back door to the manor close. I paused for a moment, listening to hear where the maid would go. *Dang, it. She's headed this way.* It was unfortunate, but my time was up. I made my way back down the first floor, hiding behind a small plant near the entrance until I heard the maid go up the stairs and proceed down the hall. Once she was gone, I used my magic to silently open the front door that Rose had left unlocked and slip outside, heading back to the academy.

SECRET SUMMONS

* * *

By the time we made it back to the academy, it was almost lunchtime. I met up with Rose along the way, keeping my distance until we were safely on the academy grounds. There was a lot to talk about, so I asked her to head back to the dorm and called Lesti and Aurelia.

"What in the world happened to you?" Lesti stared at Rose's swollen cheek, astonished. We had just walked into Rose's room in the girls' dorm. Much like Lesti's room, it wasn't filled with much besides the necessary furniture and wardrobe. Sitting at the desk with a washbasin at her feet, Rose was pressing a damp cloth against her face.

She smiled gently. "I'm fine. I just angered the baron, is all."

"So, he hit you in the face?!" Lesti walked over and pulled back the compress, revealing the full extent of the bruise. "Next time I see this guy, I'm going to have Astria beat the snot out of him."

"Mm. Fang, too," Aurelia chimed in, her mouth drawn tight in what was an unusual display of anger from her.

"Thank you, both of you." Rose smiled at the pair. "However, until my family is safe, I'd like to ask you to avoid angering the baron too much."

"Your family? So, they're alive after all?"

"Lesti, let her rest. I'll explain," I stepped in, hoping to give Rose a chance to recover, and ran through everything that had happened since this morning.

"So, to summarize, we know that Baron Arvis is holding Rose's family hostage and forcing her to try and make artifacts. On top of that, he's planning on using those artifacts to overthrow Lord Gambriel and make himself lord. Lastly, we've got that mysterious third party who gave him some other way to perform his coup and are planning to attack Elliot's birthday."

"Yeah, I'd say that covers just about everything." I looked over at Rose. "Any idea who the mystery man was?"

She shook her head, a troubled look on her face. "Sorry, no. I've never seen him before."

"That's okay." Lesti smiled at her friend before her gaze grew more serious.

"Still, I'm wondering if he's involved with Thel'al in some way. I can't imagine anyone else being able to offer Arvis a power equal to making artifacts."

"Mm. Seems likely," Aurelia said. "We should be prepared for anything."

"I agree. But we've got a bigger problem than that." I hopped up on the bed and looked at Rose. "Do you have any idea where the baron might be holding your family?"

At my question, her shoulders slumped, and her gaze fell to the floor. "I don't. Honestly, I haven't seen them since well before I joined the academy. I've been begging the baron to let me see them, but he's always refused, saying he can't bring them here."

"Well, that's a hint at least." I looked over at Lesti. "If he's telling the truth, then Rose's family is likely being held somewhere in the Gambriel territory, someplace not directly associated with the baron."

Lesti nodded in agreement. "Yeah. That's a problem, though. How are we supposed to rescue them like that?"

"Yeah. We can't exactly go all the way there ourselves." I fell into thought but couldn't come up with any ideas.

"Why don't we ask Instructor Lani for help?" Just as I was beginning to get frustrated, Aurelia chimed in.

"That's not a bad idea." Lesti snapped her fingers and pointed at Aurelia. "Lani has some pretty strong connections through her job as an instructor. She may even be able to get Frederick involved for us."

"It's worth looking into." I hopped off the bed and headed for the door. "Let's go ask her advice once classes are done for the day."

Lesti looked at me curiously. "Where are you going?"

"There's something that's been bothering me that I need to look into. I'll be back after classes are over. In the meantime, you guys should keep up your training. We're going to need to be prepared, it looks like."

Without waiting for a response, I dashed out the door and headed for the main gate. Since meeting with Dag last night, there was a suspicion I couldn't let go of in the back of my mind. Normally, I would have ignored it, but it was worth seeing if I was right with everything developing so quickly. So, I headed to the commoner market, where I would hopefully find the man himself.

Requesting Assistance

It took me far longer than I would have liked to reach the market. Despite having traveled there several times already, I still managed to get myself lost in the maze-like back alleys of the commoner district. I found my way there eventually, however, and skirted the edge of the market, heading for the area where Dag's stall should have been.

Thanks to my small body, I was able to take several shortcuts between the various stalls and head to the mostly empty area. As I walked through, I noticed several people looking at wares in the other nearby stalls, just like last time. Only this time, I recognized a few of them as the men who had been at the bar we had visited in the red light district. It made me question whether or not the other merchants were in on Dag's little ruse as well.

Walking up to his stall, I saw Dag's familiar figure sitting motionless behind the counter. I jumped straight up in front of him and took a seat. "We need to talk, in private."

"'Ell, if it 'innit Astria!" He flashed me a smile from under his hood, keeping up the fake accent that he had used the last time we had met him here. "What can I 'elp ya wit?"

"Is there somewhere more private we can talk?" I focused my thoughts on Dag so that only he could hear me. *I have a job for the Shadow Dragon Brigade.*

The smile on his face vanished immediately, the casual air he had been putting on before disappearing. He once again gave a quick series of hand signals to the men at the nearby stalls. Rather than wandering off this time, one of them walked over to join us.

"You'll be coming with me, little kitty." The man reached down to pick me up, causing my fur to stand on end. I suppressed my fight or flight instincts and allowed him to pick me up. If my hunch was right, this group wouldn't do anything to harm me.

I looked back as the man carried me straight out of the market and into the back alleys. Dag didn't move an inch or even acknowledge my presence. Once he was out of sight, I shifted my focus to keeping track of where we were going so that I could get back on my own if need be.

After some time wandering the streets, they started to grow dirtier than usual, and the stench became increasingly overpowering; we were definitely getting closer to the slums. Just as I started to worry that I would have to deal with that disgusting smell, the man stopped and looked around. Seeing no one else in the alley, he walked over to a rough-looking wooden door and knocked three times.

The sound of movement came from the other side of the door, followed by a low male voice. "The flames of the dragon…"

"Shall wash away our sins." The man carrying me finished the phrase, and the door cracked open just enough for us to squeeze inside. I found myself in a small room filled to the brim with weapons, armor, and mysterious tools. There were almost no windows in the place, yet it wasn't hot or stuffy.

The man who let us in quickly barred the door behind us. He was younger in appearance than the man carrying me, maybe in his late teens or early twenties. Once he finished securing the door, he turned and looked down at me. "What's with the cat?"

I didn't recognize him, so it made sense that he didn't know who I was, but his friend didn't seem to think so. "Idiot. This is the familiar that the commander has been going on about recently."

"This little thing?" The younger man reached out and started poking at my cheek. "She sure doesn't seem like much."

"Keep that up, and I'll bite your finger off."

He pulled his finger back but otherwise seemed unsurprised, as if he had been expecting my reaction. "So, she can talk. I guess the commander wasn't just making it all up. At any rate, what's she doing here? Did something happen?"

"That's what we're going to find out. We're going to use the secure room. You keep watch." The man carrying me turned and headed toward a door at the back of the room.

"Yes, sir." Hopping up on a box, the younger man pulled out a knife and some wood and started carving, a bored look on his face.

We entered the back room, and the large man finally put me down before shutting the door behind us, casting a spell as he did. For a brief second, the room was plunged into darkness before he finished casting, and magical lights sprung to life in the air around us. With the room properly lit, I took a look around.

It was a relatively simple affair. A desk with writing supplies sat in the far corner with a small shelf full of scrolls next to it. Other than that, the only furniture in the room was a large wooden table that sat directly in the center of the space, covered in dozens of scrolls and parchments. Hopping up on it, I could see most of them were maps of various shapes and sizes, the largest being a map of the entire region that took up the whole table.

"No one will be able to hear us in here." The large man walked over to the table where I sat and grabbed a pen and some parchment off it. "So, the boss says that you have something urgent to tell us. What is it?"

"Well, more than something urgent. I have a request." I took a deep breath, bracing myself for the conversation that would follow. "I want you to help us take down Baron Arvis."

He narrowed his eyes at me. "That's not going to be possible. I'm sure the boss told you the other night, but we've got bigger problems to deal with."

"I'm aware. Your unit is the one that's trying to track down Thel'al, isn't it?" I watched the man carefully, trying to gauge his reaction. "Well, unfortunately, it looks like the two might be linked."

A small smirk appeared on the man's face for a moment, almost as if he was pleased I had figured out what his unit was up to. But it quickly disappeared, replaced by a stern stare. "Well, I've got a few questions of my own now, but that can wait. What makes you think the two are linked?"

I relayed the event from earlier in the day to him. Unfortunately, this meant that I had to take the risk of explaining what Rose's ability was, but there wasn't much choice. We needed their help if we were going to foil the baron's plans and save Rose's family. We just didn't have enough manpower on our own.

After hearing my explanation, the man quickly scribbled down some notes and turned back to me. "So, what is it that you want us to do?"

"We can handle the attack on the party." I walked over the map and used my paws to point at several places. "I want you to raid the various estates linked to Baron Arvis, both here in the city and back in the Gambriel territory."

"Well, the estates here in the city we can handle easily enough." He tapped the spot on the map where the Gambriel household's lands were located, a thoughtful expression on his face. "However, we can't afford to send any men away while the archdemon is still at large. Besides, the commander is the only one who could get there in time."

I watched his finger as it tapped the map, my tail twitching about in frustration as I tried to think of a solution. "Do you think that Lord Gambriel would be willing to step in if we asked him?"

The man stared at the map for a moment as he pondered my question. "It's possible, but I doubt he would make a move without more concrete evidence or testimony from someone that he trusts."

"If we need someone that he trusts, then how about his own son?"

"That would definitely work." He began to scribble on the paper once more. "From my understanding, Lord Gambriel is quite fond of all of his children. I take it you plan to enlist the aid of the third son—Elliot, was it?"

I looked over at the man, slightly surprised that he knew about Elliot. Dag was one thing, but this man seemed like just an underling. I hadn't expected him to have all that much information at his disposal.

Picking up on my surprise, he grinned at me. "On the battlefield, even the slightest bit of information can mean the difference between life and death. Our unit is an elite one, so getting in is extremely difficult. As a result, our numbers are smaller than we'd like, but we also don't have to worry about leaks. Everyone in the Shadow Dragon Brigade can be trusted."

"Well, considering who your leader is, I guess I shouldn't be surprised." I swatted at a piece of paper as I recalled my treatment by the commander. "With a personality like his, I'm sure your applicants are rather limited."

"Haha! Well, you're not wrong there," the man laughed as he finished writing up his letter and sealed it. "Alright, I've got all the information I need. If the archdemon is involved, then I expect the boss will accept your request. Are you sure you can handle the party yourself?"

I hopped off the table and headed for the door. "Yeah, we'll be fine. After all, it can't be any worse than facing off against Thel'al. And this is our chance to redeem ourselves."

The man eyed me skeptically before letting out a sigh and moving to open the door. "Well, if you say you can handle it, then that's fine. Don't hesitate to call on us for help if you need it."

"I'll keep that in mind. Actually, how would I even do that?" I wasn't planning on asking for their help, but it couldn't hurt to be prepared.

He paused and thought about it for a moment. "Well, for now, just have that little master of yours cause a big enough spectacle, and we'll come running."

What kind of plan is that?! What are we supposed to do, just blow the roof off the place? I stared at the man for a moment before letting out a sigh. With reckless tactics like that, I could tell this group took after their commander. Still, I doubted we would need their help, so I decided not to bother scolding him.

With the help of Dag and his team secured, I headed back to the school. There was still a lot of work to be done, and we were running out of time. The memory of the sea of slaughtered magical beasts flashed before my eyes. Pushing down the anxiety I felt, I steeled my resolve. Elliot's party was in a week, and this time we were going to protect everyone.

* * *

When I arrived back at the academy, it was late afternoon, just around the time classes should be coming to an end. I wanted to meet up with the others and get back to training, but there was one last person that I needed to recruit. Arriving at the training grounds, I scanned the crowds of students and instructors heading in every direction until I found my target. On the far side of the field stood Lani, talking to a pair of her students.

Skirting the crowds as best as I could, I made my way over to her and arrived just as their conversation ended. "Lani, you got a minute?"

She looked around for a minute before finally finding me sitting behind her. "Oh, Astria. Sure. What do you need?"

"Let's go somewhere else to talk." I looked out over the students still hanging about the field, remembering the baron had an informant here at the school. "It'd be better if others didn't hear this."

Lani's gaze grew serious. "Alright. Let's head back to my private quarters then."

Without waiting for me to respond, Lani headed across the field in a brisk walk. The urgency in her step caught me off guard, and I had to trot along to keep up with her. At such a quick pace, we arrived at her room before long. Upon entering, she closed the door behind her and turned to look at me, her expression stern. "What has Lesti gotten herself into this time?"

So, that's what she was worried about, huh? I couldn't help but be amused by how well she had Lesti figured out. Still, now wasn't the time to bring that up. I needed Lani to be focused on our conversation. Jumping up on the bed, I started explaining everything that was happening with Rose, and how I had enlisted the Shadow Dragon Brigade's aid.

"All that has been going on, and she didn't tell me anything?" Lani's shoulders slumped. "Why do I feel like we've taken two steps backward?"

"I don't think you need to worry. This isn't like before, where Lesti didn't want to rely on you. In fact, it was her idea to ask for your help."

I tried my best to comfort her before she fell into a complete depression or, even worse, got angry. I felt a shiver run down my spine at the thought of taking the brunt of her anger on my own. "Besides, even if we had reached out to you earlier, was there really anything you could have done?"

Lifting her gaze, she smiled wryly at me. "I suppose that's true. At any rate, what did you need my help with? It sounds like you've got everything under control from what I can tell."

I shook my head. "There's one loose end that could mess everything up if we're not careful. The baron has some spies and informants here at the school."

"I see." Lani's eyes lit up a little, and she caught on to my point. "So, you'd like me to figure out who they are and make sure they don't catch onto your plans."

"That's right." My chest started to thrum in appreciation with how quickly Lani caught on. "This will all be for nothing if the baron moves Rose's family or calls off his attack on the party."

"That would be quite the problem." Lani stood there pondering something for a moment before continuing. "Still, I'm not sure that I'll be able to figure out who the spies are in such a short amount of time. I haven't looked into this Baron Arvis character before."

"Don't worry. We don't actually need to know who they are."

"We don't?" Lani looked at me like I was out of my mind.

"Nope. After all, they'll probably reveal themselves. Think about it. To learn anything useful, they'll have to keep a close eye on Rose. That will make them stick out like a sore thumb."

"Ah, right," Lani replied. "You said the baron forces her to keep her distance from the other students. Still, there are times that I won't be able to keep an eye on her, so we'll have some blind spots."

"I suppose that's true."

We both sat there in silence for some time, each pondering how we could fill in the gaps where Lani wasn't available. While our group didn't have any classes right now, we needed to use that time to train if we wanted to be ready in time for the party. We'd have to ask someone else to do it. Preferably, someone who would be able to go unnoticed.

"I've got it!" I stood up excitedly, tail flicking wildly. "We can have the headmistress's familiar cover the times where you aren't available."

Lani chuckled at my reaction, causing me to sit back down and try to control my tail. It still swished back and forth despite my best efforts. I had good reason to be happy. After all, everything was starting to fall into place. As long as nothing unexpected happened, we would be able to get the better of Thel'al this time.

"At any rate, could you ask her if she'll help?"

"Of course. Leave it to me." Lani brought her hand to her chest, eyes practically sparkling. It was blatantly obvious that she was delighted that she could help Lesti out once again.

I hopped down from the bed and rubbed against her leg, purring slightly as I made my way to the door. "Thanks, Lani. It's a big help."

"Don't mention it." She walked over to open it for me. "Just be careful. With Thel'al involved, there's no telling what could happen."

"Don't worry. We won't make the same mistakes as last time. This time, we'll win and save Rose and her family."

With a satisfied nod, Lani opened the door, and we went our separate ways. Everything was in place now. All we could do was wait and keep training ourselves to prepare for the battle to come. Praying it would be enough, I went to find Lesti and the others and fill them in on everything that was going on.

* * *

"So, that's what you've been doing all day." Lesti looked at me with a bright grin on her face. "I figured you were up to something when you ran off like that, but this is way more than I expected. Great work, Astria."

We were in the classroom we always used for our evening study sessions. By the time I had arrived, the setting sun was casting long shadows across the room, and the girls were already hard at work. Elliot was missing, but I expected that was thanks to Dag and his unit getting in touch with him.

I purred contentedly as she scratched behind my ears and praised me. "Don't mention it. I figured that we would have to do at least this much if we were going to beat Thel'al this time."

"Mm. We just have to work hard and get stronger now." Aurelia pumped her fists in a rare display of enthusiasm. Fang, seeing his master so pumped up, ran about in circles excitedly.

"I-I'll do my best as well." Rose, meanwhile, seemed anxious. "All of you are doing so much for me, I need to do my best not to hold you back."

"That's the spirit." Lesti smiled brightly at her for a moment before looking back at the tomes she had been studying, as if pondering something. "Still, there's got to be more we can do, right?"

I could tell from her expression that she was worried. The last time we had tried to stop Thel'al's plans, the archdemon had been one step ahead of us. In the end, we had managed to barely save Fang, and even that had required outside intervention. I wasn't about to let that happen again.

"Actually, I have a few ideas there." I turned my gaze to each of the girls, in turn, finally stopping on Rose. "It'll require the use of your ability, though. Are you okay with that?"

"Of course," Rose replied without hesitation, meeting my gaze firmly. "Nothing would make me happier than for the ability which has caused my family so much suffering to be used to save them."

"Great." I turned my gaze to Lesti. "We're going to need your expertise here, too. There's a spell I want you to try making. Just to warn you, it's going to be a bit different from what you're used to."

"Leave it to me." She puffed her chest out and grinned at me with all of her usual confidence. "If there's a spell that you can think of, then I'll find some way to make it a reality."

"Great, then that just leaves you two." I turned my attention to Aurelia and Fang. "I was thinking we could combine the abilities that you've both been developing. If we start now, we should make it just in time."

"Mm. If you're teaching us, then we'll definitely be able to do it."

"Alright, let's get to work then. We haven't got any time to waste after all."

Everything was officially set in motion. All that was left to do was execute our plans. With all of us working together, I was confident we could handle anything Thel'al and his minions threw our way. But there was still a bit of unease at the very back of my mind that I just couldn't shake. Trying my best to ignore it, I started our week-long training session.

Finding a Spy

Lani glanced over at the nearby first-year class as she gave her tournament preparation lesson on the training grounds. It was rather hard to keep an eye on Rose's situation and teach simultaneously, but she was managing well enough. She had carefully positioned herself to watch over the other class while addressing her own students. Thankfully, it seemed like no one had caught on to what she was doing so far.

It had been a few days since Astria had asked her to keep an eye on Rose, but so far, she hadn't seen any trace of Baron Arvis's informants. Anyone who did manage to approach Rose would probably stick out like a sore thumb. Outside of the time she spent with Lesti and the others, the girl was always alone. None of her classmates acknowledged her, and her teacher rarely called on her to demonstrate any spells. It was like she just faded into the background.

"And still, she doesn't even try to reach out."

"Did you say something, Instructor Lania?" One of the students who had been practicing her earth attack spells on the practice dummy called out to Lani, having apparently heard her muttering under her breath.

"Ah, no. It's nothing." Lani smiled at the girl, shaking her head. "That was an excellent Stone Spear spell, Natasha. It should serve you well in the tournament if you're careful about when you use it. The casting time leaves you somewhat vulnerable to counter attacks after all."

"I see. I didn't realize." The girl smiled back at her and gave a brief, elegant curtsy. "I shall keep that in mind. Thank you, instructor."

"Alright, who's next?" Lani called the next student up to show their progress, but her mind quickly drifted back to Rose. As far as Lani could tell, the girl wasn't happy about her situation. Most of the time, she looked utterly miserable. Yet, she didn't seem to put any effort into changing things.

It didn't happen often, but even Rose had to participate in her class sometimes. In those moments, Lani felt like she got a glance at what she was really like, and as a teacher, it was frustrating to watch. On those rare occasions, Rose would simply go through the motions. Her spells weren't weak or anything of the sort. But they never improved, either.

Despite her lack of effort, she always wore a pained expression whenever she was called on. It was an expression that Lani knew all too well. Just a few years ago, she had seen it whenever she had looked in the mirror. Back when Lesti was struggling with her parents' death, Lani didn't feel like she could do anything for her, no matter how hard she had tried.

That feeling had slowly eaten away at her on the inside. Even now, she regretted not being able to do more for Lesti back then. It was easy to see how Rose might be feeling something similar. After all, her family was being held hostage, and she was powerless to do anything about it.

Regardless, there was nothing that Lani could do about that right now. She'd have to leave that to Lesti and the others. For her part, she would make sure to catch the baron's spy and keep Rose safe. After all, Astria had asked her to do just that.

***

Later that evening, Lani was making her rounds of the campus. Classes had ended some time ago, and most of the students were now in the dining hall. However, there was one student still outside, toiling away despite the rapidly setting sun. Sweat dripped from Rose's forehead as she continuously worked the land under her feet.

Normally, Lani wouldn't have taken this route, instead patrolling the halls of the main building. But she had seen Lesti and the others in the dining hall and had overheard them, mentioning Rose had turned down joining them for dinner. Thinking something might be wrong, she went to check on the girl and had found her here, wearing the same troubled expression from earlier that day.

Unlike before, there was the faintest hint of determination. Whatever emotions were weighing on the young girl's shoulders, she was trying to battle them in her own way. With a slight smile, Lani began to turn and head back toward the main building. That was when she saw it.

From the shadows on the far side of the field that Rose tended to, a pair of piercing yellow eyes watched the girl. At first, Lani thought that they were nothing but an illusion or figment of her imagination. After all, eyes had to have a body, and she couldn't see one. But slowly her mind began to make more sense of what she was seeing, and a faint shape formed in the shadows.

Lani's blood ran cold at the sight of that shape. "It can't be."

Not wanting to panic Rose, Lani took a wide path around the garden, trying her best to get out of the girl's line of sight. As she moved, the yellow eyes she had spotted before locked onto her and began to follow her movements. Just as she cleared Rose's line of sight, she dashed toward the creature as quickly and silently as she could. The beast turned and ran off to the rear of the academy grounds, but not before Lani swore it shot her a toothy grin.

Giving chase, she followed the creature toward the deepest parts of the grounds, far behind the abandoned annex building. This part of the academy was rarely visited by both students and teachers and was overgrown with tall grasses and brush. The creature dove into the grass and disappeared from Lani's sight, but she didn't give up the chase, following it by sound.

A few moments later, she broke free from the tall grasses and found herself standing in the shadow of a large tree. The dog-like beast sat at the base of the tree, staring back at her with a mischievous grin. It was much larger than Lani had expected, about the size of a wolf, with much longer limbs. Its dark grey fur blended with the shadows, nearly rendering it invisible to the naked eye, but its pale-yellow eyes stood in stark contrast to that darkness. Behind the creature, four shadowy tails with barbed ends flicked through the air.

Once she saw them, Lani was finally sure. The creature sitting before her was one of the most notorious beasts in the world. The myths and legends about them even rivaled those of dragons like Skell. Before her sat a Rift Stalker, a creature that could defy the laws of time and space; the harbinger of doom.

Lani steeled herself, preparing to try and capture the creature, but before she could, a male voice rang through her head. "Now, now, there's no need to look so tense. I didn't come here looking for a fight. I'm just following orders."

"What? You?" Lani stared wide-eyed at the grinning Rift Stalker in front of her. "Rift Stalkers shouldn't be able to use telepathy. You're a familiar?"

"Yep. That's right." The voice in her head sounded surprisingly young, perhaps only a little older than Lesti.

"Since you were watching Rose, I can assume you're Baron Arvis's familiar?"

"Right again. You're quick on the uptake, aren't you, miss?" The Rift Stalker then did something rather strange—it bowed, though it wasn't the type of play bow you would expect from a dog or a cat. It was a strange, almost human gesture. "The baron calls me Shadow, but I rather dislike that name. It seems too much like something you would call a pet. I would prefer it if you called me Zeke."

"Well, Zeke, I'm sorry, but I'm going to need you to come with me." Lani crouched low in her combat stance and began to prepare a spell. "Spying on our students is a serious offense, and you'll need to answer to the headmistress."

"Sorry, I would love to, but I'm afraid that would be a direct breach of orders." Zeke stood and began to walk away. "I was hoping we could chat a little, but it doesn't seem like that will be possible, so I'll just take my leave here."

"That's not going to happen! Ice Spear!"

Not wanting to give him a chance to escape, Lani launched the spell she had prepared ahead of time at Zeke. In the blink of an eye, water was gathered from the air near her and formed into a spear shape, before having the temperature rapidly reduced to freeze it solid. The spear of ice flew toward

Zeke, but just before it hit him, the spear simply disappeared.

"Spell Jamming?! That late in the spell?" Lani stared at Zeke in shock.

"Spell Jamming? No, that's not something I can do. All I did was use a little heat and electrolysis to…" Zeke stopped his explanation midway. "Right, you wouldn't know what that is. Let's just say that I made the water not be water anymore."

Lani's only response was to snap her fingers. Suddenly, another spear of ice formed behind Zeke and launched itself at the back of his head. It was a trick she had picked up from watching Frederick back when the Ice Drakes attacked the city. If it had been a few months prior, she would have never picked up on it. However, after watching Lesti use magic circles to shortcut binding her spells to keywords, she realized she needed to reevaluate her understanding of what was possible when it came to magic.

She felt confident that her attack would land this time. Not only had she cast it silently, but from an angle that her opponent wouldn't be able to see. But one of Zeke's four barbed tails flicked through the air, and reality distorted at the last second. The spear that had been heading for him disappeared, and alarm bells started going off in Lani's head. She threw herself to the side just as the spear she had launched at Zeke came flying at her from behind.

Rolling to her feet, she glared at him. "So, that's the infamous ability of Rift Stalkers that I've heard so much about? It's not as impressive as I've heard if all it can do is redirect attacks."

"Oh, you wouldn't happen to be looking down on me, would you, miss?" The voice in Lani's head suddenly gained a dark tinge as Zeke turned to face her, his eyes narrowed in anger, "If that's that case, then why don't I give you a taste of what I can really do."

A malicious, unnatural grin spread across Zeke's face, and his tails went to work behind him. The first one flicked through the air just like before, distorting reality. But unlike last time, the distortion didn't disappear immediately. Instead, two of the other tails lashed out to the spot, sank into the distortion, and began to pull.

A sudden feeling of nausea washed over Lani as a small rift began to open in reality. It wasn't long before it was wide enough for her to see through to the other side. At first, she couldn't quite make anything out. Everything was covered in a purple haze. However, as she continued to stare into the rift, she soon found something staring back at her, with eyes as black as the void.

"Impossible. A demon?" Lani froze as feelings of shock and terror washed over her.

"That's better." Zeke's malicious grin returned to the same strange but casual smile he had before. Then, just as suddenly as he had opened it, he used his four tails to stitch reality back together and seal the rift. "I hope you understand your place now. If I wanted to, I could open a path for those creatures right here. Still, that would go against my orders, so I would rather not."

"Your orders?" Lani shook off the terror that had gripped her heart just moments before. She would have to give up on capturing Zeke for now, but she might still be able to get him talking and learn something useful. "Why would you take orders from someone like Arvis when you have that kind of power?"

At her question, Zeke's smile turned into a scowl. "Let's just say the deal we made wasn't a fair one and leave it at that. At any rate, for now, I've just been ordered to report back on what the girl is doing."

As he spoke, Zeke's tails flicked through the air once more, opening another rift behind him. This time, rather than the purple haze that had been there before, what looked like the halls of a manor appeared. "Now, if you'll excuse me, I have to report back soon, or the baron will get angry. Let's meet again soon, Miss Instructor."

"Wait!" Lani tried to call out and stop him, hoping she could squeeze out more information. But Zeke ignored her call and leapt through the rift, quickly closing it behind him before Lani had a chance to follow. For a long moment after, she couldn't hear anything but her own heartbeat as she tried to process what she had just seen.

She had always heard dreadful tales about Rift Stalkers as she was growing up, but had considered them just that—tales. As far as she knew, it had been hundreds of years since the last confirmed sighting of one. Many assumed that they had been wiped out in one of the previous wars. However, she was sure that's what Zeke was, especially after seeing his power.

Turning on her heel, Lani began to run back toward the school building. This was bigger than Rose now. As things stood, every single student at the academy was in danger. She had to tell the headmistress what had happened so that they could prepare.

Bets and Tours

Aurelia and Fang both collapsed to the ground in front of me, exhausted. Their breathing was heavy, and Aurelia's brow was covered in sweat. *Looks like they still can't use it for very long. It'll make a lovely trump card if they find themselves in a pinch, though.*

"That's enough for tonight. We don't want to exhaust ourselves before the big day tomorrow." I waited for the pair to recover before we headed back inside. It was late in the afternoon, but there was still quite a bit of time left before the sunset. Normally, I would have wanted to train for even longer, but we had already been pushing ourselves incredibly hard all week long. We needed to take a break, or we wouldn't be able to fight properly tomorrow.

Once Fang and Aurelia were back on their feet, we made our way up to the usual classroom. There we found Lesti and Rose packing up their things. Lesti looked like she was just about to fall over from exhaustion. Walking over, I rubbed up against her leg. "It looks like you managed to finish?"

She smiled at me wearily, yet still somehow managed to have all her usual bravado. "Yeah. It was a piece of cake with Rose's help. Baron Arvis and his goons won't know what hit them."

"Yeah. Your invention will most certainly catch them off-guard." Rose threw a heavy-looking sack over her shoulder, the sound of stone hitting stone coming from within. "I don't think I've ever seen magic applied in this way before."

I felt a slight thrumming sensation in my chest at her praise. "Well, it's pretty much impossible without your ability, so that's no surprise. At any rate, we should all go get some dinner and get to bed. It's going to be a long day tomorrow."

With everyone as exhausted as they were, none of them had the energy to argue, and we headed to the dining hall. There was a strange sense of tension amongst the group as they ate. Usually, they would all be chatting cheerfully, but today they ate their food in silence. I couldn't blame them. I was pretty nervous about tomorrow myself.

As soon as everyone finished their meals, we headed back to the dorm, where we parted ways and went to bed early. I had expected Lesti to be restless. Yet, contrary to my expectations, she passed out in record time. Helping Rose with her task while working on improving her magic had taken its toll on her.

I curled up next to her like I typically did and tried to sleep, but found I was wide awake. Despite being exhausted, I couldn't shake the strange, foreboding feeling in the back of my mind. But no matter how hard I thought about it, there was nothing else that we could do. After several hours of this, I grew frustrated and got up. Trying not to wake Lesti, I silently made my way to the door.

Using Wind Rake, I gently manipulated the door and snuck out. I didn't have any particular destination, so I just wandered toward the building's front entrance. But as I was moving along, I heard the sound of quiet footsteps on the stone floor. Making my way toward the noise, I found a familiar figure creeping through the darkness.

"Rose, is that you?"

Rose jumped and began looking around wildly at the sound of my voice. *Ah, right. She probably can't see me in the dark.* Even after several months of living in this new world, I sometimes forgot my eyesight and senses were now better than that of an average human.

"It's me, Astria," I called out to her once more, this time identifying myself. "Sorry if I scared you. What are you doing up?"

Hearing my name, Rose visibly relaxed, though she kept looking around for me in the dark. "I couldn't sleep. I figured I would take a quick stroll out to the garden and clear my mind. What about you?"

"Actually, I'm having trouble sleeping myself. Do you mind if I join you?" I walked up and rubbed against her leg, causing her to start briefly before she looked down and saw me.

"Of course not." She gave me a relieved smile. "I would love to have your company."

We headed out of the dorms and into the chilly spring evening. The stars and moon filled the clear night sky, giving us plenty of light as we made our way to the garden. When we arrived, Rose stopped and stared up at the night sky. "It's beautiful, isn't it?"

I joined her, taking in the countless stars and constellations. I felt a wave of nostalgia wash over me. It had been a night just like this that I was summoned to this world. Back then, I wasn't able to appreciate the stars with everything else that was happening. Sadly, tonight was much the same. While the night sky was beautiful, the sense of dread I felt robbed me of the joy I should be feeling from watching it.

We sat there in silence for a while until Rose finally spoke up again. "You know, I haven't viewed the stars like this in years. The last time I did was the night before the baron's men came along and took me away." I looked over at her and saw a bitter smile on her face. "Since then, whenever I see the stars, I can only remember the terror and fear of being stripped away from my family. For a while, I was worried that they might be dead."

"You've been through a lot, huh?"

"That's true. Still, the hardest part was being alone." Her bitter smile faded, replaced by a more genuine one. "When Lesti and Aurelia first started talking to me, I was terrified. I thought they were going to try and use me for my ability and start some sort of power struggle with the baron."

After thinking about what she said, I tilted my head to the side. "Actually, isn't that kind of what ended up happening anyway?"

She blinked once then started laughing. Unlike her usual dainty giggles, this was a full-hearted laugh. The first one I had seen from her since we had met. Eventually, she got her laughter under control and wiped tears from the corners of her eyes. "I guess you're right. Yet, I don't mind it at all. I know that I haven't known you for very long, but I really do consider you to be my friends. You've all done so much for me. It's just a shame that I won't be able to pay you back."

"What do you mean?" Suddenly, I felt the sense of dread that I had been feeling for a while flare-up.

Rose looked back toward the stars, avoiding my gaze. "Well, when all of this is over, I can't imagine that I'll stay here at the academy. I'll have lost my sponsor, and I'd like to spend some time with my family again."

I stared at Rose, utterly dumbstruck by what she had said. Her words made me realize that I had forgotten to think about what would come after our confrontation with the baron. Rose's ability was clearly useful to Thel'al for some reason. His followers wouldn't be sticking their noses in this situation otherwise.

My mind began to race as the realization that there was still more work to do dawned on me. I was almost out of time. I only had tomorrow morning and early afternoon to make any preparations. *Will that be enough time?* I grit my teeth in frustration.

"Is something the matter?" Rose, sensing my frustration, looked down at me worriedly.

No, it's nothing." I turned and started to head back toward the dorm. "Come on. We need to get to bed. Tomorrow's going to be a long day."

We headed back to the dorm and said our goodnights once more. When I returned to our room, Lesti was still sleeping soundly. Jumping up on the bed, I curled up next to her and tried my best to fall asleep. Despite having so many more things to worry about, the feeling of dread I had before was gone. As I pondered why that might be, my eyes grew heavy, and I quickly drifted off to sleep.

* * *

I stood outside in the courtyard and stared at the wooden door in front of me, wondering what I should do. It was early morning, well before most people would be awake. I needed to talk to Elliot in private, so I had come over to the boys' dorm. However, upon arriving outside, I realized that I didn't know where his room was. Not to mention, I was somewhat conflicted about barging into the boys' dorm. Despite being a cat, I was still a girl, after all.

Well, nothing is going to be solved by me sitting around out here. Making up my mind, I began to cast my magic to open the door. However, just as my spell reached completion, the door swung open, its thick wooden structure replaced by the sleepy face of Elliot. I tried to stop casting, but I was too slow. Without any warning, he was smacked in the face with a Wind Rake spell powerful enough to push open the heavy wooden door.

I stared aghast as Elliot tumbled backward. But before he could hit the ground, he tucked his chin, using his momentum to roll over his shoulder, avoiding any serious injury. Popping up into the low crouch, he glared menacingly at the door, his practice spear ready in his hand. Upon seeing me standing there, he paused and blinked a few times.

"Astria, what's going on?" He stood up and looked down at me, confused. "Did I do something to anger you?"

Why are you jumping to conclusions like that?! The fact that Elliot thought I was the type of person who would come and attack him out of the blue for upsetting me irked me more than I expected. "I was just trying to open the door!"

"Ah, right. I suppose you can't open the door normally, being a cat and all." He walked back over and closed the door behind him. "Still, try to be more careful in the future. It's not a big deal since it was me, but someone less trained in combat might have been seriously injured."

Being lectured by a boy his age was mortifying, but he was right, so I couldn't even argue back. I suddenly found that I couldn't look him in the eye and averted my gaze. "S-sorry about that. I'll be more careful next time."

Elliot gave a satisfied nod. "Excellent. Now, did you need me to fetch someone for you, or were you looking for me?"

"Right." I shook off my embarrassment and turned my attention back to the task at hand. "Can we go somewhere more private? I had something that I needed to discuss with you."

"Well, there's no one around at this time of the day." He looked around the abandoned courtyard. "Why don't we talk on our way to the training grounds?"

The idea that someone might overhear us made me a little nervous, but it seemed unlikely. It was a clear morning with no fog for a change, so we'd be able to see if anyone was following us. "Sure. That's fine."

We started making our way toward the training grounds. Once we were far enough away from the boys' dorm that I was confident no one could hear us, I started talking. "I want you to help us convince your father to let Lesti become Rose's sponsor."

Elliot glanced down at me, his face a mask that hid his emotions. His reaction caught me completely off guard. This was the first time I had seen him act like a noble in this manner. For a few seconds, the only sound was that of the dew-covered grass being crushed underfoot as we walked along. "I struggle to see how that would benefit my family or my people. Care to explain your thoughts?"

Suddenly far more nervous than I expected to be, I felt the strange desire to shred something with my claws. I took a deep breath and pushed that feeling aside, looking up at Elliot. "Once this is all over, there might be others who will come after Rose for her ability. That includes Thel'al and his demon worshipers."

"All the more reason to put her in the care of the Gambriel family, no? No offense to Lesti, but we have far more resources at our disposal than the Vilia family."

"You have a good point there." I stopped and glanced up at him. "But tell me this. Do you think anyone in your father's employ could keep her safe if Thel'al seriously went after her? The beast he turned Fang into barely scratches the surface of what he can do."

Elliot paused, his carefully constructed mask faltering for the first time. Under it, I caught a glimpse of doubt. However, he still didn't accept my proposal outright. "You make an excellent point, but you still haven't addressed my concern. If my family doesn't have the strength to defend her, then there's no way that the much weaker Vilia family will be able to."

"That's where you're wrong." I gazed at him defiantly. "Lesti and I could—no, we *will* protect her."

Elliot stared back at me as though searching for the source of my confidence. His reaction was perfectly understandable. He had missed our last week of intense training and had no idea what we were all capable of now. We'd just have to show him then. I felt my tail start to twitch about as a rather mischievous idea formed in my head.

"It seems we're at an impasse here, so why don't we make a bet?"

Elliot narrowed his eyes at me suspiciously. "A bet?"

"Yeah. This morning, you'll have a sparring bout with Lesti. If she wins, then you'll admit that we're better suited to protecting Rose."

"And what if I win? As far as I can tell, there's nothing in this for me."

"I guess you have a good point there. It's not much of a bet if there's nothing for you to win." I gazed off toward the training grounds where I could see Lesti and Aurelia starting their morning practice. Aurelia and Fang were properly warming up, while Lesti was slacking off and reading books on magic theory as usual. It was a little frustrating to see, but at the same time, it gave me an excellent idea of what I could offer Elliot.

"How about this? If you win, then I'll teach you how to increase the power of your spells."

Elliot followed my gaze, eyes landing on Lesti. "Increase their power, huh? Alright, you've got yourself a deal."

Bending down, he held out his hand. I placed my paw in it, and he gently shook it, which felt rather odd. Honestly, I felt more like a pet doing a trick than an equal making an agreement. Still, I was too busy relishing my victory to focus on that. After all, there was no way that Elliot was going to beat Lesti as she was now.

***

A while later, Elliot was sitting on his butt, his spear lodged into the ground nearby. Balls of flame and spears of stone hovered in the air around him, preventing him from moving. He stared at Lesti in disbelief, eyes wide. Meanwhile, I watched smugly.

"Want to keep going?" Lesti called out to him, her satisfied grin matching my inner feelings. "I can do this all day."

Elliot stared at her for a moment longer before smiling. "No. I know when I'm beaten. I admit defeat."

Clap, clap, clap.

Suddenly from behind me, I heard the sound of someone clapping quite loudly, as if trying to announce their presence. Turning to see who was there, I found a man I had never seen before. His chestnut-colored hair was tied back in a long ponytail, a popular style amongst noblemen.

He was perhaps just a little older than I had been before I was reincarnated, dressed in formal wear entirely unsuited for the training grounds. A rather attractive maid trailed behind him as if she were his shadow.

Lesti stared back at the man with an expression that bordered on loathing. "Augustine, what are you doing here? I wasn't expecting you until this evening."

"Yes, that was the original plan, but I simply couldn't wait to see you." Augustine smiled at her, causing a shiver to run down my spine. Though his smile was quite charming on the surface, it never reached his amber eyes. This man was clearly good at putting on airs.

"I thought that perhaps you could show me around the academy and introduce me to some of your friends." He glanced over at Aurelia, looking her up and down, causing her to glare back at him. *Wow, Lesti wasn't kidding when she said he was a scumbag. He hasn't even been here for five minutes, and he's already eyeing her friends.*

"I deeply apologize, Augustine, but after this, I have to begin preparing for the party tonight." She gave a quick yet elegant curtsy as she rejected him. I hadn't seen Lesti act so formally since I arrived in this world, so the gesture caught me off guard. The fact that Augustine was the person she was talking to made it seem all the stranger to me.

"What? After I came all this way?" At first, Augustine seemed somewhat irritated. However, he soon turned his gaze down toward me while looking like he had just come up with the most brilliant idea. "Well then, perhaps your familiar here could show me around?"

I saw Lesti start to say something but quickly cut her off. "I would be honored to show you around the academy, Master Augustine."

Taking note of Rose's manners, I tried to be as polite as possible. Lesti stared at me, completely dumbfounded. She was surely wondering why I was acting so polite and friendly towards someone that she considered public enemy number one. Honestly, I just wanted to see what he was planning. Based on first impressions, his reason for showing up early like this was undoubtedly devious.

Augustine turned and started walking toward the main building. "Excellent. Then let's get started right away. My time is rather limited, after all."

I followed after him, glancing back at Lesti as I reassured her privately, *"Don't worry. I'll be fine. Besides, this way, we can make sure he doesn't cause any trouble."*

She visibly relaxed after hearing my reasoning but still had a troubled expression on her face. *"Astria, be careful. Unless he's about to do something truly terrible, you can't attack him. The rules of the academy don't apply to him."*

Rules of the academy? I wasn't sure what she meant by that but didn't have time to ask. Augustine was already looking back at me with an annoyed expression as he pulled ahead of me with quick strides. *At any rate, I just have to make sure not to hit him. It should be easy enough.* Keeping Lesti's warning in mind, I trotted ahead of Augustine and began to show him around the academy.

* * *

An hour later, I was utterly fed up with Lesti's betrothed. We were finishing up our tour of the academy with the library, which was filled to the brim with students. Augustine spent most of our time together scoffing at how old and primitive the facilities were. Even in the library, he continued to complain about the seating not being fit for nobles.

The only time he hadn't been whining about the facilities was when he was staring at the female students and staff like a creep. The way he looked them up and down like nothing more than pieces of meat was disturbing in and of itself. However, once you considered that even the oldest students here were only sixteen, it became downright revolting. It had taken every ounce of my willpower not to claw his eyes out.

Even worse, though, was how he was clearly using my presence to make everyone aware of his "relationship" with Lesti. Whenever he would ask me a question, he would intentionally ask me as loudly as possible, while making sure to refer to me as his "fiancée's familiar" in awkward ways. It seemed my guess had been correct to some extent, and he was trying to ward off any other potential suitors that might get ideas.

Regardless, I had managed to make it through the entire tour, and my duty was going to be done soon. All I had to do now was see him off the grounds, and I could be rid of this foul man until this evening. Just as I was about to suggest we head toward the gate, a familiar voice called out from behind me.

"Astria? What are you doing here?" I turned around to see Lani walking up, a pile of books in her hands. "I figured that you would be helping Lesti prepare for the party this evening."

Augustine, noticing I was no longer paying attention, turned around, looking like he was about to scold me, but stopped short when he spotted Lani. "Familiar, who is this?"

"This is Lani, one of the instructors here at the academy." I intentionally didn't mention her being from the Vilia territory or her service to Lesti's parents. If this guy found out about that, I got the feeling that he might start acting like he owned her. Unfortunately, it turned out my efforts were for naught.

"Lani. My what a lovely specimen." He bowed gracefully and kissed Lani's hand. "I am Augustine Vanderbolt, second son of the Vanderbolt family and future lord of the Vilia territory. May I ask what family you belong to? I would like to start negotiating with them right away."

At hearing the man's full name, Lani's face grew hard. "I am sorry, Master Augustine, but I don't belong to any family, so there is no one for you to negotiate with."

"I see. You're not of noble birth." He looked somewhat disappointed but quickly recovered as he rose to his feet. "Well, no matter, you'll still make a fine concubine. Silvia, please make the necessary arrangements once we return."

The maid that had been following us the entire time, pulled up her skirt in a quick curtsy. "As you wish, Master Augustine."

"Now then, where were we? As yes, I apologize, but I won't be able to take you as my consort right away. The foolish old man running the Vilia territory keeps delaying my marriage, you see. Worry not, though. I shall settle that matter soon enough."

"Master Augustine, I do apologize, but I can't become your consort." Lani's response was calm on the surface, but I could feel a bit of the same chill I always did when she was angry. This didn't appear to be lost on Augustine, either.

He glared at her with narrowed eyes, "Oh, and why is that? You had better have a good reason."

"First, I have my duties here at the academy to attend to. Second, I already have someone that I intend to serve."

"And who might that be?" Augustine practically snarled at her. I could tell he was slowly growing angrier by the moment.

Lani simply smiled back at him, her voice growing colder. "That's not for me to say at this time. You only need to know that it's someone truly worthy of the title, lord."

I felt a smug sense of satisfaction as Lani delivered her put down. She had carefully chosen her words to not be a direct insult while still delivering maximum damage. Augustine didn't seem to share my appreciation, however; his fists curled tightly into balls, and his face turned red as a tomato.

"So, that's how it is, then?" Augustine took a step forward, causing me to tense. I knew Lesti had warned me not to hurt him, but if he was going to take a swing at Lani, I wasn't going to let that go. "You stupid peasant. I'll find this lord of yours and—"

"You'll what, Master Augustine?" An authoritative voice I knew came from down the hall. Being careful not to lose sight of Augustine, I turned to find the headmistress heading toward us, her familiar riding on her shoulder. "I would hope you weren't thinking of threatening a member of the academy? You do remember that all within these walls are to be treated as equals, yes?"

Augustine clicked his tongue and stepped back from Lani. "That only applies to the students here, and you know it, you old hag."

"As lovely a personality as ever I see." The headmistress approached our group, maintaining a calm, dismissive air. "While that may be the council's official stance, I personally intend to hold everyone, even guests, to that standard. Still, if you'd like to push the matter further, we could continue our discussion on the training grounds."

Her tone darkened significantly with those last words, giving the impression there wouldn't be much talking going on if Augustine didn't back down. Augustine simply glared at her for a moment before turning on his heel and storming off. "Enough of this foolishness. I have far more important matters to attend to. Silvia, we're leaving."

"Yes, Master Augustine." The maid quickly curtsied to the headmistress, her face just as lacking in expression as always, before scurrying off after her master.

"What a scumbag." Once he was well out of earshot, I voiced my grievances with the headmistress. "How the hell could the council pick a disgusting man like him to become Lesti's husband?"

She stared off after him, a rare look of disappointment on her face. "Yes, I had hoped I was wrong, and he had changed since his time here at the academy, but it looks like he's being set up to fail."

"You think so as well, Headmistress Rena?" Lani looked at her, surprised.

The headmistress smiled back at her wryly. "You're not the only one researching the movements and inner workings of the noble families, you know, Lania." Turning on her heel, she headed back in the direction she came from. "At any rate, everything seems to have settled down here for now, so I'll be getting back to work."

"Ah, thank you for your help!" Lani called after her, caught off guard by her sudden departure.

I looked up at Lani once she was gone. "So, care to explain what you guys were talking about?"

"Sorry, but no can do. It's too dangerous to talk about it here." Lani glanced toward the students going about their day in the library. "Besides, I need to gather more information before I can be sure."

"Alright, I understand. I'll leave it at that for now." I let out a heavy sigh as my thoughts turned toward the evening to come. "But I'm not looking forward to dealing with that jerk tonight."

"I doubt he'll give you too much trouble. If anything, he'll be too busy hounding every woman that catches his fancy to bother with you or Lesti."

"I can only hope so. At any rate, I'm heading back. Thanks for your help this week." With that, I turned and dashed down the hall to meet up with Lesti and Aurelia.

Elliot's Party

"Ugh, what a moron. I can't believe he didn't even realize who Lani was." Lesti glared out the window of our carriage. I had just finished updating her on everything that had happened with Augustine during our tour of the academy. She had told me to wait until we were in the carriage so Aurelia could hear as well.

"Mm. Incompetent," Aurelia chimed in, scratching a nervous Fang behind the ears.

"Oh, well, let's forget about that bum for now." Lesti turned and smiled at her friend. "Since we went through all of the trouble of getting dressed up like this, we should at least try and enjoy as much of the evening as we can."

Even knowing that the situation was going to be dangerous, I couldn't blame her. Both girls spent most of the afternoon getting their makeup done by a couple of maids from the Gambriel family, at the insistence of Elliot. Lesti had tried to refuse him, but he wouldn't take no for an answer, saying it was the least he could do since we were helping his family out. I had to admit, they had done a fantastic job. Lesti looked like a completely different person.

Looking her over once more, I couldn't help but tease. "You may actually have to spend some time fighting off the boys for a change, Lesti."

Her hair, usually sloppily thrown into a ponytail, had been neatly combed and styled. Her dress was a low-cut gown that showed her shoulders. Its silky red fabric glowed in the orange evening sun that flowed in from the carriage window. A golden necklace holding a green broach that matched her eyes finished off the outfit. Combined with the makeup the maids had applied, she looked like a proper noble lady for once.

"Oh, knock it off." She swatted at me playfully, her cheeks slightly red from embarrassment. "If anything, Aurelia is the one who's going to be turning heads this evening. The maids did a fantastic job with your hair."

Unlike Lesti, Aurelia typically took better care of her hair, so the maids had gone all out to elevate it to the next level. It was pulled aside in a single large braid decorated with bright, colorful flowers, which matched the color of her eyes. Her dress had a simpler design than Lesti's and featured a short skirt that ended at the knees, allowing her to move around easily.

"Rarf!" Fang barked and puffed out his chest, a tiny bow tie being his decoration for the evening.

"Yes, you look good as well, Fang," Lesti giggled as she responded to his boasting. She had been getting better lately about understanding what he was trying to say without Aurelia needing to translate.

"Mm. Astria, too." Aurelia reached over and played with the blue bow tied around my neck.

It was taking everything in me not to paw at the stupid thing. The maids had insisted Fang and I wear proper attire if we were going to accompany our masters. Although, the barely concealed grins told me that it was more about them having some fun than out of any sort of formal necessity. I felt ridiculous, but at least I could rest easy knowing there wouldn't be photographic evidence.

A few minutes later, our carriage rolled to a stop in front of a massive manor that put the ones I had seen in the merchant district to shame. A gigantic garden stretched out in front of the building. A long stone pathway, wide enough for two carriages to ride side by side, led to the main entrance where the path circled a large fountain.

We stepped out of the carriage, assisted by two well-dressed butlers who guided us to the door. There, a third butler checked a list for our names before a maid led us through the manor to the ballroom. The entire walk had Aurelia and I gawking at the pure extravagance on display. Every inch of the place was covered with high-quality materials and art pieces.

When we finally arrived at the ballroom, yet another butler announced our arrival at the party. The sheer number of staff used solely to guide guests to the party venue was making my head spin. It was even worse inside the party. Any number of maids and butlers wandered amongst the scattered groups of nobles, carrying trays of food and drink. Off to the side, more food options were piled high on long tables covered in fancy tablecloths.

"Miss Vilia, Miss Aurelia, I'm glad to see you could both make it." As I stood gawking, Elliot noticed our arrival and came over to greet us, Rose in tow.

The pair were just as well-dressed as you would expect. Elliot was wearing what looked like some sort of black military uniform with gold trim and decorations. Rose, meanwhile, was wearing a pink dress that matched her hair. Unlike the other two, her hair was short enough that not much could be done to style it differently. Instead, she wore a simple barrette set with blue gemstones that matched her eyes.

"Master Elliot, you have my heartfelt thanks for inviting us." Lesti tugged her skirt up in a quick but elegant curtsy. "May this year bring you more fortune and happiness than the last."

Aurelia quickly attempted to mimic Lesti, but lack of practice led to a much sloppier greeting. "Mm. Thanks for inviting us, Elliot."

Her simple greeting earned a slight giggle from Rose and an amused smile from Elliot. Bringing his right hand to his left shoulder, he gave a simple quarter bow to the pair. "Thank you both for taking the time to attend my humble celebration. I hope you find everything to your liking. Now, if you'll excuse me, I have other guests that I must greet. I'll leave Rose in your care."

With a slightly exhausted look, Elliot hurried off to greet another group of young nobles that had arrived at the party. Turning back to the group, Lesti clapped her hands. "Well, then, since we're here, why don't we enjoy ourselves? I'm starving, personally."

"Mm. I'm hungry, too."

"Shall we?" Rose turned, leading the others to tables stacked with food, chatting merrily as they went.

As Fang and I followed after, I took the chance to look around the party. I recognized quite a few of the faces, most likely students from the academy.

Every one of them wore their best formal wear. As for the ballroom itself, it was just as grand as the rest of the mansion. Massive golden chandeliers hung from high above, lit by magic. On either side of the room, large two-story windows ran the wall's length giving a great view of the gardens outside. Between those windows were scattered doorways, which led to a balcony.

As I glanced around, I noticed that there was one student that didn't appear to be present. "Has Alex not arrived yet? I would have expected him to get here early."

"Oh, he's not going to be here, apparently." Lesti took a break from stuffing her face with sweets, waving her fork about in an unladylike manner. "There was some business he had to take care of in the Bestroff territory, is what Elliot told me."

He went back home again? My mind recalled the first time I had ever seen Alex. Back then, he had told Frederick he had some urgent business to take care of at home and needed to take the practical exam early. That was only a few short months ago. For him to be going back again so soon, I had to wonder if something was wrong.

Unfortunately, I didn't have much time to ponder the matter. A loud clinking noise soon filled the air drawing everyone's attention to the far end of the ballroom. There I turned to find what appeared to be an older-looking Elliot preparing to speak to the crowd. He waited patiently for everyone to quiet down before addressing them.

"Thank you all for coming together this evening to celebrate my little brother's birthday. My name is Reeve Gambriel, first son of the Gambriel family. Since my father couldn't be here this evening, I have been given the honor of being your host. I may be inexperienced with such things, but I hope you will find everything to your liking nonetheless. Now, it's only proper that as an older brother, I properly harass my younger brother, and it's time for the first dance." A slightly mischievous expression crept over Reeve's face. "Elliot, would you care to lead us in the first dance this evening?"

Elliot, who had been greeting the last of the guests near the door, threw a rather annoyed smile his brother's way. "It would be my pleasure, brother."

Making his way to the center of the hall, Elliot looked around the room, searching for someone. After a few seconds, his gaze locked onto our group, and his annoyed smile turned into a playful grin. He walked right up to Lesti, who continued to stuff her face. Fortunately for her, Rose was quicker on the uptake and swiped the plate and fork right out of her hands just as Elliot arrived.

"Care to join me for a dance, Miss Vilia?" Holding his hand out, he waited for her response, seemingly enjoying putting her on the spot.

Rather than panicking like I expected her to, however, Lesti simply smiled and took his hand. "It would be my honor, Master Elliot."

Her reaction even caught Elliot off guard, causing him to blink at her for a moment before leading her to the floor. *What the heck is going on here?* I knew that the pair got along rather well, despite their bickering. However, I hadn't gotten the impression that Lesti had any romantic feelings for Elliot. I stared at her as they headed onto the floor, wondering what she was up to.

Thankfully, it didn't take me long to figure it out. With Elliot's back turned, I saw her glancing into the crowd with a wry smile on her face. Following her gaze, I saw Augustine glaring at her, face wrinkled into an utterly foul mixture of anger and jealousy. Lesti had accepted Elliot's invitation so quickly because she saw it as a chance to take a stab at Augustine's pride, and based on his reaction, it had worked. Still, I had to wonder if she should be kicking that particular hornet's nest right now.

I didn't have time to worry about that, though; I had a job to do. As the lights dimmed and the music started, I made my way out to the balcony, looking out over the front garden. Elliot's maids had informed us this afternoon of how the security for the manor was laid out. Based on that information, the most likely route of attack for Baron Arvis's assassins would be to come through this garden. I was going to keep watch and call for help when they showed up.

Once outside, I jumped up on the balcony's stone railing and closed my eyes, using my magic vision to check for threats. At the moment, everything was clear. Sitting there all evening with my eyes closed would be suspicious, so I opened them and pretended to groom myself while looking back at the party. Every so often, I would close my eyes once again and briefly check the situation.

As I did this, Elliot and Lesti continued their dance in the ballroom. I was honestly surprised by how good they were. I had expected Lesti in particular to be a complete mess, but she was keeping up with Elliot rather well. It seemed her noble title wasn't just for show.

More importantly, she seemed to be enjoying herself. Lesti was a rather cheerful and energetic girl on the surface, but I knew just how hard she was pushing herself. It was nice to get to see her relax and have some fun like this for a change. I was just a little sad that I couldn't participate myself.

My mind flashed back to the many weddings and parties I had been to throughout my human life. I had always enjoyed going out and celebrating my friends' marriages. They were fond memories for me, even if I couldn't remember who they were anymore. Yet, I had never managed to get married myself in my previous life. Heck, I hadn't even managed to get a serious boyfriend.

So, while watching Lesti dancing with Elliot now filled me with a sense of nostalgia, it also filled me with a sense of regret and uncertainty. I had never experienced true romantic love, and I wasn't sure that I ever would now. From what I knew, other Astral Cats were nothing more than wild animals. If that was true, then finding a romantic partner amongst my species was going to be impossible.

Everything had been happening so quickly since I had arrived in this world that I hadn't had time to properly consider my situation. However, for the first time, reality had thrown a cold bucket of water in my face. I continued to watch the dance, wanting nothing more than to be happy for Lesti, but all I could feel was a deep sense of loneliness.

Finally, the first song came to an end, and Lesti and Elliot struck a pose at the center of the dance floor. The other attendees applauded their performance, snapping me back to reality. *Crap! I haven't been keeping an eye on the garden!* Turning my attention back to my task, I closed my eyes once more only to find a large number of magical signals making their way through the far side.

I breathed a sigh of relief. Thankfully, my lapse in focus hadn't cost us too much time. Focusing my thoughts, I called out to Aurelia. *"They're here. It's more than we expected, though. I'd say around twenty. Are you sure you two will be okay alone?"*

I opened my eyes and looked over at Aurelia, who had already started making her way through the party toward me. Her gaze met mine briefly, and she nodded to let me know they would be fine. I still wasn't comfortable sending them out alone, but we couldn't leave the party unguarded. There could be some hidden assassins amongst the attendees after all, and we still didn't know where Baron Arvis was.

Aurelia and Fang walked out onto the balcony, staring into the garden for a moment as I directed her where to go. As soon as I finished explaining their numbers and how they were lined up, she kicked off her shoes and jumped off the balcony into the garden below. It wasn't a far drop, only about half a story, but she still looked far more comfortable jumping than anyone should. Fang trailed right behind her without a moment of hesitation, eager to follow his master into battle.

My job there done, I turned back to the party only to find a rather angry-looking Augustine grab Lesti by the wrist and drag her toward the balcony. His rough handling of her caused the stress I had been feeling moments before to transform into pure anger. Rose looked on with a worried expression. Simultaneously, several other party-goers glared at Augustine's back spitefully as he passed them. It looked like he was as unpopular amongst everyone else as he was within our group.

"Augustine, let me go," Lesti complained, pulling against his grip as they came out onto the balcony.

He did as she asked, turning around angrily and using his other hand to slap her hard across the face—well, at least he tried to. Lesti saw the blow coming and instinctively stepped back. Ironically, all the training she had done with Elliot had just saved Augustine's life. If she hadn't dodged that, I would have probably killed him.

"That's 'Master Augustine' to you!" He glared at her with a rage that didn't seem to fit the situation. "You've done nothing but disrespect me since I arrived here! Who do you think you are, dancing with another man when you're already engaged to me?!"

Lesti made the most obviously fake surprised expression I had ever seen, holding her hand over her mouth with her eyes wide. "Oh, my. Augustine, don't tell me you're jealous? It was only a harmless little dance and with the star of the evening no less. It would have been rude to refuse."

I blinked in surprise, my anger from before starting to fade a little. Lesti was laying it on so thick that I barely recognized her. Everything about her tone, posture, and expression was planned to further anger Augustine, and he was falling for it—hook, line, and sinker.

His face turned a deep shade of red, and he took another swipe at Lesti. "Don't give me that crap! I saw the way you looked at me!"

Lesti once again stepped back, easily avoiding the reckless blow. "I honestly have no idea what you're talking about, Augustine. Please do stop making a scene, though. It's rather embarrassing."

At her last jab, Augustine's anger finally boiled over, his face turning a shade of crimson I didn't think was humanly possible. "You insufferable little girl. I was going to treat you nicely since I was going to become a lord, thanks to you." His eyes grew wilder, bordering on madness. "Now though, once I'm lord, I'll have you locked in the dungeon, you wretched little wench. I'll make sure every day of your existence is pure suffering. Oh, don't worry, though. I'll take good care of your precious people that you're always going on about, especially the women."

"You weren't kidding when you said he was deranged." Elliot's familiar voice rang out in the cold evening air. Turning, I found him standing in the shadow of the doorway. "We knew he was a poor choice for the position, but this is just insane."

"Right?!" Lesti looked back at Elliot with an exasperated expression, finally dropping the act she had been putting on. "You see now why I can't trust a loser like this with my family's territory?"

"Yeah. Don't worry. With this, it should be easy to convince father."

"That's a relief. Having a strong ally like Lord Gambriel will make things much easier." Lesti turned back to Augustine and smiled cheerfully. "Well, I do have to thank you for showing just how disgusting a human being you are this evening, Master Augustine. It really helped me out."

"Huh? What are you talking about, you stupid girl?" He looked at her as though she were a fool. "It doesn't matter what this little brat says at this point. Our marriage is set in stone. You and your parents' lands will belong to me in due time."

"We'll see about that." Lesti glared back at him. "Maybe you're too stupid or too arrogant to see it, Augustine, but you're being used. Do you think the council would choose someone as notorious as you to be my husband without someone extremely influential pulling strings behind the scenes? Best case, you become their puppet. Worst case, they let the territory fail, sweep in and claim it for themselves, and execute you for some set of made-up crimes. Either way, your visions of grandeur won't come to pass."

"Y-you're bluffing." I could see the supreme confidence that Augustine had until now start to crack. "My father is the one who nominated me. There's no way that he'd do that to me!"

"I wouldn't be so sure," Elliot chimed in as glanced back at the party. "I've heard several stories from my father about how much Lord Vanderbolt struggles with his irresponsible second son. Apparently, he spent most of his time at noble gatherings before the engagement trying to find anyone to marry him off to."

"No, that can't be." Augustine started clawing at his hair before glaring over at Elliot. "Sure, I've always known that father wasn't very pleased with me, but there's no way he would toss me aside like that."

"I hate to tell you this, but he already has." Lesti's voice was calm as she spoke to Augustine. The hate and spite that I had expected to hear were nowhere to be found. Instead, her voice was filled with pity. "The Vilia territory isn't rich. Every year, the people work hard to make a meager living. Our family has never been able to live an extravagant lifestyle like the one you currently have. Even if none of what I've said comes to pass, you'll still spend the rest of your life in a small backwater territory, with little to no influence or wealth to your name."

"I see." Augustine's head fell to his chest, his entire body trembling slightly as he seemed to accept the truth of the situation. But after a moment, he began to chuckle, and then his chuckle slowly built into a loud but crazed laugh. "Yes, I see now! You're trying to trick me. You want me to give up my claim to the Vilia territory so that you can hand it over this the Gambriel brat!"

"What are you talking about?" Elliot began to walk toward the pair, clearly worried by Augustine's reaction and accusations. "I have no interest in the Vilia territory. Besides my fath—"

"Shut up! Both of you are trying to undermine the work of the council. That makes you traitors." Without warning, Augustine reached into his jacket and pulled out a large knife hidden inside, lunging at Lesti. "And traitors deserve death!"

Lesti quickly twisted out of the way, but there wasn't enough space for her to completely dodge the blow. It cut through the red fabric of her dress and into her torso. The moment I saw the wound, I snapped. Elliot had started to move, but I was far faster. Using my body enhancing spells and Air Walk, I practically warped on Augustine. Slamming my paw into him, I sent him flying ten feet across the balcony. Honestly, I was likely to have killed him, but I didn't care. He had sealed his fate when he hurt Lesti.

Elliot stared at him for a moment, completely stunned, before shaking off his shock and turning to Lesti. "Are you alright?"

"I'm fine. It's only a flesh wound." She pulled her hand aside to show us. It came away quite bloody, but she was right. The wound wasn't deep or life-threatening. "Still, I didn't expect Augustine to lose it like that."

Elliot grimaced. "Yes, this certainly does complicate things even if it does strengthen our case against him."

Lesti turned her gaze over to the fallen Augustine. "Yeah. Thanks to this little stab wound, we have evidence that he attacked me. If we play our cards right, we might even be able to get the engagement canceled entirely. Of course, that's all assuming Astria didn't kill him."

"Hey, what's with that tone?! He tried to stab you! Did you expect me to hold back or something?" I glared over at Augustine's unmoving body as Elliot walked over and pushed him onto his back. "Although, maybe I overdid it just a little."

"You think?" Lesti smiled down at me. "Still, thanks for protecting me."

I rubbed up against her leg. "Hey, what are friends for? Besides, I already promised that I would protect you."

"Well, he's not dead at least." Elliot came walking back over, looking out into the garden. "I doubt he'll be waking up anytime soon, though. I'll call some guards to lock him up for now. Keep an eye on him just in case."

With that, Elliot turned and headed back into the party. Several of the other party-goers stopped him with worried expressions on their faces, but he pushed past them. They must have seen the argument and scuffle through the window. I had to wonder, if that was the case, why hadn't anyone come to help us?

Aroooo!

Just as I was pondering that, Fang's howl pierced the evening air. A moment later, I sensed magic from down below, and five figures leapt onto the other end of the balcony, dressed head to toe in black. They immediately tried to force their way into the party, but Lesti and I weren't about to allow that. She quickly snapped her fingers. "Fireball!"

A fireball roared to life in front of her and launched itself at the invaders. I ran alongside it to intercept them. Seeing the attack coming, two of them split off from the rest of the group and moved to intercept us. They were relatively quick, making me think that they had enhanced themselves with body-strengthening magic of some sort.

But speed and strength wouldn't protect you from a fireball. Lesti's attack slammed into the figure on the left. At the same time, I boosted my agility even further and rammed my paw into the temple of the one on the right. Instead of being sent flying like Augustine, the figure barely stumbled. I stared at them, stunned as they passed right by me and headed for Lesti.

That wasn't the only thing that shocked me. Despite being hit directly in the face with a fireball, the second figure pushed through the flames and kept running. *What the heck are these guys made of?!* Unfortunately, I didn't have time to think about that. If they were this tough, then we needed to wrap this up quickly and get inside to help Rose.

Giving up on capturing those two, I pushed my Power Cat and Speed Boost spells to their maximum level and transformed into my tiger form. A moment later, I was on top of the pair of enemies. Biting down hard on the one closer to the ballroom, I threw him as hard as I could into his companion, sending them crashing into the stone railing. It cracked and crumbled under the force of the blow, but didn't give. But the pair weren't even unconscious.

"Condensed Fireball!"

Hearing Lesti's spell call, I leapt away from the pair. A massive fireball ten times the size of the one Lesti had created before roared to life in front of her before shrinking down into a small basketball-sized orb. The pair scrambled to their feet and tried to dive out of the way as Lesti launched the sphere, but it was too late. It hit the spot where they had been a moment before. A massive explosion erupted in the area. The nearby windows shattered, and the party-goers inside screamed, along with the two assassins.

When the smoke cleared, they were both lying on the ground, burned to a crisp. With an explosion like that, it was a wonder that their bodies were still intact. I wanted to know the secret to their toughness, but we didn't have time for that. We still had more assassins to deal with.

I ran over and joined Lesti. "You okay?"

"Yeah. I'm fine. Come on. We have to help Rose."

So, we left the smoldering corpses of our assailants and Augustine on the balcony and headed inside, braced for round two.

Aurelia's Battle

Aurelia dashed through the garden of the Gambriel family manor, the cool evening air rushing past her face. Fang ran alongside her, excitement overflowing. Glancing down at the little elemental hound, she couldn't help but smile. It wasn't how she had expected it to happen, but this would be their first hunt together as partners.

She couldn't relish the feeling for very long, though. They were getting close to where Astria had told them the intruders would be. She doubted they were moving so slowly that they were still in the same place, so she gave a quick hand signal to Fang, and they both ducked down in the shadow of a large hedge. With the number of enemies that Astria had told them about, it would be foolish to rush in. So, they would wait here and get the jump on their foes instead.

Aurelia decided to rely on her hearing over her vision and focused on the sounds around her. Meanwhile, Fang's eyes darted around the night, picking up on all sorts of insects and small animals she couldn't see. If this wasn't his first hunt, she would scold him for not focusing on their prey. However, he was young, and such distractions were to be expected. It would probably take at least another six months of training before he could stay focused in a situation like this.

Almost as if trying to prove her wrong, Fang's ears suddenly perked up, and his head snapped to the side. Through their connection, she could feel his thoughts. The prey was coming. A moment later, Aurelia heard it, too. The sounds of several footfalls reached her ears, despite the intruders' best attempts to keep quiet.

It was quite hard for such a large group of people to be stealthy, and clearly, this group's training was lacking. Aurelia smiled as she remembered her own mistakes from her time training with her father. As the sound drew closer, her heart rate began to accelerate, much as she tried to suppress it. This would be her first hunt since making her deal with Lord Dawster, so despite the odd prey, she couldn't help but get excited.

Getting as low as she could without lying prone, she peered around the hedge they were hiding behind. It took a moment, but her eyes were able to adjust to the darkness, and she could see the outlines of her targets. Signaling Fang to get ready, she drew the twin daggers hidden in her dress, preparing to attack.

The following seconds seemed to stretch into minutes as she waited for them to draw closer. Each movement and sound became more and more pronounced to her heightened senses. She could feel Fang's excitement building as well. His youthful vigor and natural hunting instinct poured through their connection, making Aurelia's adrenaline spike harder than usual. It was almost too much for her to handle.

Just as she was about to be overwhelmed by the sheer energy flowing through her body, the time came. Without a word, Aurelia sprang from their hiding place, heading for the closest target. Using their connection, she instructed Fang on which enemies to attack. The plan was to wipe out or disable as many of their foes as possible before they could react.

Aurelia struck the first blow, plunging one of her daggers into the throat of her target before he even saw her. She felt an odd amount of resistance as she silenced him, but paid it no heed. Ripping her dagger free, she dashed toward her next target. Out of the corner of her eye, she saw Fang dispatch his opponent, using Shadow Step to catch them off guard.

As she moved toward her next target, the group started to react to the attack. Still, Aurelia was too quick for the next victim in line. She rushed in, ducked under their guard, and swung her dagger up hard into their abdomen. She grimaced as she felt the blade once again hit a strange amount of resistance, almost as if her opponent's skin and muscles were hardened.

Still, just like before, she ripped her daggers free and turned to find the next opponent. As she did, one of the assassins leapt at her, blade raised high overhead. Aurelia didn't bother to look their way; in the next moment, Fang sprang from the darkness and knocked them out of the air, pinning them to the ground.

With four targets now eliminated, she expected her opponents to start rallying and considered ducking back into the shadows. However, as she looked around, none of her opponents were drawing their weapons. Instead, they each pulled out a small vial and began to drink from it. Such odd behavior sent a chill down Aurelia's spine. Whatever was in those vials couldn't be good news. But if they were going to give her an opening, she was going to take it.

Rushing forward, she slipped behind her next victim and slammed both daggers into his back with all of her strength. Rather than sinking deep into her opponent's flesh, the blade ground to a halt after only barely breaking the skin. Aurelia stared wide-eyed at the man's back for a moment, trying to process what had happened before ripping her daggers free with all of her strength.

Her hesitation cost her. She was still off-balance when another assassin rushed at her, far faster than their allies before them had been. Aurelia didn't have time to dodge or put her guard up as the short sword swung down toward her neck. Just before the blow could connect, it came to a stop, the attacker's arm wrenched back violently by the force of Fang's Shadow Step.

Aurelia took some distance from her opponents as they gathered, using the temporary lull in combat to her advantage. "Fang, regroup."

Hearing her call, Fang released the arm he had been tearing at and dashed back to her side, avoiding the angry swipe of his victim with their good arm. Scanning the garden, she was surprised to find that Astria's estimate of the number of opponents hadn't been far off. There were exactly twenty-one foes remaining. For a moment, Aurelia considered calling for help but stopped just as she was about to give Fang the signal.

In her mind, she knew that calling Astria now was the best course of action, but her pride wouldn't allow her to do that just yet. After everything Lesti and Astria had done for her, she was deeply indebted to them. The pair had saved Fang and her with almost no help. Calling for aid after only defeating four enemies wasn't an option.

Glancing down at the elemental pup by her side, she began to focus on controlling her magical energy. *"Fang, we're going to use it. Get ready."*

His eyes lit up with understanding, and he crouched low in a ready position. Aurelia manipulated her magical energy, forming a bridge between herself and Fang, and began to pull his magic into her. Soon their magics mixed and flowed together, giving Aurelia full control over their combined might. Using the techniques she had learned from Astria, she manipulated the massive amount of energy in Fang, causing it to swell.

Focusing, she formed an image in her mind of the shape she wanted. A faint purple aura began to wrap around Fang, growing denser by the second until it finally became a solid mass of magical energy. Her opponents stared in disbelief as a massive wolf made of pure magic now stood before them. While they tried to process what was going on, Aurelia poured her magical energy into her daggers, using what they had learned from Rose. She still couldn't store energy in them long-term, but it would be good enough for a short fight like this.

With her preparations done, Aurelia leapt at her foes, Fang moving in sync with her. Slipping into the center of the group, she began to slash at their weak points, cutting at their joints and soft spots. Her opponents tried to counter, but every time they did, Fang's wolf form would cut them off, biting and clawing at their vitals. The world around Aurelia slowly became a blur as she moved faster and faster, whirling about in a flurry of blades, fur, and fangs.

It took everything the group of assassins had to defend against their attacks. The leaders tried to shout orders and organize a counter-attack. Still, no matter how quick they were, Aurelia and Fang were faster. The magical link they shared was further enhanced by the thread of magical energy flowing between the two, binding their thoughts together more tightly than ever. Through that, Aurelia could see and feel everything that Fang did, as if she were seeing it herself.

After several seconds of continuous attacks from the pair, the assassins began to falter. While none of the wounds Aurelia landed were lethal or deep, they were starting to add up. Seeing her opening, she launched her attack in earnest, slamming her dagger into a nearby assassin's chest after Fang knocked him off balance.

Once again, the dagger stopped short, barely piercing the skin. But this time the strike was lethal. Using the technique she had started practicing on the tree, she released a burst of magical energy straight into the man's heart. Whether it burst on impact or simply stopped from the shock, she didn't know, but her opponent coughed up blood and leaned heavily on her dagger. Aurelia swiftly pulled her blade away and moved on to her next target, letting him fall to the ground.

Seeing one of their allies struck down, the rest of the group began to panic, wildly slashing at Aurelia as she drew close. This only made them easier to fell. Three more of their number lay dead on the ground in a few seconds, slain similarly to the first. Yet, just as it looked like their morale was about to break, a voice rang out from the group.

"She's a tough one. Buy me some time!"

"No, you don't!"

Aurelia and Fang both immediately turned and rushed toward the man who had given the instructions. Aurelia wasn't about to let him drink another one of those potions. Unfortunately, she didn't anticipate how willing her opponents were to die. Eleven of the remaining members leapt together, cutting off her path and slashing at her wildly. She cut them down mercilessly along with Fang but was too slow.

In the back, the man finished chugging a deep purple potion. As the last drops passed through his lips, he turned and grinned at her. "Too late, girl."

Worried he would attack her while she was still busy with his allies, Aurelia moved to quickly dispatch the remaining opponents. To her surprise, the man didn't rush her. Instead, he started to convulse, and his body began to morph. It was a terrifying sight to behold, but what scared Aurelia was the faint sense of nausea she felt in the pit of her stomach. She ducked the desperate blow of the last remaining member and slammed her dagger into the bottom of his jaw.

With all eleven dispatched, she rushed toward the man, hoping to finish him before his heinous transformation could complete. The five remaining assassins moved to intercept her, but that was part of her plan. With all the focus on her, Fang had a straight shot. Using Shadow Step, he appeared right in front of the man in an instant. Jaws made of pure magical energy opened wide, preparing to close around him when suddenly the man let out a tremendous roar.

A wave of magical energy exploded from his body, sending Fang flying backward and causing Aurelia to stagger. Thankfully, the other assassins were not immune to its effects, making them unable to attack. Unease building in her chest, she rushed to rejoin Fang.

"You okay?"

He slowly stood, shaking off the impact, and glared where the man had been standing, letting out a low growl. Through their connection, Aurelia could tell he had mostly experienced a few bruises, nothing serious. Following his gaze, she readied her blades once again.

Standing before her was a creature similar to, but more human than, the archdemon she had seen Lesti and Astria fight once before. Tough, leathery grey skin covered its entire body. Elongated arms dragged the ground below it, giving it an unsettling appearance. Eyes black as the void turned and looked at her, sending a chill down her spine. The man was no more—he was now a full-fledged demon, with the magic aura to match.

Aurelia grimaced as the wave of sickening magical energy rolling off the creature washed over her. Thankfully, the aura of this demon seemed far weaker than that of the archdemon, and she was able to handle the nausea with just a little bit of willpower. Still, she recognized the situation was dicier than before. Not only was it still six versus two, now there was a demon of unknown strength in the mix.

Aroooooo!

She gave Fang the signal, and he belted out the loudest howl he could manage, informing Astria and the others that there was a problem. However, in the next moment, the situation rapidly changed. The remaining assassins made a break for the manor without a word, giving the demon a wide berth.

Aurelia tried to chase after them, but before she could react, the monster made its move.

In the blink of an eye, it was on top of her. Its long, clawed hand swiped down at her with an unbelievable amount of speed. Throwing up her daggers, she braced for the blow, but it never came.

The creature was fast, but Fang was slightly quicker. Using Shadow Step, he rammed into the demon knocking it back.

The creature glared at Fang, a look of pure hatred smeared across its face. It lunged wildly at him, forcing him back. Aurelia wanted to jump in and help her companion, but there was nothing she could do with as fast as they were moving. She reached into the secret pocket inside her dress and grabbed onto several small stones. Pulling them out, she threw them at the demon, yelling the activation phrase. "Awaken, Mini Golems!"

At her words, the small stones sprang to life while flying through the air, unfolding into miniature stone golems only a few inches tall. They latched onto the demon and began to punch and kick at it with their tiny limbs. For those that didn't understand what was happening, it was a rather comical scene. But thanks to the magic infused in them by Rose, and the spells constructed by Lesti, the golems possessed a strength that far exceeded their tiny bodies.

Suddenly swarmed by the tiny juggernauts, the demon flailed wildly in an attempt to remove them. However, Fang didn't make that easy, using every attempt as an opportunity to bite and claw at the creature.

Aurelia began to focus on an image in her mind. The golems were meant to be her trump card, but she knew they wouldn't be enough to defeat a creature as strong as a demon. So, she took a gamble, putting together the pieces of a magic circle Lesti once showed her.

It was a dangerous move. Aurelia wasn't as good at memorizing the circles as Lesti. In fact, she was downright terrible at it. Until now, she had only managed to remember a few simple spells perfectly. If she messed up the one she was building here, there was a good chance it would kill her outright, or cripple her at the very least. Still, she had little choice. As she was now, she couldn't keep up with the demon's speed.

Sweat broke out on her brow as she quickly rushed to finish the spell. The wolf aura surrounding Fang wavered slightly as she struggled to keep up with both tasks. Her body began to feel hot, letting her know she was nearing her limit. Once the spell was complete, she would have to finish things quickly, or risk burning out.

The puzzle slowly fell into place as she inserted rune after rune into the circle in her mind, reconstructing it piece by piece. Then, just before she completed the spell, the demon smashed the last of the golems and turned angrily toward her. A sense of panic started to well up within Aurelia, but she pushed it down, forcing herself to remain calm. She was almost done. She just needed to focus.

Sensing her emotions, Fang leapt at the demon in an attempt to pin him down, but his attack was reckless and predictable. The creature quickly sidestepped it and sent him flying with a backhand. With nothing else standing in his way, he dashed at Aurelia with blinding speed and swung his long arm toward her head.

At the same moment, she finished constructing the spell in her mind. It activated, and a surge of magical energy flowed into Aurelia's body at an unbelievable speed, filling her with power. Throwing all of her strength into her legs in a panic, she jumped to the side, flying into the nearby bushes, and the demon's arm swung through empty air.

The demon stared at her with a confused expression for a moment before charging at her once more. Aurelia hastily freed herself from the bushes. Careful not to throw too much power behind each movement, she rushed at the demon. The creature, still not used to her new speed, swiped at her wildly, giving Aurelia room to duck under his guard and aim a decisive blow to his abdomen.

This time, her daggers slammed home, piercing the creature's flesh easily. However, Aurelia still wasn't entirely in control of the power her spell had granted her. Her momentum lifted the demon off his feet and caused Aurelia to stumble forward. The demon used this opening to grab onto her arms, preventing her from using her daggers to rip his belly open. Then, it opened its mouth wide, revealing rows of razor-sharp teeth that raced toward her face. Panicking, she pulled back with all her might, but the creature's grip was firm, and she only managed to pull him closer.

Just before its jaws could close around her face, another pair of jaws made of pure magical energy closed around the creature's neck—Fang had rejoined the battle. The impact knocked the demon away from Aurelia, causing it to pull forcefully on her arms. Then, it lost its grip and tumbled to the ground, Fang's jaws still clamped around its neck.

Seeing her chance, Aurelia leapt at the demon, daggers raised high above her head. They slammed into its chest with a thud, causing the creature to start flailing wildly in an attempt to knock her off. She wasn't going to let it escape this time. Planting her knee firmly on its abdomen, she used all the strength in her lower body to hold it in place. Twisting her daggers, she cut horizontally across the creature's chest, right where its heart should be. But even after what should have been a lethal blow, it continued to flail about wildly.

A sense of dread filled Aurelia as she stared bewildered at the monster. She had been hunting since she was old enough to use a bow, and had fought to defend the forest from intruders for many years. Yet, in all that time, she had never come across a foe who didn't die when you cut their chest open. In the back of her mind, she started to wonder if the creature was even mortal.

Worse, she was close to reaching her limit. Maintaining her connection with Fang was too taxing on her mind. Plus, the spell she was using to boost her strength was quickly depleting even his vast pool of magical energy. In desperation, she slammed her daggers into the demon over and over, cutting it in every way she could imagine as purple blood splattered across her dress. No matter what she did, the creature continued to struggle.

As her panic reached an all-time high, Aurelia threw her daggers aside and pressed her hands inside one of the demon's many open wounds. A magic circle flashed in her mind as she shouted the activation keyword. "Lightning Claw!"

Aurelia's hands became wreathed in lightning, sending violent electrical shocks through the demon's body. It continued to kick and scream, refusing to die as she poured more and more of her magical energy into the spell.

Fang's wolf form wavered and disappeared as his magical energy ran out and the connection between the two was severed. Exhausted, he collapsed on the ground, unable to move a muscle.

Still, Aurelia dug deep, pouring more magical energy into the spell. Even as she did, the demon slowly lifted its head, glaring at her with its jet black eyes. Reaching up, it grabbed onto both of her arms, convulsing from the electricity flowing through its body. With no other cards to play, Aurelia squeezed her eyes shut and dumped the last of her magical energy into the spell.

A moment later, the last of her energy ran out, and the spell ended. The only sound in the garden was that of Aurelia's heavy breathing. She could still feel the demon's hands wrapped around her arms, but it made no moves to attack her. Slowly opening her eyes, she saw it staring at her, mouth agape and unmoving, eyes still wide. Then, its hands slid free from her arms and fell to the ground with a thud.

The fight was over. They had won.

Heaving her sluggish body off the demon's corpse, Aurelia crawled over to Fang's side to check on him. He was sprawled out on the ground, completely exhausted due to having most of his magical energy used. Checking him over, she could tell he didn't have any severe injuries. Convinced that he was fine, she smiled gently at him and began to scratch behind his ears, pride filling her chest.

"That was great for your first hunt, Fang. Relax now. We'll leave the rest to the others."

Fang's tail wagged softly as he drifted off to sleep. Meanwhile, Aurelia looked up at the starry night sky and took a deep breath, which caused her to wince. Surprised by the sudden sharp pain, she looked down to find bruises blossoming across her limbs. The effects of her rushed spell were catching up with her. While it had boosted her strength and speed drastically, it hadn't correctly reinforced her body.

Lying back on the grass, barely able to move, she listened to the distant sounds of battle as her friends handled the remaining assassins. Though she knew they were strong, she couldn't help worrying. They still didn't know what Thel'al was after here, or where Baron Arvis was. If the remaining assassins transformed like the one she fought, then even Lesti and Astria would struggle.

But there was nothing she could do. So she laid there and prayed to the stars above for their victory as explosions echoed in the distance.

Battling Assassins

As we rushed into the party, we saw the assassins engaged in battle with Elliot's older brother. The hall around them was torn to shreds as he used earth magic to send stone spears flying at his opponents. Unlike Elliot, Reeve seemed to focus his fighting style on ranged spells.

We rushed over with Elliot to try and give him a hand. He was holding up well enough, but he was being pressed rather hard. Before making it halfway across the hall, I felt a surge of magical energy as several other attendees finished casting their spells. Fire, stone, and various other projectiles were sent flying at the assassins, forcing them to give up their attack on Elliot's brother and flee to the balcony on the far side.

Not wanting to give them a chance to escape, we rushed after, followed closely by Elliot. As we stepped onto the balcony, we were greeted with a strange sight. Not only were the assassins not fleeing, but they were chugging some unknown purple liquid from vials.

Immediately, I noticed something was wrong. Their magical energy, which was gold in most people, was a strange mixture of purple and gold, almost as if they were drawing power from two different sources. But as they drank more of the potion, the purple energy began to overwhelm the gold, surging forth at an alarming rate. Simultaneously, this new magical energy began to move with a purpose, shifting and changing their bodies from the inside.

"Lesti, take them out, quickly! Those potions are dangerous," I shouted in warning at Lesti. Whatever those potions were doing, I didn't want to find out.

"You got it! Compressed Fireball, repeat three!" At her shout, three massive fireballs sprung to life in the air before her, causing a sudden burst of heat so intense that it made both Elliot and me flinch. Compressing into dense balls of flame, they flew at their targets with incredible speed and exploded on impact, blasting the entire area to bits.

"That should take care of them." Lesti grinned triumphantly as dust and debris filled the air.

Before I could yell at her for going overboard, I felt a familiar sense of nausea as foul magical energy filled the air. Two creatures I had never seen before burst through the smoke, jet black eyes filled with rage and hatred. They were on us in an instant, elongated arms swinging at Lesti and Elliot.

To my surprise, both managed to sidestep the blows, as if on instinct. Then, in the next moment, a handful of small stones harmlessly struck the demons. These weren't ordinary stones, of course. They were the mini golems that Lesti and Rose had worked together to create.

Rose's familiar voice echoed from behind us. "Awaken, Mini Golems!"

The little stones immediately sprang to life, unfurling into tiny stone golems that latched onto the creatures attacking us, kicking and punching. Rose's surprise attack caught them off-guard and caused them to begin wildly swiping at golems. Not being ones to let a gap in their opponents' defenses go, Lesti and Elliot both launched a counter-attack.

"Molten Spear!"

Lesti launched a spell she had been working on to practice compound spells. In an instant, magic flowed from her and began to heat the stone balcony behind the creature, turning into a pool of molten rock. It then took the form of a spear, stabbing the beast straight through the abdomen. The hot stone punched through it like there was nothing there before quickly hardening, leaving the creature impaled on a heated stone pillar.

Meanwhile, Elliot activated a powerful strength-boosting spell and slammed his fist into his opponent's jaw, sending it flying into the air. He didn't stop there. Quickly muttering a chant to himself, he created a spear made of stone and leapt on the creature, slamming the spear into its chest and pinning it to the floor. Giving it a firm twist for good measure, he stood and started to walk back over toward us.

However, I immediately noticed something wasn't right. The golems were still attacking both creatures, though they should be dead. Transforming into my tiger form, I rushed past Elliot just as the monster he had impaled wrenched the spear free from its chest. Not wanting to give it a chance to recover, I activated Power Cat and bit down hard on its head, crushing it. The creature fell lifelessly to the ground, and the golems stopped attacking. I had killed it—for real this time.

Turning back to the last target, I found Lesti staring at it with disgust as the creature tried to pull itself free from the spear that had impaled it. "What is this thing, and more importantly, how is it still alive?"

"It's definitely a demon of some sort." Between the eyes and the magical energy, there was no mistaking this thing as a demon. But something seemed off about it. Most of the demons I had met until this point—while evil—were also masters of magic. These two hadn't used magic once, despite absolutely overflowing with magical energy.

But we could worry about that later. For now, I pushed aside my doubts. "Crushing their heads seems to finish them off, though."

Walking over, I closed my jaws around the creature's head, ending its life in the same way I had the other. With both targets taken care of, the golems went dormant and rolled into their ball forms again. Rose came over to join us, accompanied by Elliot's older brother.

"Demons?" Reeve looked at the two corpses in shock. "What are demons doing here?"

"That's what I'd like to know." Lesti pointed over at where the demons had come from. "One minute I'm blowing up a bunch of assassins, and the next minute demons are popping out of the smoke. That doesn't make any sense."

Glancing over at the balcony's crumbling remains that she had blasted away, I noticed a third corpse on the ground. Something about it seemed odd. Moving closer, I came across a scene that sent a chill down my spine. The body was a mangled mess, but not because of Lesti's attack. Rather, it was a strange combination of demon and human parts.

"The assassins turned into demons." I found myself having to say the words out loud because they were so unbelievable.

"What are you talking about? That doesn't make any sen—" Lesti started to argue with me but stopped short as she came close enough to see the third assassin's corpse.

"Well, this is quite the problem." Elliot joined us, looking down at the body with a worried expression. "Was it those potions that transformed them into demons?"

"Most likely. When I used my magic sense, I saw their magical energy starting to change. That's why I told Lesti to take them out."

"Elliot, you should go and report this to father. The council will need to know about this immediately." Reeve glanced back at the party with a worried expression. "Still, what really concerns me is why no one has called the guards."

"Isn't that just because most of the people at the party are mages?" I looked back at the other attendees who were glancing out at us curiously but were being kept away by the various servants. "They probably felt like they could handle it themselves."

"Even if that's the case, one of the servants should have called the guard by now." Reeve followed my gaze back toward the attendees with a troubled expression on his face. A moment later, a maid pushed through the crowd, hurriedly making her way over to us. Based on her appearance, I doubted she had good news.

"Master Reeve." She curtsied rather sloppily, clearly rattled. "I just spoke with the head attendant. He says he sent a request for aid as soon as the first disturbance occurred on the balcony. However, no guards ever came, and the messenger hasn't returned. He fears that there may still be other intruders in the manor."

"I see. Thank you for your report. Take a minute to calm yourself, then return to the party. Make sure that our guests do not catch wind of this."

"Y-yes, of course." With another hasty curtsy, the maid walked back across the balcony.

"It seems things are worse than we thought." Reeve turned back to us, gaze distant for a moment as if he were trying to decide on something. "Elliot, take your friends and go to father. I'm giving you permission to use the secret passageways."

"What about you, brother?"

"I'll be staying here. Someone has to keep our guests entertained to avoid a full-blown panic. It's already going to be quite the pain getting everyone calmed down."

"Very well, we'll send word as soon as we can." Elliot turned to us. "I'll be counting on all of you. Let's put all of that training to good use."

Without waiting for a response, he turned on his heel and headed into the garden below. Rose, Lesti, and I followed quickly, trying our best not to lose sight of him in the maze of plants. It felt strange to wander through the garden, but I assumed it had to do with the secret passageways Reeve had mentioned. A moment later, I was proved right, as Elliot took a turn into a dead-end where the manor wall was flush against the garden.

Walking up to the wall, he placed his hand on it, and I felt a small amount of magical energy trickle out. A simple magic circle glowed orange, and a section of the wall slid into the ground. Inside was a tunnel filled with magic lights that popped on one by one as the magical energy Elliot provided gave them the fuel they needed to run. Turning back, he offered a quick warning before heading inside. "Stay close. These tunnels are designed to confuse pursuers."

We quickly ducked inside after him, and the entrance closed behind us. As we followed Elliot through the tunnel, I could feel his magical energy slowly being sapped. Meanwhile, all around us, I could hear the subtle noises of the earth moving. It appeared that rather than the tunnels being designed to confuse pursuers, they instead used earth magic to change the paths as the caster passed through, making pursuit impossible.

It seemed odd that Elliot would try to keep this a secret with me around, but I didn't have time to think about it. After a few minutes and several twists and turns, we found ourselves standing before another stone wall. Elliot once again raised his hand and started to put his magical energy into it. Another circle appeared, and the wall began to slide aside, surprisingly quietly. Before it could move more than a few inches, Elliot pulled his hand away, and the wall stopped.

"Wha—" Lesti started to complain, but he clasped his hand over her mouth and signaled for us to be quiet.

Stepping forward, I peeked through the crack that had opened in the wall and felt my breath come up short. Standing in the room beyond was Baron Arvis, along with several armed soldiers, swords coated in blood. Sitting behind a desk on the opposite side of the room was a man I presumed to be Elliot's father, Lord Gambriel.

"Baron Arvis, what are you doing here?" Lord Gambriel casually interrogated the baron as if it was nothing more than a surprise visit. "I don't believe you were on the guestlist for tonight's festivities."

"Well, originally, I had planned to come here to pretend to save your brats." The baron sneered back at him. "The situation changed, though, once my spy informed me that you were here. I decided it would be faster to just kill you here and now. Then, I'll be taking over as the new lord."

"You think the council will allow that after you so blatantly waltzed in here with armed guards? You're a bigger fool than I thought."

"Yes, it really is a pain. If that familiar of mine wasn't so useless, I could have just popped in here and killed you without anyone seeing me. Still, there's nothing to worry about. It's all been taken care of."

Lord Gambriel's expression grew dark as he stared the baron down. "What did you do, Arvis?"

"Nothing crazy, really. We just made sure not to leave any witnesses." The baron stared back at him, smug as ever. "Oh, by the way, my friend here graciously agreed to provide us with all the cover we need." The baron gestured to a man I had never seen before, covered in a dark cloak. "As far as the rest of the world is concerned, you and the rest of your family will have fallen victim to assassins from the demon worshipers that have been infesting the city as of late."

For the first time since we had arrived, I saw a spark of emotion on Lord Gambriel's face as he crinkled his nose in disgust. "I knew you were ambitious, Arvis, but to think you would stoop so low as to rely on the backing of a demon and his followers... it's truly pathetic."

"Call me what you want, it doesn't matter. You'll be dead soon enough." With a flick of his head, Arvis gestured for the knights to descend on Lord Gambriel. Several rushed forward, blades raised high as they aimed to take his head. I started to move to help, but before I could, Elliot grabbed me by the scruff of my neck, holding me back.

"Not yet," he whispered, "we need to wait for the right moment."

I started to argue, but before I could, I felt magical energy swell. Turning my gaze back to the room beyond, I was greeted with a brilliant flash of light as lightning hit the knights square in the chest. A second later, a massive boom echoed as the corpses of the knights that had rushed forward fell to the ground, charred and burned.

"Lightning magic?!" Beside me, Lesti stared in shock before turning to Elliot. "Your father can use *lightning* magic? Are we even needed here?"

"Well, that depends on if the baron has done his homework." Elliot peered out from our hiding spot nervously. "Lightning magic takes a lot of magical energy to use. It's not something you can just fire off over and over, and my father hasn't totally mastered it, so it has a limited range. As long as the baron's men don't get closer, he won't be able to hit them with it."

"Why doesn't he charge them, then?" Lesti asked.

Elliot grimaced, just as confused as her. However, I could see something they couldn't. "He can't. That man standing next to Arvis prepared a spell after the first barrage. It's a powerful one too. If Lord Gambriel tries to rush in, he'll get mowed down before he can do anything."

"I see. Then, I guess we're at a standstill then," Elliot replied. However, the balance of power between the two sides was broken not a moment later.

"Lightning magic, huh?" Arvis remained calm as he took in the sight of his fallen knights. "That's quite the powerful spell you have there. I guess it's a good thing that I came prepared. Do it!"

Several knights pulled out vials of purple liquid at his command, preparing to drink them. I felt a sense of panic welling up in me. There were a good twenty knights still standing, and almost all were pulling out vials. If all transformed into demons, we'd be in serious trouble. It seemed Elliot had the same thought; Before I could say anything, he dropped me and began to dump magic into the circle on the wall once more, causing it to rocket open.

Arvis and his men turned to stare at us, eyes wide with shock. Not wanting to give them time to recover, I immediately activated Power Cat and Speed Boost and leapt into action. Using the mobility of my smaller form, I darted about the room, slipping between the legs of the knights while avoiding their awkward attempts to cut me down. Whenever I got the chance, I would knock the vial out of their hands or trip them up, anything I could do to keep them from drinking.

"Earth Tomb!"

Behind me, Lesti began disabling the guards using her earth spells. It was a rare display of restraint from her. Usually, she would have started firing off fireballs despite the tight quarters.

Meanwhile, Rose fired a barrage of simple wind-based spells at the knights. They didn't do much damage, thanks to the knights' armor, but it was enough to slow them down. Finally, Elliot stood in front of the pair, taking on any knights that managed to approach. With his enhancement magic, he was more than a match for them despite the age difference.

With their ranks thrown into chaos by our surprise attack, most of the knights abandoned drinking their potions, instead focusing on trying to take us down. However, just as soon as I thought I could relax, the cloaked man next to Arvis made his move. His magical energy swelled and moved as he formed his spell, muttering the incantation under his breath. I tried to use spell jamming to cancel it, but I couldn't focus on the task while dodging the knights' attacks.

The spell finished, and the ground beneath my feet began to shake. A moment later, huge spikes of earth exploded from the ground. To dodge them, I was forced to leap back into the corner, but that seemed to be part of the man's plan. Several spikes shot up and slammed into the wall forming a cage around me. Yet, the rumbling in the ground didn't stop there.

Time seemed to slow down as I looked around desperately for a way out of my stone prison. Unfortunately, there were no gaps large enough for me to squeeze through. I thought about shrinking myself down for a split second, but knew it would be too slow. I didn't have enough practice with that form. So, I decided to take the only option left open to me. Crouching down, I gathered up as much power as I could in my legs and threw up a magic barrier in front of me.

Right as I felt the ground burst beneath my feet, I leapt forward, smashing into the stone cage. With the extreme speed I was traveling at, I crashed through the barrier in an instant. I felt a large chunk of my magical energy drain as my defenses absorbed the impact, but at least I was free. Looking around the room, I saw similar traps had been laid for the others, as well as Elliot's father. Although, in his case, it looked like he had simply used a spell to blast his way out, similar to me.

As I was taking all this in, Lesti's voice rang out from behind the wall that hemmed them in. "Hail of Stone!"

A second later, the stone spikes blocking the secret entrance we had come through broke into hundreds of stone shards. Those shards were launched across the room, pummeling nearly everyone within. Thankfully, I still had my magical barrier up and avoided taking any damage. The hooded man next to Arvis threw up his own defense in the form of a stone wall and pulled a vial from his cloak, thinking he was safe.

But just as he moved to undo the stopper on the vial, I reached out with my magical energy to manipulate the projectiles Lesti was firing. I altered the course of several, curving them around the stone wall the man had set up in every direction I possibly could. He tried to throw up more defenses, but couldn't block them all. The rough-edged stones slammed into him from multiple directions. Since he wasn't protected by heavy armor like the knights, his body was turned into a massive pincushion full of stone needles.

The vial in his hand fell to the ground with a clatter, and the room finally fell silent. As the dust settled, Lesti stepped through the doorway of the secret passage, a grim expression on her face. "Looks like that did the trick."

Behind her, Elliot had an arm slung over Rose's shoulder, a deep gash in his side. It looked severe but not life-threatening. Rose seemed fine, but there was a pained look on her face. Most likely, Elliot was injured covering for her. That was about the only way I could see him getting hit by that spell, with as much room as they had to maneuver in the tunnel.

But I could worry about that later. For now, we needed to finish things up. Turning my attention back to Arvis, I prepared to finish him off, but just as I did, Lord Gambriel spoke. "Surrender Arvis! You can't win."

I felt a tingle run down my spine at those words. It seemed so cliche that I couldn't help but see it as a bad omen. Unable to brush off that sense of foreboding, I began to slowly creep closer to the baron, just in case. As I did, Arvis started to look around the area, clearly panicked, until his eyes fell on several vials of the purple potion lying nearby. Practically throwing himself onto the ground, he swept them up.

"This isn't over!" He held the potions up with a mad look in his eye. "Once I drink these, I'll be unstoppable!"

"And what makes you think that I'm just going to let you drink them?" I asked.

Arvis froze at my words. While he had been distracted by Lord Gambriel, I had walked right up behind him. There wasn't a chance in the world he could drink the potions before I knocked him out cold. However, before I could make my move, a loud explosion echoed from above, and the ceiling came crashing down where we were standing. I leapt back to avoid getting crushed by the debris, but Arvis wasn't fast enough. I watched as a giant slab of stone fell directly on top of him, sending a massive cloud of dirt into the air.

As the dust settled, a familiar voice called out from above. "Looks like I made it just in time."

Looking up through the hole in the ceiling, I found Malkael's brother, Ulrich, staring down at me with a satisfied expression. On either side of him stood two demons unlike any I had seen before. They had the same leathery grey skin and pitch-black eyes as their brethren. However, their bodies had much more human proportions, and large jet black horns protruded from their heads.

The most significant difference, though, was the amount of fouled up magical energy they were both putting off. It still wasn't nearly as much as Thel'al himself but was far greater than anything that transformed assassins or imp-type demons put out. I knew I couldn't let my guard down around them, so I crouched low, preparing to pounce at a moment's notice.

"Hey, you're that guy that was leading the beasts when they attacked the academy!" Lesti pointed an accusing finger up at Ulrich. "Perfect timing! I've got a score to settle with you."

"Sorry to disappoint you, little girl, but I don't have time to play with you this evening. I'm simply here to make sure that our experiment is complete."

"Experiment? You mean those people that turned into demons?" Lesti swept her arm across the room in front of her. "Too bad for you. It looks like you took out the last person you could use when you caved in the ceiling."

"Ah, you mean Baron Arvis?" Ulrich smiled knowingly down at the pile of rubble. "I assure you, he is quite alright."

Ulrich glanced at one of the nearby demons and nodded. When he did, I felt the creature's magic begin to swell. A moment later, the pile of stone that had fallen on top of Arvis floated into the air, turning into stone spears that launched themselves at me. With not much room to move, I used my magic barrier to deflect some of the spears and created a gap to break through the barrage.

All in all, it was a rather half-hearted attack with no follow-up. However, when I finally broke free, I was stunned to find Arvis standing there, a small magical barrier protecting him as he looked around in confusion. The rubble cleared, he looked toward the hole in the ceiling and spotted Ulrich. A look of relief washed over his face as if he had already been rescued from his fate.

"Ulrich! Where have you been? The men you sent me were completely useless, I'll have you know. Not only did they fail in their mission, but they let these brats escape and ruin my plans. Don't worry, though. I'll forgive you." Arvis swept his arm about, gesturing toward the rest of the room. "Just clean up this mess for me, and all will be forgotten."

Ulrich glared down at him, the disdain clear to see on his face. "Baron Arvis, you seem to be sorely mistaken about your position here. I'm not here to help you. I'm simply here to ensure that our experiment goes as planned."

"What do you mean, you're not going to help me?!" Arvis shouted, turning red in the face. "After everything I've done for you, all the funding I've provided, you're just going to abandon me here!?"

"Well, I suppose I could offer you one last chance to get out of this mess on your own." Reaching under his cloak, Ulrich pulled out a fresh vial of the purple potion and tossed it down toward Arvis. As it tumbled through the air, I noticed there was something different about this batch. It was packed with so much foul magical energy that I could feel it, unlike the others.

Not wanting to let Arvis get his hands on it, I leapt toward the vial as it fell. But before I could reach it, one of the demons jumped in my path at an astounding speed and landed a powerful kick, sending me flying back into the wall. I was able to throw up a magic barrier in the nick of time and absorbed most of the impact.

"Drink that potion, and you may still be able to escape from here with your life."

"And if I refuse?" Arvis looked up at Ulrich, eyes full of suspicion.

Ulrich shrugged. "Then you can die here and now."

"Don't do it! That potion will turn you into a monster," I called out to Arvis, hoping he didn't know what the potions actually did.

He glanced over at me briefly before returning his gaze to Ulrich. "Is that true?"

"Some may consider the form that you'll take that of a monster," Ulrich replied, the wild madness I had seen in him before returning to his eyes. "However, I choose to view it as an ascension. The next step in moving mankind toward our ultimate destiny!"

"I see, so I'll become one of them, huh?" Arvis glanced over at the demon blocking my path to him. "Well, I guess it's better than being dead."

"No!" I tried to force my way past the demon by transforming into my tiger form and running straight through it, but it managed to catch me. Putting me in a headlock, it forced me to the ground. I boosted my Power Cat spell to maximum output and threw the demon off, but it was too late. I watched in horror as the last drops of the potion passed through Arvis's lips.

"Let the ascension begin!"

As Ulrich's frenzied shout rang out from above, Arvis began to change. Almost immediately, I felt his magical energy become tainted and begin to swell, triggering the familiar sense of nausea that always came with it. His eyes turned pitch-black, and his body morphed, bloating like a misshapen balloon. Once it had grown to about five times the baron's original size, it stopped and turned a familiar leathery gray color. Finally, a pair of jet black horns similar to those on the other demons burst from his head.

Before me now stood a thirty-foot tall monstrosity that could barely fit in the room. What was truly horrifying, though, was the insane amount of magical energy that flowed out from it. There was so much that it fouled the air, making me feel even sicker than I had when fighting Thel'al. If it kept pumping out magical energy at that rate, we were going to find ourselves in trouble pretty quickly.

"Gruaaaah!"

The massive demon let out a guttural roar, which grated on my ears, forcing me to flatten them against my head. Then, without warning, it swung its massive deformed arm in a wide arc. As it struck the walls, they crumbled, sending a shower of debris cascading down into the room. I dashed toward Lesti and the others, racing against the wave of debris raining down behind me. "Get back in the tunnel! Go!"

Hearing my cry, Lesti slipped under Elliot's other arm and helped Rose carry him into the tunnel. Elliot's father rushed in shortly after. Once he was inside, I felt magical energy begin to build within the tunnel as someone cast a spell. Worried they were going to seal me out, I ramped up my Speed Boost spell and flew into the tunnel. As soon as I passed through the opening, Lord Gambriel finished casting.

"Earth Wall!"

A wall of stone several feet thick sprung up at the tunnel entrance and slammed into the roof just as the demon's arm swept overhead. The walls above the tunnel came crashing down, causing the ground around us to shake. The ceiling started to buckle in several places. Just as it looked like it was about to give, several stone pillars shot up from the ground and slammed into the weakened spots, reinforcing them.

Right after, the lights went out, causing the entire tunnel to go pitch-black. I quickly cast a Magic Light spell and checked to make sure everyone was okay. Lesti let out a relieved sigh as she lowered Elliot to the ground along with Rose; it didn't look like he could keep fighting. Lord Gambriel, on the other hand, seemed to be just fine.

The ground rumbled and shook as the giant demon continued to rampage outside, causing dirt and dust to occasionally fall from the ceiling.

"We need to hurry up and get back out there." Lesti looked worriedly toward the sealed entrance of the tunnel. "That thing is going to destroy the entire manor at this rate."

"Don't bother." Elliot's father walked over and picked his son up, throwing him carefully over his back. "I threw a few lightning bolts at the beast as I ran over here. They didn't do a damn thing. We need to get out of here and call for reinforcements."

"You're just going to run away?" Lesti looked over at him in disbelief. "What about all the people who were at the party? Don't you have a responsibility to protect them?"

"You don't need to worry about them. Reeve will make sure they're evacuated, along with the staff."

"Do you honestly think they'll be able to get away from that thing!?"

I stepped between the two, cutting their argument short. "Lesti, let it go. We don't have time to argue about this. Lord Gambriel, can we trust these two to you?"

"So, you really are going to try and fight it." He looked between the pair of us, almost as if he were assessing us in some way.

"I told you they were interesting, didn't I?" Elliot smiled weakly from his father's back.

For the first time since we had arrived, Lord Gambriel smiled ever so slightly. "So you did. Alright, we'll leave it to you then. I'll take these two to safety and come back as quickly as I can with reinforcements."

"Thank you." I watched for a moment as they headed down the tunnel before turning back to Lesti. "This is going to be incredibly dangerous. That thing has even more magical energy than Thel'al did. Stay close to me, okay?"

"You've got it. You be my legs, and I'll be your firepower." Lesti smiled and thumped her chest. "That thing won't know what hit it."

I transformed into my tiger form, and Lesti hopped onto my back. "So, how are we going to get out of here anyway? If we're not careful, we'll just collapse this whole thing on our heads."

"Don't worry, I have an idea." She patted me on the back. "I'm going to use an earth spell, and I want you to redirect my magical energy and make sure it uses the stone we want it to with spell jamming. That way, we can carve a tunnel out of here without bringing the whole thing down on our heads."

"Wait, will that really work?" I asked as I looked back at her nervously.

"Only one way to find out! Hail of Stones!"

Without giving me a chance to object or even prepare, Lesti cast her spell. I watched as her magical energy began to reach out at a rapid rate and gather the stone. I panicked and started to reach out with my magic to redirect it, but quickly realized I didn't need to. For some reason, the stone she was gathering was forming a perfect tunnel directly in front of us, as the spears she molded floated in the air nearby.

"Oh! Nice job, Astria. It's exactly how I imagined it would work." Lesti scratched behind my ears gratefully, despite me doing nothing.

I stood there for a moment, pondering why her spell had acted in the way that it had, but before I could come to a conclusion, our escape path was complete. As soon as the end of the tunnel opened, the stone shards floating about flew outside and darted into the sky. Not wanting to be left behind, I raced after them, out into the ruined room.

Rose's Resolve

Rose followed Lord Gambriel through the dark tunnels beneath the manor, glancing around nervously. The magic that had moved the walls of the underground maze had ceased to function; Some places had partially caved in as well. Still, Lord Gambriel navigated the labyrinth without any hesitation. Even Elliot seemed surprised by his father's confidence.

Outside, the sounds of the demon's rampaging echoed, causing the tunnels to shake and debris to fall on their heads. The idea that it could all come crashing down at any moment nearly caused Rose to panic. The only thing keeping her calm was Lord Gambriel's steady stride. Still, she wanted nothing more than to exit the tunnel and get as far away from the massive demon as possible.

Just as she had that thought, Lord Gambriel came to a stop before a stone wall. Reaching out, he touched it with his hand, but it didn't react. "No good, huh?" Turning, he walked past Rose and set Elliot on the ground, then looked Rose in the eye. "Wait here for just a moment."

Without waiting for a response, he walked back toward the wall, stopping a few feet before it. Closing his eyes, he took a deep breath and muttered something. For a moment, Rose wondered what he was doing, then the image of Lesti sitting over her books scribbling onto parchment as she mumbled flashed through her mind. Lord Gambriel was creating an instruction-based spell on the fly.

The notion sent a chill down her spine. If something went wrong, he could seriously injure or kill them. It was incredibly dangerous. She was still amazed by how confidently Lesti could craft her spells. She would never have the courage to try something so reckless. Even in the academy's controlled environment, she hadn't tried the spell Lesti had made for her. She was simply too scared.

Finally, Lord Gambriel finished the long set of instructions for his spell. A moment later, a loud explosion sent dust and debris flying everywhere as the wall in front of him was blasted open. Pebbles pelted Rose's arms as she covered her head. Thankfully, none were particularly large or had enough speed to do any real damage.

When the dust cleared, she looked up to find Lord Gambriel standing over them with a slightly annoyed look on his face. "I forgot to give the force proper direction. It looks like you're not injured, but you still have my apologies."

"Ah, no. It's fine, my lord." Rose looked at him, utterly bewildered. He had just done something as dangerous as crafting an instruction-based spell on the fly and made a mistake while doing so. But he was acting like it was no big deal. Was he out of his mind?

"Come on, the exit's open." Lord Gambriel picked up the injured Elliot once more, and they headed out into the night. Once outside, Rose immediately recognized that they were in the same place where she had entered the tunnels with Elliot and Lesti. Looking around, she couldn't see the giant demon, but could hear fighting in the distance.

They quickly made their way through the garden, heading away from the sounds. That alone should have helped Rose feel more at ease, but with every step, she felt a tightness growing in her chest. Slowly, fear and anxiety she didn't understand began to build up inside her.

"Rose, are you okay?" Elliot called out to her from his father's back as they walked along.

Rose's head snapped up, and she was surprised to find herself slowly falling behind Lord Gambriel. It wasn't that he was walking too quickly for her. Instead, she had slowed down. Unable to sort out the feelings in her heart on her own, she decided to try and voice them out loud.

"It's strange. I should be relieved, getting away from that horrible monster."

Rose's feet came to a complete stop as she started to talk. "Yet, the further away we get, the more scared I feel. It doesn't make any sense, right?"

"I don't think it's strange at all," Elliot replied without a moment's hesitation.

His straightforward answer completely caught Rose off guard. She started to ask him what he meant, but before she could, Lord Gambriel turned and glared at her. "Enough chatter, you two. I don't have time for your nonsense. I have to get reinforcements as quickly as possible, or your friend and her familiar are gonna wind up dead. Do your soul searching while we walk!"

Rose knew that she couldn't argue with him, so she swallowed her words and followed after him quietly. Yet, the storm of emotions raging inside her didn't cease. In fact, she was so focused on her own thoughts that she didn't notice the path that Lord Gambriel took, one that very intentionally brought them into view of the battle.

They rounded the corner and Rose froze, attention firmly on the chaos in the distance. The massive demon was surrounded by tornadoes, rocks, and lightning that lashed out at the much smaller figure darting around it. It was this figure that Rose's gaze was firmly locked onto.

Astria ran through the storm so fast she could barely keep up. But despite her speed and powerful magic, she was walking a fine line. One that, if she stepped over it for even a moment, then her life would be forfeit. Even so, she didn't back down or hesitate. She threw everything she had at the creature, all to protect her friends and buy time.

For a long moment, Rose stood there, gaze fixed on the battle, until Lord Gambriel's voice called out to her from behind. "Are you coming?"

Unlike before, his voice didn't carry any anger. Instead, it felt like it was pushing her forward, encouraging her to go to her friends. Rose knew that was crazy, though. There was nothing she could do. She had been too scared to master the magic Lesti had taught her, and she wasn't any good at hand to hand combat. If she went, then not only would she have to face down those terrifying demons, but she would most likely be in the way.

Despite all that, she found herself taking a step toward the battle on shaky legs. Memories of the last few weeks flashed through her mind. Ever since she was separated from her family, she had been alone without an ally or friend in the world, but they had come crashing into her life to change all that. They had filled her days with fun and laughter. For the first time in years, she had been happy, even if it was only for a little bit.

The fear of losing all that again moved her feet forward. It drew her towards that battlefield where terrible monsters, misery, and pain awaited her. Whenever she hesitated, memories of the days she had spent alone and scared, worrying about her family, pushed her forward. She was still frightened. Maybe she always would be, but doing nothing and losing her friends scared her more than anything else.

"I'm going." Without realizing it, the words slipped from her mouth, and she broke into a jog that quickly turned into a full-on sprint. Lord Gambriel made no move to stop her. Even if he had, she wouldn't have listened. Rose had found her determination and was taking the first step toward a new future for herself.

Decisive Battle

The entire space around us was completely decimated. Not only was the room leveled, but the whole manor in front of it was flattened. The massive demon had apparently crushed it as it passed through into the garden. For some reason, it hadn't headed over toward the party. Instead, it seemed to be wandering aimlessly, destroying everything in its path.

"If it keeps going that way, it's going to end up wandering out into the city." Lesti pointed out to the glowing lights beyond the demon's massive form. "We need to get its attention and keep it here until reinforcements arrive."

"Alright, I'll see what I can do. Hang on tight."

I took off, leaping over the rubble of the manor as I headed for the demon. As I drew near, I took to the air using Air Walk, jumping higher and higher as I went. Soon, we found ourselves in the air directly behind the demon's head. "Hit him with everything you've got!"

"You've got it! Fireball, repeat twenty!"

Twenty massive fireballs flared to life in front of us and launched themselves at the demon. On impact, they exploded across its body, causing a deafening roar. However, the damage appeared to be minimal. The tough leathery skin was barely burnt at the point of impact, much less the surrounding areas. Still, Lesti's attack seemed to do the trick. The massive creature turned to face us, eyes filled with rage.

Raising its massive, deformed arms overhead, it swung them down toward us with a frightening amount of speed for a creature so large. But it wasn't nearly as fast as the demon that had been with Ulrich. Using Air Walk, I changed the direction of our descent, easily avoiding the blow. The demon's arms smashed into the ground with a massive bang, creating a small crater on impact and sending dirt and debris flying.

"Well, it looks like we've got its attention at least," I shouted as I dodged another swipe of its arm. "Now, we just have to keep it busy."

"Don't worry. I'll take care of that." Lesti fired off another round of fireballs, pummeling the demon's thick skin. "You just keep us from getting hit."

As quickly as I could, I moved us back down to the ground. I didn't know how long it would take for help to arrive, and my magical energy wasn't infinite. If I used Air Walk the whole time, there was a chance I'd run out. So, I raced around on the debris-filled ground, dodging the demon's blows while Lesti continued to nail him with spells. It looked like we'd be able to hold the line, then things took a turn for the worse.

After I dodged the creature's strike for what felt like the hundredth time, it let out a frustrated roar. As soon as that happened, I felt a spell forming at lightning speed. A massive amount of magical energy began to swirl about the area, and the wind picked up. I tried my best to use spell jamming to stop the casting, but the sheer amount of magical energy at play made it impossible.

Soon, small tornadoes began to form, and the debris littered around the area lifted into the air, floating around the creature. On top of that, lightning arced through the night sky, striking the area around it at random. It was a terrifying display of power, but it didn't seem to have any direction. Almost as if this monster were nothing more than a child throwing a tantrum.

I continued to dodge around the area, using my ability to sense magical energy to predict where the lightning would land. Just as I felt I was starting to adjust, the demon began to mix debris into its attacks. Massive slabs of stone and earth came flying out of the storm that circled the creature, peppering the ground around us. Worried I would throw Lesti off my back if I moved any faster, I took some distance from the creature, retreating to the roof of the ballroom where the party had been held.

"This is bad. I won't be able to keep dodging this thing forever. It's burning through my magical energy too fast." I turned and looked at Lesti as she crawled off my back. "I think we need to try and take that thing down. Got any ideas?"

"Maybe." She glanced over at the demon nervously. "It's going to take some time, though. I'll need to build the circles on the fly, and there's quite a few of them."

"You're not thinking of using your blood to draw them again, are you?" I glared at her, remembering what she had done when we fought Fang.

She smiled mischievously back at me. "No. I have a better idea this time. I'll need to be on ground level, though."

"Alright, I can set you down over there." I gestured toward the garden in front of the ballroom. "I'll try and draw the demon's fire, but I don't know how long I'll be able to keep it busy, so work fast."

"I will."

Lesti hopped up on my back again. Then, we leapt down to the garden below, which she immediately began destroying by uprooting all the plants with magic.

"What in the world are you doing?"

"Don't worry about it. I don't have time to explain." She pointed back toward the demon. "Just make sure that thing doesn't toss any of its spells over here."

"Alright, be careful."

I jumped over a nearby hedge and ran toward the demon. As I ran, I thought over how I could try and land a blow on it with all the attacks it was throwing around randomly. Based on what I had seen from Lesti's attacks, regular spells weren't going to do anything. I'd need something with quite a bit of power behind it.

With that in mind, I transformed back into my standard form and stopped my Power Cat spell to save on magical energy. I would focus entirely on Speed Boost for the time being, then ramp up my power whenever I got a chance to land a blow. It was a similar strategy to the one I had tried to use in my training against Skell. This time, though, the ending would be different. I had way more magical energy at my disposal than I did back then.

If I managed everything correctly, I didn't have to worry about running out at the last second.

With my plan set, I accelerated and charged at the demon like a bolt of silver lightning. Soon large slabs of stone from the manor and bolts of lightning began to slam into the terrain around me, forcing me to zigzag to avoid them. The wind whistled past my ears as I drew closer to the magic-fueled tornadoes swirling around the demon. They weren't enough to slow me down. I aimed for the middle of the gap between them, where the wind was the weakest, and charged through.

I leapt up using Air Walk, bounding higher and higher until I was far over the creature's head. Then, I created a foothold for myself and cast a spell as I transformed into my tiger form. "Stone Armor!"

All around me, giant pieces of stone came flying in my direction, shaping and molding themselves as they did. Soon, I was coated in a layer of stone armor that protected my chest, head, and legs. Once it was complete, I launched myself downward like a bullet. The demon, seeming to have sensed my spell, looked up as I came rocketing down towards its head.

Debris glanced off my freshly-made stone armor as I descended. At the last moment, I activated Power Cat and twisted in the air, using the motion to add extra force to my blow. At the same time, I shifted the shape of the armor protecting my leg, turning it into large stone claws. With all the power I could muster, I slammed them into the demon's head.

My body was jarred by the impact, causing me to wince. Rather than skin and flesh, it felt like I was driving the claws through concrete. Still, my attack managed to break through, and purple blood flew from the demon's skull, causing it to let out a pained roar. It wasn't nearly enough to finish it, but at least it proved that we could injure it. Leaving the stone claws behind, I leapt away, barely dodging the lightning bolt that passed through the air where I had just been.

Well, that seems to have made it mad. I was forced to evade a lot more as the stone and lightning that were being randomly thrown about before became focused on me. As I dodged, I gathered more stone, replacing the bit I had left behind in the demon's skull. *If that's the case, then let's do it again!*

Over and over, I repeated the pattern, slowly turning the demon into a pincushion full of stone. With each blow, the demon's attacks became more focused on me. It was getting to the point where I could barely keep up the attack, so much of my time was spent dodging. That was fine, though—as long as I kept it from attacking Lesti, I didn't need to do any real damage.

Just as I thought that, the battlefield shifted. I felt a small flux of energy coming from Lesti's direction that quickly exploded in scale. In an instant, it ballooned into something that rivaled the magic flowing around our opponent. I started to panic, thinking maybe Ulrich had summoned another demon of some sort, but my fears were quickly laid to rest.

Looking toward the source of the magic as I continued to dodge about, I found Lesti at its core. She was standing in the center of a large magic circle that had been carved into the earth. It was unlike anything I had ever seen before—a single massive spell comprised of a dozen smaller magic circles, chained together by connecting runes.

One of those circles glowed with intense light and pulled in the foul magical energy the demon had been filling the air with. As that energy entered the circle, it flowed through the ground, filling the rest of the spell with power. It began to gather any metal it could find nearby, molding into something larger.

I stared in shock as the spell continued to work. The sheer scale was astounding. Due to that, it was going to take quite a bit of time to complete. Even worse, I wasn't the only one who had noticed what was happening. Suddenly, the attacks that had been pushing me back came to a complete halt, and the demon turned its gaze to Lesti.

The stone swirling around the beast began to gather, forming into a large ball. At the same time, I sensed the flow of magical energy change, collecting at the same spot. I immediately set to work, trying to slow it down with spell jamming. At the same time, I gathered my own energy, desperate to do anything I could to stop it.

Racing toward the growing projectile, I gathered all the stone I had used for my armor and transformed it into a miniature wrecking ball. Packing it as tightly as I could, I slammed it into the giant ball of stone, shattering it to pieces. But that didn't end the spell. Instead, it shifted, transforming into something new. The shattered stone fragments formed into a barrage of spears that launched themselves at Lesti.

"Oh no, you don't!"

With Lesti unable to defend herself, I dashed in front of the barrage, blocking the first round and causing my magical energy to plummet. Shifting tactics, I began to divert the projectiles, changing their course just enough to avoid hitting us. Even with that adjustment, I could tell it would be tough to hold out against such an attack long enough for Lesti's spell to finish. Still, I dug my heels in and hardened my focus. I would hold out, no matter what it took.

For several seconds, I continued desperately swatting aside projectiles while Lesti's spell continued to form behind me. Then, the demon let out a screeching high pitch roar that didn't match its massive body. Simultaneously, the demon's magic surged, using the enormous amount of energy it was generating for the first time since the fight had started.

Rather than attacking, it did something I didn't understand. The magical energy I could see reached out and seemed to writhe in mid-air without doing anything. For a moment, I could only watch, confused—until I saw the first signs of change as the air began to warp. A moment later, the first rift was torn open, followed by a dozen others.

I stared in horror as swarms of demons poured out of the rifts with an increased amount of corrupted magic. I panicked for a moment, worried the overwhelming amounts of magic would stop me in my tracks. Thankfully, between Lesti's spell absorbing large amounts of magic from the air and the immunity I had built up, I was able to hold out.

While I battled back the roiling feeling in my stomach, the demons hung in the air, seemingly disoriented. That didn't last long, and they quickly locked onto Lesti as their target. Dread washed over me as they raced toward us.

I was still pinned down, batting projectiles out of the air, but I couldn't let that stop me. In my mind, I formed the image of a magic circle that Lesti taught me. Fireballs sprang into life in the air around me and launched themselves at the demons. I wasn't nearly as practiced at this spell as Lesti, and I couldn't afford to pump tons of magical energy into it, either. So, instead of trying to take out the creatures, I used the spell as a deterrent to force them back.

For a moment, it seemed like it would work. The first members of the swarm eyed me cautiously and were careful to avoid my attacks. But it all fell apart when the first fireball landed. It collided with a mid-sized demon, causing a powerful explosion. I carefully watched the spot out of the corner of my eye, praying it would fall from the sky, but when the smoke cleared, it was floating there, a wicked grin on its face.

"Kyihihi! Weak! So weak!"

I grit my teeth as I saw the realization that I couldn't hurt them spread through the swarm. Their familiar high-pitched cackles swelled as they accelerated toward us. Knowing I wouldn't be able to buy Lesti any more time, I gathered my magic for a desperate counter-attack. We'd have to abandon defeating the demon, but I could at least make sure we escaped with our lives.

However, I was too slow. Before I could gather the energy I needed, one of the demons raced past me. It dove at Lesti, claws and rows of razor-sharp teeth bared. At that moment, I forgot everything else. The stones raining down on me, the other demons, everything.

I diverted the magic I had been gathering into my Power Cat and Speed Boost spells, pushing them to their limits. Without a second thought, I gave up on blocking the shower of projectiles and dove at the demon bearing down on Lesti. I was on it faster than lightning. Shifting into my tiger form, I swiftly used my jaws to remove its head from its body, tossing it aside.

With the immediate threat disposed of, I threw myself directly in front of Lesti. As her familiar, I had sworn to protect her above everything else, and I intended to do just that. Closing my eyes and throwing up the best barrier I could, I braced myself for the onslaught of projectiles to pummel my body, but they never came.

"Living Wall!"

An out of breath shout came from nearby, quickly followed by an explosion of plant growth. Massive roots and vines erupted from the earth and intertwined themselves into an enormous wall. The sheer size of it was absurd, but even more ridiculous was that the entire thing moved as if it had a will of its own. As demons tried to fly over the wall, vines reached up to swat them from the air like flies.

"What in the world?!"

I looked around for who could have possibly cast such an insane spell, only to find Rose collapsed nearby. A rather complicated magic circle was sloppily drawn into the earth below her. Immediately, I feared the worst—magical overload. For her to cast such a powerful spell, she must have pushed herself too far.

"Rose! No!" I ran over and flipped her onto her back, expecting to find her eyes dead and empty. I instead found a relieved but exhausted smile. "Wait, you're okay? But how?"

"I-I used these." She reached over to the edge of the circle fueling her spell and grabbed what appeared to be a small stone. I recognized the rolled-up shapes as the mini golems she had worked with Lesti to create. Looking at them now, they were nothing more than lifeless stone, drained of all their magic.

"You used the magical energy in the mini golems to activate the spell." I felt anger flare up inside me. "Why would you do something so reckless?! You could have died!"

"I had to do something. You couldn't hold all of them off on your own, right?"

I stared down at her, wanting to argue but unable to find any words.

Rose didn't give me a chance, either. Reaching up, she gently stroked my fur. "Besides, you've all done so much for me, going this far to help me save my family. I'd never have been able to live with myself if I just ran away now."

I stared at her, completely stunned. It was the first time she had ever touched me. When we first met, she had been so scared of Fang and me that she ran away screaming. Yet, here she was, putting her life on the line to save us. She had grown so much in such a short time. Seeing her like that, I couldn't help but feel strength welling up inside me.

Leaning into her hand, I latched onto that feeling. "You did great, Rose. Now, get some rest. I'll take care of things from here."

As I turned to face the wall, the first of the demons managed to break past the living mass of vines. I threw myself at the creature with everything I had. It saw me coming and tried to cast a spell to defend itself, but I didn't allow it. Before the magic could begin to form, I used spell jamming to forcefully scatter the energy swirling around it. Caught off guard, the demon couldn't do anything to defend itself as my jaws closed, crushing the life out of it.

I didn't have time to rest. More demons were making it past Rose's wall and heading straight for Lesti. With an angry roar, I threw myself into the fray, jamming their spells as I went. I could feel my magical energy rapidly draining, but I didn't care. I threw myself at them with reckless abandon. Even if it burned me out, I wouldn't allow us to fail this time. Not after everyone else had pushed themselves so hard.

Still, the numbers began to slowly overwhelm me. I felt myself being pushed back further and further, lashing out desperately at any demon that tried to make it past me. Behind me, I could feel Lesti's spell close to completion. The magic began to shift, entering the final stages of preparation. I just had to hold out a little longer.

I was in rough shape. I had been slowly accumulating wounds of my own, and they were starting to slow me down. Cuts and bruises covered my body, and a mixture of purple demon blood and my own red blood covered my fur. I grit my teeth and prepared for a final desperate push when suddenly I heard a familiar howl. A second later, Fang's tiny form darted into the swarm of demons, biting and clawing at their weak points.

"Fang! What are you doing?" I yelled at the pup as I continued to tear through the demons in front of me. "You're going to get surrounded like that!"

Just as I voiced my concern, a volley of spells came flying in from behind me. Lightning, fire, and stone combined to pummel the demons, who were unable to defend themselves. The chaos caused by the unexpected attack gave Fang the chance to slip out and retreat to my side. Looking back over my shoulder, I searched for the source of the bombardment.

Standing behind Lesti was Lord Gambriel, a beat-up looking Aurelia propped up by his shoulder. Accompanying him was Dag, with several of his men. We had done it. Despite the odds, we had managed to hold out long enough, and help had arrived. Now all that was left to do was finish the fight.

With a triumphant roar, I leapt back into the horde, and we began to push back the demons that had made it past the wall.

Fang ran rampant through their ranks, sowing chaos with his speed and precision attacks. Meanwhile, I corralled the demons, preventing them from spreading out. Any that tried to surge forward or drifted too far from the group were put down swiftly by my fangs and claws. At the same time, spell after spell from Dag and the others slammed into the swarm. Slowly but surely, we whittled away at their numbers.

"It's ready!" Finally, Lesti's shout echoed through the chaos. "Get clear and take down that wall so I can see."

"Fang! We're leaving!" I called out to the pup, who quickly joined me in retreating behind Lesti. At the same time, the wall of vines twisted and shifted, causing a massive hole to open in the center. On the other side of that hole, I could see the gigantic demon Arvis had become. He was still surrounded by portals, more demons pouring out of them with each second.

Seeing the wall was open now, the creatures began to swarm toward the opening. Simultaneously, I felt the demon begin to gather its magic for a massive attack. Stone gathered into an enormous spear in front as lightning sparked around it. But Lesti only smiled.

Above her floated a spear formed of pure polished metal, its tip sharpened and deadly. The spear began to rotate faster and faster. Electricity filled the air, causing my fur to stand on end. Layers of magic formed around the spear, creating protective barriers and reinforcing its structure. Then, just as the massive wave of demons started to clear the wall, Lesti waved her arm and launched her spell.

"Take this!"

The spear surged forward so fast it was nothing more than a streak of light to my eyes. In an instant, it tore through the swarm of demons, ripping them apart with its passing. Just then, the massive demon fired its spell, a powerful combination of stone and lightning. The spells collided in mid-air, but the demon's attack was swept aside so easily that it may as well have not been there at all. The magical barriers placed around the spear easily deflected the lightning and stone.

The streak of light continued onward, plowing into the massive demon's chest. Ripping straight through the creature, it continued into the distance. For a moment, the monster stood there, a gaping hole in its chest, unmoving. I feared the worst and prepared to throw myself back into the battle—then the first change happened.

The storm of lightning, wind, and stone that had raged around the creature began to dissipate. At the same time, the portals that filled the sky around it started to close. The magic that had once flowed from the terrible beast stopped, and its eyes turned from a deep pitch-black to a dull shade of grey. Finally, the creature toppled backward, falling to the ground with a massive thud. Dead.

I felt a sense of elation welling up within me, unlike anything I had felt in either of my lives. So powerful was the emotion that I couldn't contain it. I let out a mighty roar that was echoed by the cheers of Dag and his companions.

We had done it. We had won.

Reunited

"Well, then, let's get down to business." Lord Gambriel's gaze drifted around the small, hastily prepared tent we were in. It was a few hours after we had managed to fell the massive demon that had once been Baron Arvis. We had only recently finished cleaning up the remaining demons that had been summoned. Even now, soldiers called in from the city guard were outside, gathering up the bodies and preparing to burn them.

As for us, we had stepped onto a completely different battlefield. In addition to Lord Gambriel, all the other actors I had pulled into our crazy battle were present. Dag sat on our right. Behind him, standing at attention, was the man who had been running the bar when we visited the red light district. Off to our left sat Elliot, Aurelia, and Rose, each looking more nervous than the last. Finally, standing behind Lesti, whose lap I was sitting on, was Lani, who had rushed over from the school. Like Dag's companion, she stood at attention, back rigid, eyes focused. Despite our victory, the tension in the room was palpable.

"First, I'd like to hear your report," Lord Gambriel said, turning his gaze to Dag. "I know through my son that you were raiding the baron's manors. What did you find?"

"Yes, my lord." Dag's reply came out far more formally than I had expected. "First, it appears that the demon worshiper Ulrich managed to escape. Oddly, none of the guards posted throughout the city saw him; even our best scouts were unable to find signs of his passing."

Lord Gambriel grimaced at the news. "It's rather troubling that he managed to avoid our scouts so thoroughly. Still, with all the chaos this evening, it's to be expected that he escaped. What about the raids?"

"Yes. The raids, on the other hand, were rather fruitful and mostly peaceful. Most of Arvis's troops that were in the city were sent here, it appears. We found several documents detailing his dealings with the demon worshipers, though most of them had been destroyed. Additionally, we were able to locate the girl's parents."

"You found Mother and Father?!" Rose shouted frantically as she bolted up from her seat. "Are they alright?"

"Rose." Elliot placed a hand on her shoulder, gently pushing her back down. "I understand your worry, but you mustn't speak out of turn."

"It's fine." Lord Gambriel waved his hand dismissively at Rose's apparent breach of protocol. "I'd have to be a monster to get angry at a girl for being worried about her family's fate." He glanced over at Dag once more. "Well, how are they?"

"Yes. They are alive and well." Dag dropped his stiff attitude from before and addressed Rose directly. "They were a little underfed. However, it doesn't appear they've been tortured or anything like that. A little rest, and they should be good as new."

"Thank goodness." Rose began to sob quietly into her hands. I purred contentedly on Lesti's lap, happy to know she would soon be reunited with her family.

Lord Gambriel glanced at her, a brief smile softening his rough features for a moment. Then, as though it had never been there at all, he was back to his usual stern self. In fact, he seemed ever more intense than before, gaze now firmly fixed on Lesti and me.

"With that out of the way, shall we begin our negotiations? My son tells me you would like my backing in the council?"

Lesti glanced over at Dag. "You seem to be more familiar with Dag than I expected, but is this really something that we should be discussing in front of him?"

"Dag and his men serve the alliance as a whole. So long as your goals aren't treasonous, you should be fine."

"Very well." Lesti took a deep breath, preparing herself. Meanwhile, behind us, I could feel magic flowing from Lani as she prepared a spell. Her reaction caused me to tense up myself. Was she really that worried about what Lesti was going to say?

The silence filled the air for what seemed like far too long, until finally, Lesti began to speak again. "I assume you're aware of my engagement, Lord Gambriel?"

A rather irritated grimace came across Lord Gambriel's face. "To the young Master Augustine, yes? I am aware."

"Well, to be rather blunt, I simply don't think that man is worthy of ruling over my family's territory. He is an unstable, selfish, and egotistical man." Lesti gestured to the small cut in her dress. "Even tonight, he cornered and attacked me. Elliot can testify to this fact as well."

"Is this true, Elliot?" he asked, glancing over at his son.

"It is, Father." Elliot recalled the incident on the balcony with a look of pure disgust on his face. "The fool grew so enraged over Lesti simply dancing with me that he threatened to throw her in the dungeon once he gained the lordship."

"I see. Then I take it you want the council to select a new partner for you? If that's all you want, then it should be a simple matter to get the votes."

"No. That's not my aim." Lesti shook her head before meeting Lord Gambriel's surprised expression with a steady, defiant gaze. "It is clear to me that the council cannot be trusted with selecting someone to run my parent's domain. Which is why I intend to take the title of lord for myself."

At Lesti's words, the tension in the air became so thick, it was practically suffocating. Even Elliot stared at her in shock, unaware of her intentions despite his involvement in her plan.

Dag, meanwhile, seemed to be the most relaxed person in the room. He simply watched Lord Gambriel, a bemused smile on his face. It was as if he had already known what Lesti was going to say.

"You know that's impossible." Lord Gambriel's response shattered the silence at last. "Only a man can inherit the lordship in the alliance. The council will never allow you to take over your parents' lands. Not even I have the power to change that."

I felt my fur start to puff up in anger. This idea that a woman couldn't inherit the lordship didn't sit right with me. Seemingly sensing my growing irritation, Lesti ran her hand through my fur gently. I looked up to find her smiling back at Lord Gambriel. "I'm well aware that the council will never be swayed to allow me to inherit the lordship. However, I intend to take it, whether they grant me their blessing or not. When that time comes, I would like your assistance, Lord Gambriel."

"My assistance? Are you asking me to rebel against the rest of the alliance with you?" He glared at Lesti angrily. "If so, then there's absolutely no way I can support you. The Elstian Empire would descend on us at the first sight of in-fighting. Not to mention what the Kingdom might do. We'd be crushed in an instant."

"Actually, Lord Gambriel, it's the exact opposite. I don't want you to fight with me, but to not fight at all."

"Not fight at all? Explain."

"It's rather simple, really. I intend to use my time at the academy to gather as much power as I can. Enough power that it will make any reasonable lord second-guess turning against me on their own."

"I see," Lord Gambriel cut in as he realized Lesti's intentions. "If you manage that, then the only option left to them will be to gather enough of the combined might of the alliance to bring you to heel, and that's where I come in, correct?"

Lesti nodded. "Yes. I'm glad to see that you're as quick on the uptake as I've heard. Rather than fighting, I would like you to simply refrain from fighting and convince your allies within the council to do the same. That should be reasonable enough, no?"

"True. If that's all you need, then I believe it could be accomplished easily enough." Lord Gambriel leaned back in his chair, his gaze shifting away from anger towards something more like curiosity. "Still, my block isn't so large that their lack of assistance will prevent the other lords from descending upon you like a pack of wolves."

"That's very true. However, I believe we have some options there." Lesti glanced up at Lani, who still stood rigidly behind her. "Lani, if you would be so kind."

"Yes, my lady." With an air of formality that she didn't usually have, Lani stepped forward, pulling out a map and placing it on the makeshift table in front of Lord Gambriel. "As you have said, Lord Gambriel, it would certainly be impossible for you to garner enough support within the council to prevent other lords from banding together. However, based on the information I've gathered, you and your allies possess a certain soft power I don't believe anyone has noticed."

Lord Gambriel looked down at the map, curiously. "Oh, and just what would that be?"

Lani's hand quickly traced an arc across the map, practically cutting the alliance in half. "You and your allies control the very heart of the alliance, minus the special territory controlled by the academy. As you know, no military can pass through the city without the express permission of the headmistress, and she has a strict policy about remaining neutral in political matters."

Lord Gambriel's eyes widened slightly. "I see. So, that's what you're after. That's rather shrewd of you."

On the other hand, I was baffled. "Care to explain for those of us who aren't experts at politics?"

"Ah, yes. Sorry." Lani turned and faced the rest of us before continuing her explanation. "There is a rather old, but still widely observed, law in the alliance. That law states that none of the member territories may send troops through another's territory without receiving the consent of that territory's lord. Not even the council has the authority to override the lord's decision should they decide to refuse."

"Ah, so that's your plan." The realization finally hit as I remembered the line Lani had drawn across the alliance lands. "Lord Gambriel and his allies will refuse to get involved and refuse passage through their lands. Since they basically cut the alliance in half, it'll significantly cut down on the number of foes that can come after us."

Lani smiled at me briefly before putting back on the stiff, serious expression she had been wearing this whole time and turning back to Lord Gambriel. "That's right. So, what do you think? Will you lend us your aid?"

"I do have to say that I'm rather impressed. To think that you would have planned things out this far in advance, it's quite admirable. Still, there's one flaw in your plan." Lord Gambriel turned his gaze toward Lesti. "Do you think you'll survive long enough to make all of this happen?"

I felt Lesti tense a little under me. Looking up, I could see her mouth set in a hard line. "I see. You think they'll choose to eliminate me as a threat."

"Exactly. There's already been some trouble within the council thanks to that Bestroff boy. Though, in his case, he has the backing of the most powerful and influential family in the alliance, so he should be fine. Your situation will be much more dire, though. Not only is your magic far more absurd than that brat who only has raw power, but you're also from small backwater territory. I can only imagine how many people are going to try and have you assassinated from here on out."

"Let them try." I fixed Lord Gambriel with a stony glare. "I'll rip anyone who tries to lay a finger on her limb from limb."

"You really think it's that simple? Assassins aren't the type to just walk up and announce themselves. They'll use all sorts of underhanded means to get at your master. They'll befriend you and earn your trust, poison your food, or even take your friends and family hostage. Do you really think you can protect her from all that?"

I grit my teeth a little, frustrated because I knew he was right. No matter how strong I was, I wouldn't be able to defend Lesti from everything on my own. Still, I was her familiar, and it was my job to keep her safe. Even if I had to take her and flee from the alliance, I would make it happen somehow. Just as I started to tell Lord Gambriel that, Dag stepped in and cut me off.

"Perhaps I could be of some assistance in this matter?" Still leaned back lazily in his chair, he glanced over at Lani. "The best way to counter assassination attempts is to keep a close eye on your enemies and their pawns. While Lani here has done an excellent job thus far on filling that role for you, it won't be enough going forward. With my resources, I could make sure no assassins get within striking distance of you so long as you're at the academy."

Lord Gambriel looked at Dag, surprise clearly written on his face. "You intend to give her your protection? There's no way the council will approve that."

Dag merely shrugged. "So what if they don't? The commander has ordered me to help her out if I can, and that's what I intend to do. If the council has a problem with it, they can take it up with him."

"I see. He never was very good at taking orders." Lord Gambriel rested his chin on his hand, mouth set in a hard line. "Still, why would he go so far just for her?"

"If I could venture a guess." Lani hesitantly raised her voice once more to offer her opinion, "I believe the commander has some concerns about the alliance's ability to deal with the archdemon Thel'al. He may view Lesti as a valuable asset in that fight."

"I see. That certainly is a possibility." Lord Gambriel fixed his gaze on Lesti as if he were trying to assess her abilities. "Not only does she have a high-level familiar, but she also uses magic, unlike anything I've ever seen before. Yes, now that I think about it, I can clearly see why Commander Frederick would want to protect her."

At Lord Gambriel's last statement, Lesti's hand, which had been gently stroking my fur, suddenly stopped. At the same time, a suspicion of mine was finally confirmed. Frederick's military position, the unit banner in his office, the name of Dag's unit, and several other smaller details finally came together like a puzzle.

"Wait, Frederick is the commander that you've been talking about?" Lesti turned her gaze toward Dag, "Then that means you work for him, right?"

"You're just now figuring this out?" Dag stared at her with a slightly disappointed look. "I thought you would have realized that after I told you the name of our unit. Isn't your familiar Skell's apprentice?"

"Well, I had my suspicions, but I didn't really have any hard evidence. Besides, I haven't really seen much of Instructor Frederick since Thel'al showed up. Actually, why isn't he here? We could have really used his help against that thing that Baron Arvis turned into."

"He was on a separate mission." Dag shrugged. "We got an anonymous tip about a group of demon worshipers holding up in a village near the city. The report suggested they were on the cusp of summoning several greater demons, so the commander went to take care of it personally."

"Greater demons?" I cocked my head to the side, wondering if there was some sort of classification system I wasn't aware of.

"Greater demons are the tier just below an archdemon," Lord Gambriel offered me an explanation with a concerned look on his face. "They normally act as commanders or generals for the archdemons. The two demons that were guarding that man who gave Arvis the potion were greater demons."

"They're normally like commanders?" I thought back to my brief fight with said demon. Its strength definitely lived up to the title it was given. Still, something was bothering me. "If they're so strong, why didn't they just take us out themselves?"

"Yes. That was quite odd," Dag said. "Based on what I've heard from you all, it seems like they were more interested in testing that potion than actually doing any harm. Normally, demons are all about destruction and chaos, so what gives?"

"I don't think that's quite right," Lesti replied. "Most demons don't seem to be simple chaotic beasts. They're vile creatures, to be sure, but I think they're smarter than you're giving them credit for. Not to mention, they're actively working with Ulrich, a human. We should be careful not to underestimate them."

"Well said." Lord Gambriel nodded in agreement. "Regardless, thinking about it too much won't get us anywhere. We'll need to gather more information before we can come to any conclusions. In the meantime, if Dag is willing to offer you his protection, then I would be a fool not to offer you my aid. I'll play along with your plan, but don't expect me to get involved if things go sour. You won't be receiving any military aid from me."

I felt the tension that had been present in the air since the beginning of our conversation finally start to dissipate. Lani released her spell, and Dag's companion seemed to relax a little as well. Oddly enough, it felt like a pair of lead weights had been removed from my own body. Apparently, I had been tenser than I thought.

"Now, then." Lord Gambriel walked to the entrance of the tent, looking back over his shoulder with a softer smile than I would have expected of him. "With that out of the way, I think it's time that we return Rose to her family, wouldn't you say?"

Rose stood, a mixture of excitement and nervousness apparent on her face. "Yes, my lord."

* * *

Sometime later, we arrived at one of the Shadow Dragon Brigade's safe houses on the other side of the city. It was quite a distance, so Dag arranged a carriage for us. Apparently, they had moved Rose's parents there in case the demon worshipers had some interest in kidnapping them, but it had been unnecessary. According to Dag, it appeared they had utterly abandoned Baron Arvis. In the end, he had only been a convenient tool.

As I hopped out of the carriage, I paused. We were once again in the commoner district, but this time it appeared we were in an area dedicated to various types of craftsmanship. In front of us sat a rather sturdy looking building, smoke billowing out of the chimney above. From inside, I could hear the loud ringing of metal striking metal; by all appearances, it was a normal smithy.

"Are all of your safe houses random businesses, Dag?" I looked back at the masked man as he stepped out of the carriage.

"Not all of them, but quite a few." He continued past me toward the entrance. "It serves two purposes. First, it makes the safe house less likely to be found. Second, it gives us some good connections throughout the city. For example, in case we needed some weapons or armor made quickly, we could rely on the smithy here."

"A very convenient arrangement." Lord Gambriel glared at Dag's back as he stepped out of the carriage. "However, I was under the impression the council had already provided you funds and craftsmen to use?"

"Yeah. That was all fine and dandy until we found out the council members were getting kickbacks from those craftsmen." Dag glared back at Lord Gambriel over his shoulder. "At any rate, we can save this discussion for another time. This is meant to be a happy moment." Dag's gaze softened as he looked over at Rose, who was waiting anxiously nearby. "Follow me. Your family is downstairs."

After entering the smithy, we walked into a separate side room that looked like it was used for business meetings. Once everyone was inside, Dag pulled aside the simple table and the rug beneath, revealing a wooden door built into the floor. Pulling it open, he started down the ladder, signaling for Rose to follow. She began to take a step forward but hesitated. It was understandable. After all, she hadn't seen her family in years. Anyone would be nervous, given the circumstances.

Seeing her hesitation, Lesti reached out and gave her a push on the back. "Come on. How long do you intend to keep your parents waiting? I'm sure they've been worried sick about you this whole time."

Rose looked back at her for a moment before finding her resolve and heading down the ladder. I glanced up at Lesti as she went. She had been unusually quiet since arriving here. I got the feeling something was bothering her, but whatever it was, she wasn't showing it on her face. *Putting on the tough act again, huh?*

Once Rose was down the ladder, we followed after. There was a relatively small space at the bottom, with a simple wooden door leading to another room. Once everyone was gathered, Dag knocked on the door twice. From inside, a voice called out, "The strength of our armor."

Dag glanced back at us briefly before replying, "Is nothing before a dragon's claws."

There was a brief pause, followed by the sound of the door being unlocked from the other side. A moment later, it swung open, and a man I recognized from that night we had visited Dag at the bar stood before us. There was a brief flash of surprise on his face when he saw us, but he quickly recovered.

"Sir, I take it you've brought the girl?" the man asked.

"Rose? Is Rose here?"

From somewhere deeper in the room, a woman's voice called out. The desperation, anxiety, and longing in her voice were nearly enough to break my heart. For Rose, it was too much to bear. Tears began to roll down her face, and her mouth opened and shut several times before she finally managed to find her voice.

Through the tears, she barely managed to squeeze out a single word. "M-Mom?"

A moment later, a woman bearing a striking resemblance to Rose pushed past the guard. Her blue eyes frantically scanned the unfamiliar crowd before her as her long pink hair swayed about. It only took her a moment to find her daughter, and there was no hesitation when she did. She ran up and threw her arms around Rose as she fell to her knees, sobbing.

Not a step behind her was another man who must have been Rose's father. Unlike his wife, he was clearly trying his best to hold back his emotions, though losing the battle. Tears streamed down his face. For a long moment, he simply stared at his daughter in disbelief. Then, Rose looked up at him, and whatever willpower he had been using to hold himself back was blasted away by the sight of his daughter's face. He threw his arms around the pair and began to quietly sob himself.

I watched on with strangely mixed feelings. I felt I should be happy, and I was, but there was also a tinge of sadness. As I tried to sort out my emotions, I glanced up at Lesti only to find she was wearing a similarly conflicted expression. Tears formed at the corners of her eyes, threatening to spill over as she fought them back.

Seeing her struggling made me realize what I was feeling was loneliness. While we were both happy that Rose had been reunited with her family, it was something we could never expect for ourselves. Neither of us would ever see our families again. In both cases, they were somewhere far beyond our reach.

The realization didn't help me push those emotions down. If anything, it only made them worse. I rubbed up against Lesti's leg and began to cry for the first time in a while. At the same time, Lesti broke down. Kneeling, she swept me into her arms.

We cried along with Rose and her family, our tears a mixture of happiness and grief.

Epilogue

"To think they would be able to take down a siege demon without any casualties." Ulrich looked over the aftermath of the battle through the eyes of the imp he had left behind. "I can see why the master is so fixated on them."

"Kyihihi. I must say, Master Thel'al does play around a bit too much," a high-pitched voice that failed to match the body of the creature it came from echoed behind him. "The fact that such a weak familiar managed to wound him is truly amusing."

Ulrich glanced back at the greater demon, narrowing his eyes in irritation. He couldn't stand how arrogant these creatures were. Mere servants of an archdemon had no right to be so boastful. Still, it had a point. In the brief exchange from earlier, the Astral Cat hadn't been able to even touch a mere greater demon. How in the world had she managed to put an archdemon like Thel'al on the ropes? The only answer Ulrich could think of was that the archdemon had been holding back.

But that seemed like far too simple an explanation. Mulling over the problem in his mind, Ulrich turned his attention back to the projection displaying what the imp saw, only to find said Astral Cat glaring right back at him. "She can even see through the invisibility spell? How?"

The projection cut out as the imp turned and fled the scene to avoid being captured. Ulrich stood from his seat and turned to leave the barren stone room he had been using. While the Astral Cat's strange ability was annoying, it was a problem for a different day. The imp being spotted didn't really matter at this point anyway. He had all the information he needed from

EPILOGUE

their experiment.

"Well, what do you think? I delivered the results as promised." Ulrich glanced over at another smaller presence that sat in the deep shadows of the room, only his yellow eyes giving him away. "Will you accept my offer?"

"If I'm being honest, I still don't trust that you can do what you say." The bright yellow eyes narrowed at him before an amused grin spread across the creature's face. "Even so, you managed to free me from that wretched pact, so I'll play along with you for now."

"Excellent." A smile of his own crept across Ulrich's face. "I look forward to working with you, Zeke."

"Likewise," Zeke replied as his tail twitched in the shadows. The air behind him seemed to warp; in the next moment, he was gone. For a second, Ulrich stared at the spot where he had been before giving an amused snort. The Rift Stalker had a strong personality, but it was nothing Ulrich couldn't handle.

That matter out of the way, it was time to put the next of his plans into action. Ulrich exited the room and walked down a dim stone hallway, lit only by the occasional flitting magic light. The two greater demons followed a step behind. Eventually, he came to a large, sturdy wooden door, guarded by two lesser demons.

Ulrich stopped before the pair. "I'm here to see our guest. I assume he's awake by now?"

"Kyihihi. You'll find the wretched little man shivering in the corner of his cell," replied one of the guards while the other began to unlock the door.

Ulrich eyed the pair angrily. "I hope you didn't do anything foolish. He's a valuable tool that we need for our master's plans."

"Kyihihi. No, much as I would have loved to." The demon smiled, imagining the horrible acts it wished it could have performed on their prisoner. "I just went to give him food and water as instructed. When he saw me, he shrieked like a little girl and huddled up in a ball."

"Did he, now? This might be more difficult than I thought then." Ulrich clicked his tongue before looking back at the greater demons that were following him. "You two, wait here."

The other lesser demon opened the door, and he went in without waiting for a response. Inside was a single long row of cells. Ulrich slowly walked toward the end of the hall, taking his time as he thought about how to approach his target. He needed to find some way to convince the man to cooperate with them, despite being obviously fearful of the demons. Unfortunately, it didn't seem like his previous offer of power and fortune would be enough to convince his target as he had thought.

Unable to come up with anything, he arrived at the man's cell. As the guard said, he was huddled in the back corner, hiding in the shadows. Ulrich fought the urge to gag as the strong scent of urine assaulted his nose. The man's fear was worse than he had imagined. He certainly hadn't thought him a brave warrior or anything of the sort, but this was far below his expectations of the proud Alandrian nobility.

"W-who are you? Are you with those horrid creatures?" The man finally noticed Ulrich standing there and hesitantly called out to him, voice cracking with fear.

"Calm yourself, my friend. I am no ally of demons." Ulrich put on his most soothing voice and tried to ease the man's fears. "My name is Ulrich, and I'm a researcher—of sorts."

"R-researcher? Are you being held here against your will too, then?"

Ulrich noticed a shred of hope in the man's voice. He was desperate to have someone he could relate to. Sensing an opportunity, he decided to play along and see where the momentum took him. "That's right. Although they seem to consider me useful and give me some amount of freedom."

"Do you know what they want with me?" the man asked as he finally managed to look Ulrich in the eye.

"Most likely, they want to use you as a subject for one of their deranged experiments. They've been having me develop all sorts of strange potions and test them on humans."

"W-what do those potions do?"

"Mostly, they turn whoever drinks them into a mindless beast." Ulrich recalled the early prototypes of his potions, which had turned dozens of demon worshipers into uncontrollable lesser demons. "Although, they do seem to have the side effect of greatly boosting the user's magical energy."

EPILOGUE

"No! No! No!" the man shouted as he clawed at his hair. "It wasn't supposed to be this way. If it weren't for those two, I'd be sitting pretty right now."

Ulrich's eyes lit up as the man's anger flared. It had thoroughly blasted away his fear of the demons. Plus, if Ulrich was right, the targets of that anger were a pair he was very familiar with. Not wanting his chance to escape him, he desperately probed the man for more information.

"The pair that you speak of." Ulrich stepped closer to the cage, grabbing the bars for effect. "It wouldn't happen to be a red-haired girl with an Astral Cat familiar, would it?"

At his words, the man paused before turning to glance at Ulrich with wild eyes. "How do you know that?"

"How could I forget it?" Ulrich scrunched his face up in disgust, recalling how the girl had managed to thwart his last set of plans. But he had no intention of letting this man know about that. "That girl and her familiar are the reason I'm here in the first place. I was there when the demons attacked the academy, seeking shelter from the storm. I begged them to save me, but they betrayed me and gave me up to the demons so they could escape."

"Those cowards." The man finally crawled out from the shadows of his cell, revealing the dirty and tattered clothes of a noble. "They betrayed me as well. They'll try and frame me, but I know the truth. They're the real criminals here. That's why I need to get out of here as soon as possible. If I stay here too long, they'll ruin my good name."

Ulrich could tell that the man was lying—either that or he was delusional. The Vilia girl was clever, and like other nobles, she would manipulate people to get what she wanted. However, she wasn't the type to go around committing crimes and framing others. Whatever the case, the man's story was precisely the opening he needed.

"I see. That does sound like something they would do." Ulrich furrowed his brow pretending to think about something. "Perhaps..."

He paused, waiting for the man to take the bait, and a moment later, he did. "Perhaps, what?"

"Perhaps, I could earn you your freedom, and you could exact our revenge on that girl and her familiar." Ulrich observed the man carefully as he said these words, waiting to see how he would react. It seemed he had found the right buttons to press. Whatever the girl had done to him had clearly lit a fire of hatred in his heart for her. His eyes lit up, and he leaned forward like a child hearing their favorite bedtime story.

"How?"

"Work with the demons here. Their leader, like us, has a hatred for those two." Ulrich chose his words carefully. He couldn't afford for the conversation to end too soon. "If you agree to act as a spy and field agent for them, they'll surely let you free and provide you with assistance."

The man froze, but didn't completely withdraw into his shell this time. "You want me to work with those disgusting things? I-I can't do that. They're demons!"

Ulrich hastily leaned in closer, glancing back toward the door. "I agree, and that's why we'll sabotage them. If we work together, we can get our revenge and foil their plans at the same time. We can be heroes."

"I see." The man seemed to still be struggling with Ulrich's proposal. "How will we do that, though? You're a prisoner here, right?"

"There are others like me. Those who work with the demons only out of fear for their lives. I can use them to get instructions to you, though they will officially come to you as demon worshipers."

The man looked at the floor for a moment, considering his options before looking up at Ulrich with a fire in his eyes. "A-Alright. I'll do it. We'll stop these wretched demons and get our revenge at the same time."

"Excellent. I'll work on getting you released right away." Ulrich looked back at the door, feigning fear. "Remember, from here on out, you're a double agent. If you mess it up, dying will be the least of your worries."

The man swallowed hard and nodded, his face growing pale. Satisfied he wouldn't go running his mouth once released, Ulrich prepared to make his exit. "Alright, I have to go now. If I spend any longer here, they'll get suspicious. Stay strong, my friend."

"You as well."

Ulrich quickly averted his gaze and walked back down the hall, struggling to control his expression. The fool had fallen for his act. He could barely contain the joy building up inside him. Finally, he had a pawn on the board that was his and his alone. Hands shaking from excitement, he began to plan his next move in his head.

Things were about to get much more interesting.

Newsletter & Social Media

Thank you for reading my book! If you enjoyed it, please consider leaving a review. Want to know more about the latest releases, giveaways, and other news? Sign up for my newsletter now!

https://ranobepress.com/newsletter-signup/

If newsletters aren't your thing, consider following me on any of the following social media sites.

https://twitter.com/d_s_craig
https://www.facebook.com/dscraigauthor

Artist Information

Yura's arts is a talented freelance artist with a focus on anime-style illustrations. She is available to hire for both personal and commercial commissions and can be contacted via her Twitter.

Twitter
https://twitter.com/yura_s_arts